BETA
VULGARIS

BETA VULGARIS

A Novel

MARGIE SARSFIELD

W. W. NORTON & COMPANY

Independent Publishers Since 1923

Copyright © 2025 by Margie Sarsfield

Printed in the United States of America
First Edition

For information about permission to reproduce selections from this book, write to Permissions, W. W. Norton & Company, Inc., 500 Fifth Avenue, New York, NY 10110

For information about special discounts for bulk purchases, please contact W. W. Norton Special Sales at specialsales@wwnorton.com or 800-233-4830

Manufacturing by Lakeside Book Company
Book design by Beth Steidle
Production manager: Lauren Abbate

ISBN 978-1-324-07873-9 (pbk)

W. W. Norton & Company, Inc., 500 Fifth Avenue, New York, NY 10110
www.wwnorton.com

W. W. Norton & Company Ltd., 15 Carlisle Street, London W1D 3BS

10 9 8 7 6 5 4 3 2 1

To my family, chosen and unchosen

BETA
VULGARIS

You Are a Sugar Beet

YOU HAVE SPENT MONTHS BECOMING: PUSHING YOUR-self free of hard shell, snaking your newborn fibers through the soil, sprouting leaves, amassing, absorbing, aliving yourself into something fat and bulbous and full of candied potential. You are already a survivor. You were not consumed by sugar beet maggots. You did not succumb to root madness. All that good, hard, organic work, just to wind up dead and frosted over on concrete. Not even any dirt beneath you to remind you of home.

Some say you can feel it when the machines exhume you. When your leaves are sliced off and your taproot is plucked from the ground, ripping out all your lateral roots with it. That it is a kind of pain. We don't care if you can feel it or not. We're going to do it anyway, because we are more important than you. We are your creators. We wanted certain things from you, and we made it easy for you to give us those things. It was not manipulative. It was for your own good, your species propagated like a prairie fire, more than you could have managed on your own. You are bigger, too. Heftier, and denser. You are primed for sweetness in ways that would baffle your ancestors. At some point you stopped being purely natural. When you are the way we made you, you are the way we want you. This is symbiosis: replaceable things are happier than rare things, because replaceable things do not go extinct. You have no choice but to trust us on this.

The question, ultimately, is why. You are not cheap: land and water, furnace maintenance and good press, pest control and payroll. We are one corrupt EPA inspection away from becoming another Michigan Sugar, $13.2 million in revenue kissed goodbye. Why spend so much money to bring you to life, then kill you, five billion times over? Why carve you up, boil you, dismember you, shave you into strips, rupture you, and beat you to a bland pulp? How did you go from a wrinkled clay-coated seed to a monstrous corpse, bled of all worth, subsumed into a greater mass of vegetal waste, a product of duplication rather than reproduction? What is so special about that other part of you, the part we siphon off, crystallize, and purify for profit?

It's sugar that we want. We want the soft and supple sweetness. We want those tiny dissolvable bodies. We want enough of it to rot our teeth away. We want every cell to bloat with energy, we want all the dopamine released at once. And, yes, of course, such a fierce want will cause suffering. If the price paid to indulge this hunger seems high, that's only because you haven't yet accepted the impossibility of overcoming it. There is no overcoming it. It's lust: innate, insatiable, as deep and earthen as a grave.

1

SHE WOULD NOT TELL TOM THAT THE ROOM WAS $20 more than the price advertised on the highway billboard. $59 was about one-third of Elise's bank balance. She'd have $135 left, but $25 needed to go to her credit card payment, so she wasn't counting that in her total.

The night before, they'd slept in the car in a Walmart parking lot, bundled and stuffed in their respective sleeping bags with the front seat backs lowered as far as possible, which was not far enough. Tom kept making jokes about Elise's lifetime ban from Walmart. This ban was real, but back in Brooklyn, where there were no Walmarts, it had taken on a pathetically mythic quality, something to whip out as evidence that Elise was at least a little bit punk. Last night, she had not been in a joking mood, her energy focused on tamping down the desire to whine about sleeping in the car. Not that she got much sleep. Elise kept shivering herself awake, the windshield blurred with condensation from their breath meeting the predawn freeze. She could have extricated herself from the sleeping bag, dug through the pack in the backseat for more layers. It was one of those things, though. The prospect of brief but blunt suffering stopped her from investing in her future comfort.

Here she was doing it again: spending money she ought to be putting toward her debt or saving for emergencies just because she didn't want to spend another night sleeping in the car in a Walmart parking lot.

Their room was almost comforting in its familiarity; exactly what she expected from a motel overlooking a stark, acne-scarred highway in middle-of-nowhere Wisconsin. A queen bed with a thin comforter tucked with hospital corners, a pilly brown blanket folded into a band at its foot; a small television hanging in a corner that was, cruelly, hard to watch from the bed; the bedside table with a corded phone topped with a small clear globe, blinking red, and a notepad with only one page left, a stubby golf pencil beside it. The notepad and the pencil both bore the gilded script Marriott logo. This motel was not a Marriott. There was a menu for a Chinese restaurant in the drawer, but no Bible. This made Elise uneasy. Aside from an academic interest in Buddhism that stemmed mostly from having had good experiences on psychedelics, Elise was not religious. But it was wrong for a motel room to lack a Bible. Tom sat on the bed and stared at the television. The room was shitty but much better than a Walmart parking lot.

"We always stayed in places like this on vacation," Elise said, suddenly nostalgic for family trips to Mystic, Buffalo, Ocean City. It had always been just as exciting to watch HBO on the TV at the Motel 6 as it was to go to the aquarium. Tom looked around the room. Tom's family were Marriott people, not Motel 6 people. Did Marriotts have Bibles?

"Where's the remote?" Tom asked. He was annoyed because they were behind schedule. They had given themselves three days to get from New York to Minnesota, planning back-to-back shifts at the wheel that would get them to Robber's Bluff just in time for orientation at the piling site. If anything went wrong on the road the next day, they could be genuinely screwed. Nothing was going to go wrong, but what if something did? What if they missed orientation and were kicked out of the sugar beet harvest altogether and had spent the last of their money on this extremely unpleasant cross-country trip to nowhere for no reason?

Not really the last of *their* money, though. Tom had plenty of money, even if he refused to touch most of it. It was the last of Elise's money; Elise, who touched all the money she could get her grubby hands on. And Tom didn't know it was the last of Elise's money.

"I'll ask the front desk," she offered. Tom stood up and walked toward the television while she picked up the receiver. On the first ring, Tom waved to get her attention, holding up a remote he'd just pulled from the shelf where the television rested. Purple duct tape held the bottom of the remote together. But Elise also wanted to get rid of the red blinking light on the phone. On the fifth ring, the receptionist picked up.

"Hi, our message light is blinking," Elise said, putting her finger in her free ear as Tom turned on the TV, *Seinfeld* blasting at top volume.

"Dial 7 to listen to your messages," the receptionist said.

"Oh, but it can't be for us. We just got here."

"I can't do anything about it from here, ma'am, you'll have to erase it yourself." The receptionist hung up. Tom fixed the volume and lay back on the bed, diagonal so he could watch the screen, a limp pillow folded over on itself propped beneath his neck. Elise dialed 7. A woman wailed at her.

"Please," the voice hiccupped. "Burt, please come home. You don't know, know how much—oh, I'm so, here with the girls— girls, say something to your daddy—"

Elise wasn't sure how to delete the message, so she had to keep listening, and anyway she was intrigued. Had Burt sat right where she was sitting now? Maybe he had stared at the phone as it rang again and again, let the red blinking light blink all night.

"Hi, Daddy, we miss you," said a not-crying little girl. Elise held the receiver away from her ear; another child's voice was warbling happily in the background before the woman came back.

"You hear that, you miserable bastard?" The woman did not sound like she was crying anymore. "I know what you're doing in that place, and I swear I'll burn this house down before I—oh"— now crying again—"Burt, PLEASE!"

The message ended then, and the phone told her to press 1 to delete it, which she did.

"What was that about?" Tom asked, scratching his stomach where his shirt pulled away from the top of his jeans. There was lint in his belly button. She reached for it, and Tom laughed and rolled onto his side and said "That's mine," which is what he always did when Elise pretended she was going to steal his belly button lint.

"I don't know, weird message," Elise said. "For whoever was here before. I think he was cheating on his wife."

"Cheating in a motel room. How boomer," Tom said, moving his hand from his belly to his face, scrubbing at his eyes.

"Guess what his name was?" Elise asked. Tom shrugged. "Burt."

Burt was also the name they had given the pop-up camper they were towing behind their car.

"It's a sign," Tom said. Elise didn't ask what it was a sign of. Sometimes Tom just said things. Sometimes Elise just said things, too.

"Should I get some ice? For drinks?" she asked, thinking of the duty-free booze they'd bought on the Canadian border way back in Michigan, a dozen or so hours ago. Tom nodded.

There were little flecks of something like black paint inside the ice bucket. Elise washed out the ice bucket in the bathroom sink, imagining that she was really making a big environmental impact by not using the provided plastic sleeve. Elise the eco-warrior. She shook her head. She'd looked up the environmental impact of the sugar beet industry: pesticides, soil erosion, fertilizer runoff, millions and millions of gallons of water. And that was just the farming; forget about the factories. But she needed the money. Or she wanted it. People lived on less than what she had. People lived in motels like this one because apartments required background checks and deposits. Whole families lived in motel rooms. Elise's head hurt just a little, but it was enough for her to give herself permission to stop thinking about all that.

Elise avoided looking at the snacks in the vending machine next to the ice machine; her brain would just fill itself with calorie counts, skipping like a record over anything she didn't have memorized. She caught a glimpse of puffy Cheetos (160) and cringed. Elise could only eat crispy Cheetos because a younger Elise had successfully associated puffy Cheetos with caterpillars: cute, fuzzy, squirming caterpillars that would explode white guts against her tongue if she bit down on them.

In the room, Elise put the ice bucket down beside the plastic cups on the dresser; before she could unwrap the cups or get the liquor bottles from their green plastic bag, Tom beckoned her over. The harsh lighting coated the ice in the bucket in a cold fluorescent glimmer.

"We've never fucked in a motel room," he said. This was true, and exciting in the way banal things can be exciting so long as they are new. They'd been together five years but never been on vacation together—not that this was a vacation. Elise straddled him. He put his hands on her waist, moved them under her shirt. They kissed. Rubbed, pulled, loosened and tightened each other. He squeezed his hands around her neck and she panted into his ear, her thigh muscles burning. She came, then he came, both experts at each other's pleasure, both still mostly clothed, Tom's pants stretched around his thighs and Elise's hanging from one ankle. The credits to *Seinfeld* played in the background. The ice had hardly melted at all. Elise nudged her head under his hand, the way her childhood dog used to do when he wanted his ears scratched. Tom spidered his fingers, moved them through her hair, rubbing up and down across her scalp. Elise pictured her skull softening, expanding, relief flooding into newly opened spaces between gray matter and bone.

"*What's* the *deal* with my girlfriend's hair?" Tom said. "*How does* she get it so soft? I've seen her shampoo. It says it smells like *summer rain*. I've *smelled* summer rain, okay? My girlfriend's hair smells much better than summer rain."

"*What's* the *deal* with my boyfriend's Seinfeld impression?" Elise mimicked back. "*Why is* it so bad? *How does* he sound so much like William Shatner?"

"That's it, no more head rub," Tom said, though he didn't pull his hand away. "You go call up Billy Shatner and see if he'll come over and rub your head."

"No, please." Elise rolled closer into Tom's body. "I'm sorry. You sound just like Seinfeld. You should do it more. Do it onstage between songs."

"*What's* the *deal* with mosh pits? You ever notice there's never a woman breastfeeding her baby in the pit? Why not? It's *natural*! And they say punks are so progressive!"

Elise pulled Tom off the bed so he could continue to massage her head as she poured them drinks. Tom fell asleep with a half-drunk cup of gin in one hand and Elise's head in the other.

Elise tried to figure out what channel HBO was on, but wound up distracted by a crime thriller with Morgan Freeman on FX. The volume was only just audible, so as not to wake Tom, captions on, identical commercials playing in a different order every fifteen minutes: mesothelioma, Gerber Baby Grow-Up Fund, Honda Dollar Days, Obamacare sucks so vote Republican. It'd been a while since Elise had been exposed to cable commercials. They didn't have a TV, only watched Netflix and Hulu and illegal torrents, so when Sarah McLachlan started crooning over stock footage of scared dogs, Elise, embarrassingly, teared up a little bit. She was tired and tipsy and bored and kept thinking about the vending machine. There was a time when Elise would have felt driven back to the machine by an insurmountable anguish. And another time when not giving in to her hunger would have filled her with a vapid, painful pride. Those versions of herself were still inside her, but only as echoes.

On the television, Morgan Freeman's female partner was shading a pencil over a yellow legal pad to see the last thing it'd been used for. Elise picked up the golf pencil and the pad with its single sheet and tried it. She was surprised when it worked. Someone had written *I <3 Oblivion*. The handwriting looked a lot like her own.

In the morning, while Tom was at the continental breakfast, Elise used the Wi-Fi to fill out her "on-boarding paperwork" on her phone: she had to e-sign workers' comp and state-mandated insurance forms and submit pictures of her ID and Social Security card. She should have done this several weeks ago, when it was first sent over—that's when Tom did his. But Elise had not done it several weeks ago, she was doing it now, at the last minute, using the frustratingly slow internet, her clumsy fingers forever choosing the wrong option, her thumb scraping over and over against the crack across her phone screen. She frowned at the "application" portion—there had been no application process, really, just a brief form she'd filled out and a phone interview that boiled down to: "Are you sure you want to do this? Because it really sucks, especially overnight shifts." Elise imagined that no one was ever turned away from the sugar beet harvest. But now she was being asked strange and personal questions: *What is your blood type? Do you believe that sugar consumption is inherently patriotic? Are both your parents still living? Are your parents still married to each other? Have you ever thought your parents would be happier if they got divorced? Have you ever had a pet you did not love? Have you ever caused (directly or indirectly) the death of a creature larger than a cockroach (INCLUDING HUMANS)? Describe your experience with sugar.*

Why hadn't Tom told her about this portion of the paperwork? Her hand was cramping. Elise wrote: "I have eaten sugar before." A dust-sized sliver of glass from the crack in her phone screen stuck into her index finger as she e-signed her name for the last time.

Tom returned from the continental breakfast empty-handed. He had promised to bring her back a waffle.

"They wouldn't let me take anything back to the room," he said, shrugging. Elise had never heard of such a rule, but whatever. She was sure Tom wasn't lying.

"Why didn't you tell me about those weird questions on the application?" she asked as they gathered together their luggage and detritus.

"What?" Tom asked.

"On the application," she said. Tom looked confused. He was impatient to get on the road again. "In the paperwork they sent. For the harvest."

"Huh," he said. "I don't remember. You ready?"

Now, that *might* have been a lie. But it wasn't worth pressing. Elise let it go. That lie, if it was a lie, was nothing compared to Elise pretending to be a responsible adult with whom Tom could and should build a life. She felt guilty. She really should check her bank account, open that haunted little app that only ever served to tell her she'd fucked up that month, shouldn't have made that second trip to Trader Joe's, didn't need that ironic vintage T-shirt. She was never going to get back to school if she spent all her money on bullshit.

She wouldn't check her bank account, though. She'd just hang on for dear life to the idea of $110.

2

ELISE LIT A CIGARETTE AS TOM TRIED, AGAIN, TO BACK
the car out of its parking spot. It was an easy job made impossible
by the green camper, currently folded in on itself into a neat rectangle, attached to Tom's sedan by an old trailer hitch. There wasn't
enough space in the parking lot to just back up and then turn, and
the camper refused to participate in the reverse-maneuvering Tom
was trying to execute. Elise had tried to be useful and direct Tom
in steering things one way or another, but, clearly, whatever she
was doing was not helpful. She didn't want to sit in the car beside
him, expose herself to his mounting frustration. Elise, for some
reason, did not enjoy the company of angry men.

It was as good a morning as anyone could hope for in late September, the sun cheerfully present. She ate the last of the spana-
kopita (200) their friends had sent them off with—Elise insisted
on calling it spank-o-pita, repeating it even though it didn't make
Tom laugh, thinking that eventually he would find her persistence
funny although the joke wasn't. But he hadn't and now there was
none left, no more reason for Elise to say spank-o-pita. There was
only the parking lot and the September morning sun and Tom,
hitting the steering wheel, repeating the same useless motions
until Elise's cigarette was done and she leaned in the window and
told him they should just unhitch the camper, pull the car out, and
re-hitch it. Tom was unhappy with this alternative, but he agreed
to it, and in this way they finally managed to leave the parking lot.
Elise could feel Tom's nerves in her own stomach. They had ten

hours to get to Robber's Bluff, which was seven hours away. His shoulders were high and tight—Elise reached over to rub the one closest to her.

"We're gonna get there early," she said.

"I know," Tom said.

All their friends, especially the couple who had recommended the harvest to Elise and Tom after doing it the year before, had expressed great enthusiasm for this trip they were taking across America, but most of the highways so far looked identical: kudzu and trees and billboards that advertised Jesus as the bread of life (caloric content unknown). And it wasn't a proper road trip with fun roadside-attraction detours; they'd given themselves only a little more than the bare-minimum time to get there so they could keep working at their real jobs for as long as possible. Even stops to pee were precious. Elise drove first, gladly. As a passenger on such a trip, you could only sit and stare at the dull landscape and try not to read every billboard aloud. As a driver, you at least got to think about practical things like when to pass and how fast you could get away with going on a particularly empty stretch of interstate. Wisconsin was nice enough, a forested country peppered with advertisements: gun stores, antiques, chain hotels, fudge (70). A surprisingly equal split between handmade Romney signs and Obama bumper stickers. The wind tugged playfully at the tree-tops, psychedelic and sensual.

"I don't get fudge. Like, why is it the thing?" Elise wondered aloud. "Every vacation town has fudge, but who even likes it? It's like a chocolate bar and a brownie had a baby that grew up dumber than its parents."

Tom snorted but didn't look up from his book, a brutally thick tome on Lucretius, Epicurus, and nothingness. He'd written his thesis on nothingness. She'd read it; it was really good. Elise had barely understood a word even though she was also majoring in philosophy. She'd written her thesis on surveillance and shame, arguments about stock footage of the "obesity epidemic." The hard copy of that thesis was stored in some box in some basement on the SUNY campus. No one would ever read it. Tom was more invested in their shared major; he would go to law school someday for sure. If Elise—when Elise—went back to school, it wouldn't be for that. Law degrees were too expensive, though she knew, of course, that the whole point was that you could make enough as a lawyer to pay back your loans. Otherwise, people would not do it. A limiting factor of Elise growing up without money was how hard it was for her to imagine a life with money. Her brain could not wrap itself around the idea that she could ever, even as a lawyer, someday earn more than $40,000 a year; $40,000 being the amount she'd heard growing up was what you needed to earn to be comfortably middle class. Elise had grown up just a tad bit under comfortably middle class, though her parents had gotten there by the time she graduated high school. Elise didn't know what to consider herself now, suspended between the safety net of her parents' suburban home and the trapeze of the post-recession job market. Usually, she just considered herself stupid.

"Peanut butter fudge is even worse," she said, lowering the volume on the music so they could talk. It was one of the McVie songs on *Rumours*—skippable.

Elise's ambitions for grad school were more modest than Tom's; most of them weren't actually grad school at all. She might decide to be a paralegal or a vet tech, for instance, which were technically lesser degrees than her bachelor's. She sometimes fantasized about getting her MFA in theater, though that seemed like even more of a rich girl's game than law school. She thought, sometimes, about going back to school for therapy—in her wildest dreams, she was some sort of movie-of-the-week guidance counselor who fortified the hearts of her students. Elise fantasized about being the kind of adult she'd needed as a teenager, which felt a little pathetic, veering too close to "inner child" territory. Realistically, Elise could not be trusted with anyone's heart, not even her own.

"But also you can just make fudge at home. It's easier than making, like, a cake, so why would you buy it on vacation?"

She talked about going back to school a lot, but, realistically, what Elise needed most was a job with health benefits so she could go back on antidepressants. She wanted something office-y. A job where she could spend a day clearing out her email inbox and no one would get on her ass for wasting time, the way every boss she'd ever had bitched if she wasn't spending every minute being useful even when there was nothing that needed to be done. How many times had she wiped down a counter that was already clean because she couldn't get caught standing around not wiping anything?

"And only on vacation—that's the only time anyone ever thinks about fudge. When your family splits up for an hour and you already went to the only store you wanted to go to, so you have all this time to do nothing so you're like, okay, fine, fudge."

For now, it was enough for Elise to imagine making it back to Brooklyn after the harvest, flush with the $12-an-hour, time-and-a-half-on-Saturdays, double-time-Sundays, eighty-four-hour-workweek paychecks that Salt of the Earth Sugar offered their temporary workers. Her job at the grocery store was good enough, and good enough was better than she usually dared to ask for. Probably a symptom of her depression. Lots of people worked full-time and went to school; her own mother had, which led to a lot of frustrating dead-end discussions about something that her parents only barely avoided calling laziness. But Elise was already tired all the time. She didn't want to do that; she just didn't fucking want to.

She turned the volume dial up again but the album was nearly over. She was worried that she was being annoying. Tom fiddled with her phone, the aux cord hanging umbilical between it and the radio. Maybe he'd put on one of his hardcore albums, a sure sign that he didn't want to talk to Elise anymore. Tom wasn't going back to school yet because he was having fun, playing house with Elise in between band practice. Elise had to work hard not to resent him: the student loans he didn't have to take out, the money just waiting there for him to decide he was ready to go get his law degree, the fact that he actually could go and be a public defender or sue corporations on behalf of newts or whatever environmental lawyers got to do. She refused to indulge in fantasies about how much easier their life would be if he'd use some of his trust fund money. They split everything but groceries straight down the middle; they each bought their own groceries, since Elise didn't eat meat and Tom didn't drink soy milk. They worked the same hours, for basically the same pay. If Tom didn't want to touch his family money, who was she to tell him to? For what? So she wouldn't have to break her back to pay rent like every other twenty-something she knew? Elise didn't deserve to have it better than her peers just because of who she was dating. Tom felt insecure and ashamed of his silver spoon; Elise felt insecure and ashamed of her fiscal irresponsibility. The relationship just worked better when they kept their financial travails to themselves. And if Tom were to embrace his wealth, maybe he wouldn't want Elise anymore. He'd be able to afford someone better.

The only time they'd had a conversation that somewhat acknowledged this fissure was when Elise first brought up the possibility of being a vet tech. Tom had laughed, incredulous.

"What? Why not just be a vet?" he'd asked. And Elise, uncharacteristically, had answered honestly. She even looked him in the eye when she said it:

"Money."

He had paused, then looked away, cloudy. Elise thought this was the closest he'd ever come to betraying some fear that, ultimately, he would be wealthy, either through inheritance or otherwise, and that, just as ultimately, Elise would never be wealthy. She would never catch up to him. *It* would always be between them. But he could not, now, with the beans and rice in his cabinets and cheap ground beef in his freezer and Miller High Life in his fridge, with the Anti-Flag patches on his jacket, with the zines on his bookshelf, with the Bad Brains set list thumbtacked to the wall, admit this could be a problem. Ever since then he had been enthusiastic—overly so—whenever she mentioned getting a technical degree.

And now, instead of Earth Crisis or Discharge or some bootleg basement-show Drug Church mixtape, Tom put on a playlist of nostalgic indie pop from their mid-aughts college days: Passion Pit and MGMT and Fleet Foxes. Tom would not have picked this playlist to listen to if he were alone.

Elise shook her shoulders and sang along while Tom drummed his fingers against the glove box, contributing when a verse called for a tenor. When they crossed the state line into Minnesota, they both said "Minnesota" aloud in *Fargo* accents. Tom often seemed like a better partner than Elise could afford, his affection for her a debt she could never pay off.

3

THE SMELL HIT THEM FIFTEEN MILES OUTSIDE OF town: dirt and chemicals alchemied into something sinisterly vegetal but sharply inorganic. The processing plant sprawled behind a barbed wire fence; thick columns of smoke rose from its bulky towers into the sky.

Robber's Bluff had a population of just under eight thousand. Elise wanted to call its downtown bleak, but wasn't sure if that was fair; it wasn't built for tourism, no cobblestones to speak of, no grand courthouse sitting pretty in the center of town, no benches in the shade of yellowing trees. But it wasn't blighted, either. It was just small. There was an antiques store, a women's clothing store, a card shop, an employment agency, an American Legion, and a block-long bar called Shooters. Vacant storefronts aplenty, but none of the empty windows were broken. They turned left at a Sunoco, off the main street and onto Central Park Boulevard, named after the municipal park that was their destination. Salt of the Earth Sugar, their employer, ponied up for campsites, evidence of the symbiotic relationship between corporation and town. A church near the campground offered free meals to the "workampers," though Salt of the Earth Sugar did not pay for that. Jesus did, or whatever. They'd brought some food from home: packets of tuna for Tom, Pop-Tarts for Elise, ramen and Knorr Pasta Sides and a camp stove to cook them on, but not nearly enough to get them through the harvest.

The campground was tucked, bowl-like, between two hills,

invisible until they reached the park entrance. A topographical secret, like something the county was ashamed of: *Don't look at what we need to do to stay afloat*, it seemed to say. *Don't look at who we have to host.* There were a hundred small towns just like this: unhappy grumblings about Spanish becoming an unofficial national language, Fox News playing at Supercuts, reporting that the children at the border could be carrying diseases. Was Elise being a snob? Was this coastal elitism? People everywhere would always give Elise the benefit of the doubt, a white girl with a white boyfriend. She was not obligated to do the same. But why did Elise assume there'd be immigrants working the harvest in the first place? Was she just as bad as the imaginary racists in her head?

The pavement turned to loose gravel, then to dirt as Tom slowed the car into the campground. Each campsite had a picnic table and fire pit and a half-bare tree, muddy autumnal leaf litter carpeting the ground. They turned into one, and Tom turned off the car. Elise wasn't tempted to call it home even as a joke.

Almost all the other campsites were occupied already: converted vans, RVs, small trailers. There weren't many people around—one guy fiddling with the roll-out awning over the door of an Airstream, three people at a picnic table eating tortilla chips and salsa. In the campsite behind them, two crust punks sat outside a van: both with dreads, one with a beard, tattered black hoodies, septum piercings, dual lip piercings, dirty bandannas, patches and patches and more patches, all black and white. They were sitting on camp chairs, a thirty-rack between them, a pair of dogs lying on their sides at their feet. Everyone Elise saw was white, deepening her sense of shame: she'd been wrong, after all, about the people who would be at the harvest. She really was *that* racist.

Elise could feel her stomach existing, a sensation that wasn't nausea but wasn't the absence of feeling that she preferred. She didn't like meeting new people, was convinced that strangers were just people who didn't yet know that they didn't like her. She couldn't believe that they'd have to go to work in a matter of hours. Actual, honest-to-god *work*. They were there. They were doing it. Tom was already out of the car, stretching. The sedan bounced slightly as he fiddled with the hitch, his pointed gaze through the rear window telling Elise to join him. It was cold and windy.

Setting up the camper was not unlike pulling out a sleeper sofa, a configuration of folding metal poles and wooden platforms on rollers, all covered in the canvas top that snapped into place around and under the body. The door had a zipper. The zipper was broken. Just a little bit, just at the bottom, where it wouldn't fully close, leaving a triangle exposed. They had only noticed after paying for the camper. They'd agreed to just figure out how to fix it once they got to the harvest. Well, now, here they were. Time to figure it out.

Not quite yet, though. Soon but not quite yet.

There were two single beds, thin vinyl cushions smelling vaguely of mildew on raised planks of wood that doubled as storage, one on either side of the interior. Elise fitted an oversized sheet onto one cushion, laid out their pillows and sleeping bags. It made the bed marginally less dismal. Elise emptied her backpack, folding her clothes in piles on the other bed. Tom plugged their space heater into the outlet at the campsite and ran the cord under the canvas. The rusted box rattled and hummed as it pumped hot, stale air. Elise turned it off, her lips already chapping.

"Home sweet home," Tom said when they were finished, lying back on the bed and hiding his eyes under the crook of his elbow, making the joke Elise had avoided.

Elise sank down beside him. His proximity was a comfort even if she was not, in that particular moment, feeling the love she knew she had for him. The love had not gone missing, at some point it would make itself known again, filling her up like a hard-won orgasm, so shudderingly satisfying that it almost hurt. It was just that sometimes Tom was less the Tom she loved for being Tom, handsome and funny and smart, and more a body she took solace in because it had chosen to keep her own body company for several years now and showed no signs of choosing otherwise anytime soon. Elise wondered if this was yet another personal deficiency. Was everyone else walking around constantly feeling *L-O-V-E* for their partner? She fell asleep beckoning to the love like a dog, calling it home so that she could stop wondering what the fuck was wrong with her.

She was alone when she woke up.

4

SHE WAS STILL WEARING HER JACKET, AND HER HAIR was sweat-stuck to her flesh. Tom had turned the space heater on, in case she got cold. Didn't they have to be at work? But then, Tom wouldn't have just gone without her, he would have woken her up—she looked at her phone. Not late, not even too late for free dinner at the church. Disoriented and thirsty, she unzipped the door and looked out at the campsite. It was still bright out. The cold was a relief compared to the cloying dryness of the space heater. There were dogs running all over the place. People were out, chatting and laughing. Tom's voice carried from the other side of the camper, where the crust punks were. He was so friendly, so much more at ease with people. He had not been bullied in high school. His band had come in second at Battle of the Bands. It was one of the more selfish and embarrassing reasons Elise liked being with Tom: she liked dating a popular boy. When the self-hatred reached a fever pitch, she could look at Tom and tell herself that he wouldn't have tolerated her this long if there was nothing redeemable in her. Tom liking Elise gave Elise at least one reason to like herself. He certainly wasn't with her for her money. Ha ha.

Elise's hands were cracked and dirty in the cracks. There was no mirror anywhere for her to check how she looked. She didn't like having no control over how others saw her. She needed coffee, something. There was the gin; Elise was better off with water. Bravely, she stepped out of the camper and filled an empty Gatorade bottle with water from the pump next to their picnic table. No one paid attention to her.

Tom's back was to her as she approached, with the two crust punks and seven new people all standing in a circle. She put on a smile.

"Hey," she announced herself, interrupting some laughter.

Tom turned; he was holding a puppy, a little sleepy thing, black-and-white fuzz over very pink skin.

"Puppies!" Tom exclaimed. He introduced her to the crust punks, Aya and Chet, who were from California and were doing the beet harvest for their third year, and to Cee—short for Elsie—and her partner, Sam, and their friends Dan, Eric, Jai, Ryan, and Ash, and to Iko, the mama dog, and Bingo, her neutered cuckold of a boyfriend. Cee and Sam and their friends, whose names drizzled out of Elise's sieve of a brain, were from Maine, and were working the same overnight shift at the same site as Elise and Tom. They would be spending twelve hours a night, every night, together for the duration of the harvest. Elise wished, more than ever, that she could have fixed herself up in a mirror before meeting them. They were familiarly hipster in knitted wool caps, faded T-shirts and flannels and Doc Martens. Cee, especially, was bright and magnetic, with a full head of frizzy brown hair. Elise felt simultaneous surges of attraction and envy, pushing both down as far as she could.

In the middle of the circle was a cardboard box full of puppies, four weeks old and making high-pitched whining pleas as they tumbled over each other. Cee scratched the head of the puppy in Sam's arms. The one Tom held was snoring. One tricolored puppy in the box kept falling onto her back as she tried to stand on her hind legs; Aya picked her up and handed her to Elise. As these new humans handled her progeny, Iko watched with a doleful trust Elise felt she had done nothing to deserve.

The group made banal, pleasant conversation about good names for dogs.

"I've always liked a dog with a human name," Elise said. "Kevin. Dolores. Bruce Springsteen."

Cee laughed at that, an ugly, charming guffaw. Cee was hot. Elise's sternum hummed. She turned her attention back to the puppy, who was warm and nibbly. The puppy took the index finger Elise had been using to stroke under her chin into her mouth, sucking and jawing with the nubs of her milk teeth. Elise lifted the bundle to her nose, sniffed it, a small warm life that still smelled sweet. The puppy's stomach was huge, though, bloated and tight like something about to burst. Elise peered at the other puppies, all similarly potbellied.

"It's too bad our apartment isn't pet-friendly," Tom said, shifting his puppy's weight in his arms. The firmest plan Tom and Elise had ever made for their shared future was someday adopting a dog. Not yet: not with their current budget, jobs, apartment. But someday. They each occasionally looked at shelter dogs online, sending each other links to particularly appealing options. They would play-fight over whether to name the dog Minor Threat or Bon Iver.

Elise's puppy started to shiver. Her lips pulled up at the edges like a smile. Before Elise could do anything about it, the puppy opened her mouth and released a yellowish cream that ran down Elise's forearm and dripped onto the grass below. A small, thread-like worm dangled from her arm hair; several more worms were visible in the puddle on the ground. Elise thought some were moving. Worse, almost, than the worms were the streaks of blood mixed into the bile like oil paints. The group recoiled. Iko lifted her head, staring at her puppy as she passed again from Elise to Aya, then stood up to sniff the puke. Chet grabbed Iko's worn black collar and dragged her away, told her not to eat it. Aya produced a towel from somewhere inside the van, and Elise wiped her arm clean, saying that it was okay, she was fine, it was just a puppy, poor thing. Nobody said anything about the blood. Maybe the blood was normal? The puppy had a little pink streak on her white-furred chin.

"Puppies get worms, it's just a fact of life," she said. "They have pills for that, right?"

Chet said, cryptically, that they were "working on it." Elise nodded. She wouldn't be able to afford a whole litter's worth of deworming pills, she guessed, if she had to buy them right now. But she also didn't have a dog. A pair of dogs, with a litter of puppies. She didn't want to judge the crust punks. Tom held the puppy in his arms at a distance, as though it was defective. Elise looked at the puppy looking back at Tom, wondered if the puppy was wondering why it was suddenly colder than it was a minute ago, where all that human heat had gone.

Aya kicked grass and dirt over the vomit. Elise had to, again, temper her feeling that the crust punks were not doing things correctly. What did she know? Maybe it was like fertilizer; maybe all the earth ever really wanted was worms, bile, blood.

5

CHURCH BELLS CHIMED, DULL AND ATONAL AND LOUD and clear. It'd be dinnertime. Elise inventoried her stomach: empty. If she was anything but starving, she had to scan herself for hunger symptoms. Whatever bridge between brain and stomach other people had, it'd burned away in high school when her brain, colonized by Tumblr posts about hip bones, was coached into ignoring the signals sent from her gut. Now, she found herself unable to tell when she was hungry until the hunger expressed itself as fatigue or bitterness. Elise realized this by paying attention to Tom, who only expressed that kind of moody hunger when food was unavailable. If there was food, he just ate it. Tom, and other people, knew when to eat and had no problem doing so. Astounding. It was sort of nice, then, to have to eat at 5:30 p.m. every night, for it not to matter whether she was hungry because this was when it was time to eat. Tom, for his part, seemed to think that Elise's need to be told that she was hungry when she started acting bratty was endearing, a charming naïveté, a way that he could take care of her better than she could take care of herself. He got to be the Adult, a role he quite liked. His asking if she needed a snack was like a more practical form of a forehead kiss. Elise preferred for Tom to think of it this way than to know the truth. Being a little bit helpless really was much cuter than having an eating disorder.

They entered through a back door, far from the ornate wooden entrance facing the street. Elise had been in rooms like this many times in her life: it was the kind of rec room you could rent for cheap for a wedding or a wake, with stackable chairs arranged around circular tables spaced out on the institutional linoleum. There was a swinging door in one wall behind a table of aluminum heating pans, a busy kitchen revealed in measured flashes as people came and went with plates, bags of chips, more aluminum heating pans to switch out with the empty ones. A perpendicular table against the adjoining wall held cold foods. A smiling, sandy-haired man stood in front of the swinging kitchen door, eyes bright. This, Elise realized, was a soup kitchen. Of course it was; why hadn't she made the connection earlier? Perhaps it was the cognitive dissonance: Elise was the sort of person who *volunteered* at soup kitchens, not ate at them. Which meant there was a sort of person who ate at soup kitchens. And what sort of person, exactly, did Elise think was the soup kitchen sort?

The church also housed a shelter, rules for which were printed on white computer paper and taped on various walls throughout the cafeteria: no weapons allowed on the premises, residents not allowed to enter the kitchen or dining room during posted times, no drugs or alcohol permitted, do not use this door, residents only beyond this point, etc. One of the signs said, "The beets can only hurt you if you LISTEN to them!!!!" in Papyrus font. It was laminated, the only laminated sign in the room. Elise assumed "beets" was a typo, but couldn't figure out what the word was supposed to be: maybe beasts? Maybe it was a church joke that Elise wasn't meant to get.

There were a few dozen people—mostly white, Elise noticed—serving themselves cold food, being served hot food, or sitting with their flimsy plastic plates around the tables. Elise hated buffets: the anxiety of reaching, of deciding while others watched and waited, the clumsiness with which she spooned salad or chased French fries around with tongs, the conspicuousness of standing for seconds.

It was a highly visible form of food consumption. Back in high school, on the lunch line, boys would cough and say "TrimSpa" and cough again, purposefully failing to hide the word inside the coughs, or tell her point-blank she needed to go on Hydroxycut.

The paucity of choices at the mission made it easier to manage the anxiety: a limp iceberg lettuce salad (40) with only ranch dressing (145) to put on it; loaves of white Wonder bread (79) beside pats of cold butter (102), apples (95) and oranges (45) in a clear plastic bowl, snack-size bags of Lay's chips (120). The heating pans held watery green beans (31), buttered corn kernels (135), and two identical casseroles composed of hot dog bits in a cream-of-something soup topped with tater tots (she couldn't begin to guess, and didn't need to, since she didn't eat meat).

The enthusiastic blond man loudly introduced himself to everyone as they walked by, so Elise knew his name was Mike well before she and Tom reached him; he guessed that they were there for the harvest, an easy guess, and told them to see him after dinner so he could take down their names and shifts, have lunches ready for them each night. Mike welcomed them to Robber's Bluff, and to dinner, and was so happy they were there, wanted them to have whatever they needed.

Elise was already concerned about how she was going to show Mike that she was grateful for what he and the rest of the folks in the kitchen were doing. Elise didn't need this help, not really. If anything, Elise accepting this help was taking food away from someone else who did really need it. After all, this was charity, wasn't it? Elise and Tom didn't deserve charity. They were college-educated and rented a studio apartment in Brooklyn. It was the same reason Elise wouldn't go on Medicaid even though she qualified for it; it felt, somehow, like taking away from people who really needed it.

That buying the camper, $350 split evenly between them, had cost all of her surplus funds for a month and a half did not strike Elise as evidence of financial need. She should have been saving that money, anyway, for GREs and application fees and tuition, for the post-secondary education she kept saying she was going to get once she was in a little less debt and had a little more firm of an idea about what she wanted to do with herself, her life. Realistically, it would have just gone to concert tickets and maybe some drugs to do at the concert and probably a couple of nights of takeout—those thin luxuries that she always regretted as soon as it was too late to get the money back. Buying the camper was kind of like saving. It was an investment? For the people in the kitchen to be cooking free food for Elise just didn't feel right. *Then don't eat it*, Elise thought. But not in the way she used to think about not eating food.

Mike called the hot dog casserole "hot dish" and questioned Elise when she passed on it. She hadn't planned on making a thing of her vegetarianism—had planned to make do with what she could eat and supplement with the food they'd brought from home. But when she found herself blurting out the words "I don't eat meat," Mike responded with an embarrassing amount of concern, told her to be sure to come see him after dinner so he could be sure she got what she needed because he sure didn't want her to go hungry. Elise was relieved when Cee, at her elbow, also said she was vegetarian; Elise wasn't alone, then. She was not the only person making someone else work harder for her moral comfort.

Elise and Tom sat down with their new coworkers, Elise next to Cee and Tom next to Ash, distinctively dressed in a wool beanie and overalls and boots Elise associated with fishermen. He was the only one among them who had done the harvest before. He filled them in on gossipy details, including the fact that Mike, who ran the soup kitchen, was a recovering alcoholic, and that several pedophiles on the sex offender registry lived in the shelter, and had to eat separately from everyone else because of it. Elise looked over her shoulder—there were, indeed, several families with children eating at the mission.

"I don't understand," Elise said. "Why would a church harbor sexual predators?"

Cee laughed, louder and longer than Elise thought the joke deserved. It was kind of low-hanging fruit. But Cee's laughter got Elise laughing, too, which felt good. The two of them laughing in harmony, Cee no better than Elise and Elise no worse than Cee.

"You guys are gonna be operators?" Ryan asked from a few seats down, leaning halfway across the table to look at Elise and Tom. He wagged a plastic fork toward them.

"Just me," Tom said while Elise shook her head. The applications for piler operator and sample taker were identical, but piler operators made a couple more dollars an hour and got to work in the relative comfort of a booth on top of the machine instead of fully exposed to the elements outside. Elise hadn't applied for the position, unsure she'd be able to do it. She envied Tom's confidence. Friends who had done the beet harvest the year before assured Elise that it was easy, but she still didn't want to fuck with a big machine. True, the extra money would have helped her pay off her debt faster. But Elise was a coward. Or, she had an undiagnosed anxiety disorder. Either way, she didn't want to mess everything up and be laughed at.

After eating, they took turns writing their names and shifts on a clipboard Mike handed them. He turned to Elise and Cee, singling them out.

"We're gonna make sure you two are taken care of," he said. "It's hard work, and cold, especially night shift. You need your energy. We're gonna take care of you. We don't have anything for you two tonight, but tomorrow. Feel free to take a lunch anyway, okay?"

He reminded Elise of an uncle. Not any of hers, but someone's. He had the reformed addict's energy—that born-again craving for betterment.

"Thank you," Elise said, again. "Thank you so much. Really, you don't need to go to any trouble for me."

"It's no trouble," Mike said, smiling. "We're gonna take care of you." Elise believed him—or at least she believed in his intention to do so.

Elise wanted to show Tom the weird sign about listening to the beets, but now she couldn't find it on any of the walls. The wall she'd thought it had been on was bare. Elise thought she could see a lighter rectangle on the wall, cleaner and less faded than the paint around it, as if the sign had been there for a long time before someone took it down.

6

ELISE TRAILED A BIT BEHIND THE MAINERS AND TOM
on the walk back to camp. She was typing out a text to her mom,
letting her know that Elise and Tom had made it "safe and sound!"
to the campsite. Her mom replied in less than a minute, saying
thanks for letting her know they'd arrived and wishing Elise luck.
It rang a little bit false. Elise's mother had made her position on
the beet harvest clear: Elise was wasting her time and it was stupid
to risk losing her job at the grocery store. Elise's boss had actually seemed begrudgingly pleased to not have to pay Elise for a
month, but it wasn't unthinkable that he'd replace her. She wasn't
that valuable an employee. "You're living in a fantasy world," her
mother had said. Her go-to critique for anything Elise did or said
that she didn't like. As though Elise and Tom had not sat down
and done the math: just one of their paychecks for a week of harvest work would nearly cover rent for a month. The harvest lasted
four weeks; combined, they could make six and a half months'
rent. It usually took Elise three weeks of work to come up with
one month's rent. Plus, Tom's cousin from Pennsylvania, or maybe
Connecticut, Elise couldn't remember, was supposedly looking
for a job on Wall Street and an apartment in SoHo, so his parents
were paying a token amount—much less than a hotel room—for
him to stay in their apartment while they were gone. This had
been Tom's mother's doing. Elise imagined her hammering out
the details with her sister-in-law.

"You know, Tom's in this whole Beat poet phase," Mrs. Henry

would have said. "He doesn't think about practical things like this."

"Jeffrey needs to be down there anyway, you're doing *us* a favor," her sister-in-law would have assured her.

The way it worked out with Tom's cousin felt like a favor, but it wasn't, at least not to Elise. Somehow, in a way Elise couldn't quite untangle, it felt like a rich person favor. In her family, it would only have counted as a favor if they'd let Jeffrey stay for free; they'd originally planned on just eating the cost of rent for the month. That still would have left them with enough to cover five months.

Having a good portion of their rent covered while they were gone, in addition to the high pay, had been enough incentive to make up for the risk of losing her shitty, extremely replaceable job. Plus, it had sounded like fun, kind of. A real life experience. Something they could say they'd done when they got back to Brooklyn, where hardscrabble Steinbeckian authenticity was social currency. It would sound cool. Elise felt cool. That was, like, her favorite feeling.

Her mom signed off the text as though it were a note: I love you - Mom. Elise sent back an emoji of a heart. She'd have to call her mom soon. Elise made a concerted effort to call her mother regularly. It was an easy way to be a good daughter.

When Elise looked up, she was surprised to find Cee at her side. Sam was looking at their own phone, a few paces ahead.

"Are you ready?" Cee asked.

Elise opened her mouth but faltered over a response. She wanted to say something to make Cee laugh again. Cee was cute when she laughed, and Elise was hot when she was funny.

"As I'll ever be," she finally managed, once the silence had grown so long that no joke would make up for it. She looked down, embarrassed, then back up again. She caught Cee eyeing her. Was Cee checking her out? The possibility was thrilling, but she'd never grown out of the instinct that anyone looking her up and down was doing so with derision rather than approval.

"I'm excited," Cee said. She punched the air in front of them. "I'm ready to fuck up some beets."

Elise laughed, admiring or envying Cee's ability to pull off silliness. Sam looked over their shoulder at Elise. Tom, at the front of the pack, looked over his shoulder, too. It looked like he was looking at Cee.

"Wow, you have really nice hair," Cee said. She reached out, gently grasped Elise's ponytail, first lifting it, then letting it run through the tunnel of her fist, then giving it one fast twirl around her index finger. Elise's mouth went dry, sweat gushing from the glands in her armpits. It was a five-second interaction. Less, even. Women touched each other all the time in innocent ways. It was like summer camp, braiding hair.

Elise was supposed to say something: "Thanks," or "You too," or something. Anything. She wasn't saying anything, and too much time was passing. Fuck.

"Yeah," she finally managed. Then, "Thanks." Her phone chimed. She was grateful for the excuse to look away; grateful, too, because Elise receiving a text would broadcast, to Cee, that someone thought Elise was worth texting. Elise was normal; she had friends. It might have just been her mom again, but Cee didn't have to know that.

Leave, the text said. It was not from Elise's mom; it was from her friend Carly. Elise was confused. Leave what? Leave the harvest? She did not want to leave, actually. Her phone chimed again.

*leave yet? lol sorry hit send too soon, i don't want you to leaveeeee but if you did leave then I hope you're having so much fun!!! Carly wrote. Elise replied with a string of emojis and pocketed her phone. She was hungry, and gut-wrenchingly nervous about the first shift, and cold, and had to keep telling herself that she had no reason to think the Mainers already disliked her, but still. She was glad to be on this adventure, and she was gladder still to be on it with Tom.

I am allowed to enjoy things sometimes, Elise heard herself think. She was finding, the older she got, the more she had thoughts that were not entirely catastrophic in nature. She didn't put much stock in them, yet, but it was a pleasant change of pace. She could have so much fun, if she tried. She was going to try.

7

THEY STOPPED AT THE GAS STATION ON THE WAY TO
work; Tom filled the tank and Elise bought a noxious $3 shot of
caffeine and legal chemical uppers, bringing her probable account
balance to $107. She peeled the plastic from the top of the tiny bot-
tle and downed it like hard liquor. It made her instantly thirsty. It
tasted like Dimetapp. Did they still even make Dimetapp? They'd
had a little vial shaped like a dog that Elise's mother would tip
down Elise's throat. She blamed it for her hatred of grape-flavored
candy. Or perhaps it was the reason she was secretly fond of mixing grape juice and vodka—the medicine hadn't tasted good, but
there was something in the way she'd been mothered through
those illnesses, cared for completely.

The jobsite was west of the campground, so they were driving
into an otherworldly sunset: a yellow glow sandwiched between
the darkening land and flat, sturdy clouds, which gave way higher
up to cottony hills, lit from below in all the desperate places light
could reach—gray and pink and painful. When they turned off
Robber's Bluff's main street onto one of the county roads, the sky
turned with them.

Elise had heard about roads like these, mostly in country
songs: straight, flat, and uninhabited. Somehow, though, she
had never quite been able to imagine them the way they really
were. Twenty good miles of nothing but farmland and far-off
houses. Around them, machines rolled over dirt. Industrial-size
sprinklers sprayed water. Airborne particulates hazed the hori-

zon. Overwhelmingly open. Endlessly empty. It was different, somehow, from the farmlands back in Albany, where there were, usually, mountains in the distance. When she thought about all the mouths that needed to be fed in America, it made sense that so much land would be humanless, devoted to growing food. It made sense but had been abstract to the point of mythology. Elise thought of the word *desertification*.

It wouldn't be that long before they needed to gas up again, given the long drive to the work site and Tom's old car. She had enough, for sure, for another full tank—maybe even two. She had $107. For sure she did. For sure, for sure. But what if something else happened before payday? How much money, exactly, was in Elise's bank account right now? She was afraid to check. Always afraid to check.

"They all seem cool," Tom said, snapping Elise out of her spiral. He was talking about the Mainers. She nodded. A black sedan appeared in the rearview; Ash's car.

"Uh-huh. Okay. Do you think it's weird that . . ." Elise faltered, wanting to get the question exactly right. She wanted to know if he had also noticed that most of the workampers were white. Not all of them; Eric was Korean, and Jai was Black. She'd seen a couple of people at the mission who looked Indigenous, a few who appeared to be Latinx. But not many, and Elise wanted to know if she had been wrong—racist—to expect otherwise.

Tom was waiting for her to finish her sentence.

"I just, I don't know. There are a lot of white people here, right?" Elise cringed. That was certainly not the most thoughtful way to put it.

Tom hummed.

"You're not wrong," he said, adding nothing else.

"Do you think it's racist that I even noticed?" Elise asked.

Tom snorted.

"No," he said. "For all we know, the town tells their corporate daddy not to send any brown people their way."

Elise and Tom talked about politics a lot; gleeful, sardonic incredulousness over conservative talking points. Elise liked that Tom listened, and considered, and agreed when she talked about the ways she was materially affected by sexism and homophobia. She liked that he was open with his experiences being raised as a man, and told her how men talked about women when there were no women around. It gave her insights that were sometimes painful but always validating.

"As a dude, you grow up thinking that, like, you only cry on the worst fucking day of your life. So when chicks cry, we're like, 'Oh my god. *This* is the worst fucking day of her life? She's crying because I was *in a bad mood*? She's so dramatic,'" he'd told her once. It made her glad that Tom had cried in front of her before. It felt good to be loved by a man who could cry.

Tom also did a very good impression of George Bush. Sometimes, out of nowhere, like if he was washing his face while she was peeing, he would say "BOTSWANA!" and she would giggle and he would look at her, grinning the way he did whenever he made her laugh. Knowing that making her laugh made him happy would, in turn, make Elise feel blessed beyond reason. Did Elise love Tom, or did she love how Tom made her feel? Was there a difference?

"I think I've heard of Dan's band," Tom said, redirecting the conversation after a moment of silence. "And I think I haven't heard great things."

"Oh really?" Elise scrunched her nose, then chastised herself for her reaction. Elise had never told Tom, but she was actually a little bit embarrassed of *his* band, Pane. She didn't really know what made good or bad hardcore, but it certainly seemed like Pane was in the latter category. Of course she still went to see his band play, standing by the bar so she could avoid the mosh pit and drink her way through the noise. She always told him, afterwards, how good he'd done. She liked dating a musician, thought he looked hot onstage; she did feel a little bit hurt that in five years Tom had written several songs about his friends, about his high school breakup, and about getting laid, but none about Elise.

"You've heard them?"

The closer they got to the site, the lower and lower the sky seemed, until it was like they could have scraped the top of the car against it.

"No, just from people telling me," Tom said. "'Cause they're kinda doing what we're doing. Synth-y."

To be clear, Elise thought that Tom was an excellent musician, but this band, for whatever reason, through whatever confluence of creative differences between him and his bandmates—blew. Elise did, however, envy Tom's commitment to his band; even more, his ability to not see all the painfully obvious ways Pane sucked. Elise couldn't find anything good in anything she did, and was committed to nothing, and couldn't even make *bad* art. She didn't have the right to judge. Maybe Pane was actually destined for greatness and she was just too uncultured to see it.

If Elise actually believed that, she would have to spend much more time anxiously fantasizing about Tom leaving her for a groupie.

"You should listen to it before you decide it's bad."

"No," Tom said. "You can't make me."

"Maybe I'll listen to them," Elise said, a joke. Elise sometimes wondered if Tom secretly wished she were a true fan, instead of a fan by proxy. Elise was always trying to identify the wedge that would drive them apart: something that had been there all along, a current that had been dragging them in separate directions ever since they got together.

"What's that?" Elise pointed to the field on their right, where a statue stood in the middle of an acre of nothing. "Is that a Big Boy?"

It was. She didn't even know how she recognized it, some American genetic memory: the chubby-cheeked kid in red-checkered overalls holding a hamburger over his head with one hand. Standing in the middle of a seemingly abandoned field, one of the few tracts of land not tilled and irrigated and pummeled into agricultural submission. They hadn't even passed a house in miles. The Big Boy's eyes were slanted downward to the right, and Elise had to convince herself that the eyes were not actually lit from within, were not casting a weird blue glow on the ground they looked at.

"That's . . . weird," Tom said as the Big Boy receded from view.

"Maybe a restaurant used to be there? Or someone who owns that land is just a big fan, I guess," Elise offered.

"Or he walked there from downtown," Tom suggested. "Got tired of the ol' hustle and bustle of the city, got himself a place in the country."

"Looking for a home in the heart of the country," Elise sang.

More miles, more fields, until they passed a metal sign announcing ELDRITCH.

"At least we have a nice commute," Elise said as they turned onto a gravel road.

"I mean, not really," Tom said. "In an hour it'll just be dark."

"Oh right," Elise said, forgetting that a usual shift started at eight, not six thirty. For the rest of the harvest, it'd be dark before they even started the drive.

8

A MAN WAS WAITING FOR THEM, STANDING OUTSIDE A white clapboard building that could have passed for a tiny house. Hands in the pockets of his Levi's, amiable smile on his face. He was tall but stood with a forward stoop. White hair, white skin, red flannel shirt—he could have been a healthy sixty-five or an unfortunate forty-five. A blue port-a-potty stood beside a set of metal stairs leading to the door.

"Hi, folks," he said. "You made it!"

Elise forced a smile to match his. Behind them, the sound of tires on gravel; the three waited in silence for Ash, Ryan, Eric, Dan, and Jai to park and get out.

"Hi, folks," the man said, again. "You made it!"

"There should be another couple people arriving here in a minute," Ryan said. "They were right behind us."

"Alrighty," Jeff said. "That's no problem. I'm Jeff, by the by. I'll be your foreman here at Eldritch."

Stray locks of Elise's hair lashed her in the face. She tried to contain them by redoing her ponytail but it was a losing battle.

"Is it windy enough for ya?"

An uneasy, polite chuckle from the group. Jeff's smile didn't falter. He dripped sincerity. Maybe even more than Mike. He and his wife were retirees who lived out of their RV, traveling to seasonal work to supplement their pensions. Elise tried to imagine Jeff's wife: plump in an apron, same smile as her husband, fond of game shows and *My Name Is Earl*. There was nothing wrong with the portrait Elise's mind had drawn for Jeff's wife. Elise liked game shows, too. But her instincts, always, leaned toward patronizing caricatures of "simple country folk." They were not instincts she was proud of, proved wrong more often than right. She wanted to be rid of them but did not know how to do that except for berating herself whenever they made themselves known.

"So, are we ready to pile some beets?"

Elise wondered if Jeff imagined his crew putting all their hands palm-down into the middle of the huddle like a football team. But he seemed just as happy at the halfhearted nodding and single "Sure" he got.

"Let's go on inside and get your PPE and I'll show ya how to clock in."

The scalehouse hosted a coffee urn and watercooler, a card table with metal folding chairs, and a filing cabinet covered in OSHA posters and numbered lists of protocols and two printed-out pictures of overturned trucks, beets spilling out around them, each with years (*2004* and *2008*, the years Elise started, then graduated high school) written in Sharpie. An old-fashioned time clock was affixed to the wall. There was also a tall table and a stool set up underneath the far window, where a computer and small gray printer sat at an angle. A white girl was sitting on the stool, smiling as she slowly rotated in half-circles. A South Asian girl wearing a green hard hat sat in a folding chair in the opposite corner, picking at her fingernails. She did not look up at their group entrance.

"Hi," the smiling girl said. A thick textbook sat on its side next to the computer, spine exposed: PESTS & DISEASES.

"That's Sydney," Jeff said. "Her job is to record the trucks coming and going, their weights and whatnot. Farmers get paid by the pound. And by sugar content, which is why we take samples. More importantly, she's responsible for keeping the coffee fresh."

"I'll sure do my best," Sydney said. She was wearing a University of Minnesota sweatshirt.

"And that's—oh shoot—wait"—Jeff was staring at the corner girl, rubbing his hand over his lips. She blinked up at him. She had a scorpion tattooed on her cheek. She was very pretty. "Don't tell me, don't tell me. Jessica, is it?"

"Close enough," she said. Instead of saying what the right answer was, she turned her head and tapped the side of her hard hat, where she had written BLESS UP in block letters. It took Elise a second to realize this was her name and not a life motto. Jeff snapped his fingers.

"That's right, yep, I'm sorry," Jeff said, then turned back to the larger group. "I promise I'll get your names. Just might take a while."

Elise guessed that Bless Up was the other, heretofore absent, piler operator. Elise hadn't seen her at the Robber's Bluff campsite, but there were other campsites scattered throughout the region. There'd be no way to accommodate all the workampers in one town park.

Jeff, digging through a large metal cabinet, handed out hard hats and safety vests and yellow gloves, keeping up a monologue about the importance of keeping track of your PPE and how to go about replacing lost PPE (cost of replacement PPE would come out of their paycheck), and how they'd also be getting a padlock that'd be their padlock to keep track of for locking out the piler during cleaning (cost of losing a lock would come out of their paycheck). This monologue was close to over when Sam and Cee finally arrived, Cee laughing as she opened the door, cheeks red and eyes bright. Sam was smiling, too, both hands dug into the front pockets of their Levi's. Jeff poked his head out from the open door of the cabinet.

"Ope! You made it!"

"Sorry, we got a little turned around," Cee said.

The route to Eldritch from the campground had a total of three turns. Maybe they'd pulled over for a quickie. Elise wondered if she thought about sex a normal or abnormal amount. She remembered Cee's fist around her ponytail, a tickle at the base of her neck. Her envy, for the first time, was directed toward Sam.

"That's fine, not to worry," Jeff said. "Although, if you're late three times during the harvest, you'll be asked to go home. So try to be on time for your shifts."

Finally, everyone had everything they needed: time cards, hard hats and gloves, and padlocks with zip ties attaching the key to the lock so that they weren't constantly losing one or the other.

"Looking good," Jeff said. "Well, seems to me like we can go on out to the pilers if we want. What do you say?"

It was just like the "ready to pile some beets" question—Elise couldn't tell what reaction Jeff hoped to get, but he seemed pleased with their lukewarm agreement.

It was easy to forget about the wind inside the scalehouse— outside, it was hard to think of anything else. The hard hat refused to sit properly on Elise's head; whenever she tried fiddling with the rubber band that adjusted the fit, it was too loose or too tight.

The pilers sat idling in the near distance: machines whose shapes were still impenetrably abstract. Beyond them, lumpy walls of the beets that had already been piled during the brief preseason harvest. Everything smelled like soil and starch. Everything was hit by the wind.

Elise glanced over her shoulder at Bless Up, trailing purposefully behind the group. She wished she had Bless Up's boots:

beaten-up but sturdy, with thick treads. Elise's feet were already aching in the cheap old boots she'd bought along with her cheap red ski jacket at Goodwill. They were supposed to be snow boots but they felt thin and were half a size too small, cramping her toes. *What did I expect? They're used, and not even brand-name to begin with. Waste of money.* She should have accepted her parents' offer of new boots as an early birthday gift. She'd said no because cash made a better gift. Cash, a.k.a. rent money. Whenever Elise thought about money, her heart rate increased. $107 in her bank account. She had the sudden urge to grab Tom's hand in both of hers, pull him back toward her, as though they were walking toward their doom and this was her last chance to save them, by convincing him to turn around. Let everyone else move forward while they stayed in place, forever only knowing exactly what they currently knew about each other and only seeing exactly what they currently saw in each other.

It was a weird impulse and she shook it off. The gales hitting her face made her eyes water.

Up close, the piler looked like the Loch Ness Monster: a dinosaur with a long neck and wing-like flippers. The flippers, one on either side of the machine, were metal platforms whose sides lay flat when a truck was driving up beside the piler, then lifted to form a container into which the trucks vomited their beets. The neck was a conveyer belt that carried and jostled the beets up to a thinner, mobile conveyor belt that shot the beets into the pile. The pile of beets would freeze over the winter, the northern cold doing the job better than an acre of walk-ins could, preserving the beets until they could be processed.

Jeff led the group to the front of the piler, pointing out the operator box at the top of a metal staircase, an electrical panel protruding from the side of the main conveyer belt, and another staircase leading to something he called "the dirt box," which they'd have to clean nightly; when that happened, they had to lock down the piler's power switch so that it couldn't be turned on when there was someone working on or in the machine. Jeff made them practice locking out the piler with their padlocks. Everyone's lock had to be on the switch. If you weren't there to put your padlock on the switch, you might be on or in the machine. Elise did not think that Salt of the Earth Sugar cared if one of their employees was eaten by the machine, they just didn't want to get sued. And a dead body in the piler would hold things up for a while.

Jeff demonstrated the right buttons to push for sample-taking and activating the conveyer belt that would return the dirt shaken off the beets into the bed of the trucks, because Salt of the Earth Sugar wasn't paying for dirt. As Jeff said the words "return the dirt," Elise heard, in her head, another voice saying *Return the dirt*. It was not Elise's voice. It sounded almost like a chorus: many different voices coming together in perfect pitch and harmony to disguise itself as a single voice. Elise shook her head as though she could toss the voice out through her ears.

It wasn't the first time Elise felt like there was someone else's voice in her head. There was a reason the girls in online eating disorder communities talked about how Ana "told them" not to eat, or Mia "told them" they had to get rid of every bite. This voice wasn't the same, but the sensation was familiar.

". . . the most important thing is that when the trucks are loading their beets, stay away from them," Jeff said. "You wouldn't want to be too close if they tip over. Now, I need two people trained to be relief operators, too. Anyone?"

Eric and Cee raised their hands, and Jeff led Tom and Bless Up and the two volunteers up the ladder into the piler box, directing everyone else to go back to the scalehouse and stay warm until the trucks started coming.

"'Cause right at eight we're starting for real," Jeff promised. "Sound good?"

Judging by the response from the workers on the ground, it sounded terrible. This didn't bother Jeff, who was walking backwards up the stairs so he could continue talking to the group. The wind carried his words away; Elise strained to hear him. Craning her neck, she had to hold her hard hat in place.

"People think this job is easy, and it is, but you can't take it for granted. You can't be letting your guard down. I been doing this a decade. I've seen a lot. You'd be surprised. A lot of people don't make it. They don't get their bonus. And then there's the people who go, you know, they don't know what they've gotten themselves into and they're not up to the task. I hope you folk prove me wrong, but in my mind, I'm thinking, more than one of you won't make it to the end of the harvest."

Elise's gut twisted. She told it to calm down.

"Sometimes it seems like the beets just swallow—"

Jeff turned his head, then, to check his footing as he reached the platform, rendering his last words unintelligible. Jeff wasn't saying what Elise's mind told her he was saying. Elise stole a glance around her, trying to find someone else who was thinking what she was thinking: Did he mean that more than one of them was going to quit, or that more than one of them was going to die?

9

WITH TOM AND BLESS UP IN THE PILER OPERATOR boxes, the remaining crew were left to divvy themselves up between the two machines. Elise felt, keenly, her role as outsider as the Mainers grouped off together according to preexisting preferences. Ash was the boom operator, meaning that he monitored the smaller conveyer belts that shot the beets into their piles. He also got to drive the skidsteer, a sporty little go-kart with monster truck tires and a big hydraulic shovel that could scoop beets out of the way. Cee and Sam migrated to Bless Up's piler, followed by Dan and Jack; Jai and Ryan paired off, leaving Elise and Eric to work the left side of Tom's piler. It was a vaguely last-one-picked-for-the-kickball-team situation, though Elise recognized it was worse for Eric, who was here, ostensibly, with his friends.

Elise was disproportionately nervous, given how low the stakes were. Eric, certainly, seemed amused at her keyed-up energy.

"Even if you mess something up, which you won't, who cares?" he asked. "You don't owe these people anything."

But Elise, to her great shame, felt that she did. They were paying her, weren't they? It was not very cool and punk and flannel of Elise to feel indebted to a corporation. All that safety talk and training wasn't for her own good. It was so Salt of the Earth Sugar didn't have to pay workers' comp or worry about litigation. Elise knew that. But she also saw the way her parents shamed people who didn't "work hard," had picked up through osmosis if not direct indoctrination the belief that job performance was moral performance.

At eight, the first trucks turned off the dark road, headlights like monstrous eyes. Elise let Eric take the lead. The driver leaned out the window, passing down a white slip of paper. Eric studied it, scribbled the piler number on it, and handed it back. Then he came to stand beside Elise. They watched, interested because it was new, as the truck's bed began to lift. The world got louder when the beets began to drop into the piler; thirty seconds later, it got louder still as the beets avalanched from the conveyor belt into a funnel feeding them onto the boom. It was too loud to talk over. The boom rotated slowly from the left to the right and back, evenly distributing the beets on the pile.

When the truck was empty and the bed went back down, Eric walked out in front of the truck, waving it forward until the bed lined up with the short conveyor belt that would return the dirt; Eric motioned for the driver to stop by holding up his fist. Elise pressed the *dirt return* button. A wave of dirt shot smoothly from the conveyer into the bed. The voice spoke in her head again: *Return the dirt.* Debris fell onto her hard hat, small plinks she heard but didn't feel. Eric waved the truck off and another truck rolled into place. There was a line of trucks waiting. Already, it was too busy to worry about the voice.

The job did prove to be unfuckupable. Taking a sample, the most complicated part, consisted of putting a piece of paper into a transparent pocket on a thick, sturdy vinyl sack, fitting the sack around a chute, waiting for a light to turn on and pressing a button. A metal shovel would clang against the chute, vibrating into Elise's arms, then the beets tumbled down into the sack. Elise was a body chosen solely for its ability to eternally repeat the same actions with little to no thought. There was something painful about how the weight of the beets yanked the sack downward through her clutched fingers, but it wasn't a lasting pain and in fact might have only been the feeling of anticipating pain without the pain ever actually coming. The sacks were hard to close; one had to manually cinch the top and wind a thin yellow strap around it, tugging until the snap lined up to lock it into place.

The trucks hemorrhaged beets, stray bulbs bouncing off the piler, littering the concrete. Some beets stayed intact, others exploded under truck tires, got crushed when Tom lowered the platform walls to admit a new truck. When they could, they'd clean up around the piler, shoveling beets onto the conveyor belt. They had to move fast, there was always a line of trucks. Elise's arms hurt by the end of the first hour.

It was work, laborious and banal. So far, she'd made $12. Minus taxes. She'd paid off about one-quarter of the motel room. In five hours, she'd have paid off the whole thing. Two days and she'd be halfway to paying off her lowest credit card balance. A single weekend could almost net her share of a month's rent. Maybe she could even splurge—Doc Martens, or a new tent or tattoo, or maybe tickets to Governors Ball. She could buy Tom a hand-tooled customized guitar strap, a Christmas gift she'd always wanted to get him but could never afford.

Even in her imagination, frivolous spending turned knobs that responsible, conservative fiscal allocation could never reach. She'd promised herself that every cent from this would go toward getting out of debt and starting to save: for going back to school and/or the new apartment Tom wanted for them. She was afraid of her future self breaking that promise, could see herself in a couple of months no better off than she'd been before the harvest, surrounded by useless *stuff* that only served to distance her further and further from the person she needed to be. Maybe this influx of cash would only expedite Tom's understanding of Elise as someone incapable of planning for the future, hers *or* theirs. He'd know how much she'd made, and he'd watch every cent carried away by roaches, and he'd give up on her. He'd leave.

"You okay?" Eric yelled to Elise from where he stood, holding down the dirt return button. She was standing there, vacantly rubbing her neck with her dirty gloved hand and taking quick shallow breaths. She probably looked insane.

"Just overwhelmed by all my dreams coming true," she said as a sheet of dirt flew from the piler into the bed of the truck. Soil clinked against her hard hat. Her feet hurt. "I feel like a Kennedy."

Eric chuckled. They waited for the next truck to pull in front of them.

"So, what's your vibe?" Eric asked. "What're you into?"

It could be hard for Elise to think of things she was "into." It felt, sometimes, like the world was an amorphous blob of tolerable and intolerable things. Elise understood this as a symptom of her depression. If Elise stared at any one of the beets on the ground for too long, the harsh lights would play tricks with her eyes and the beet would start to throb and pulse. Elise used to think that about beets, if they were on her plate at dinner: to keep from eating them, she saw their red juices as blood, pictured them beating like hearts. She'd forgotten about that.

The effect went away when Elise blinked. These beets weren't edible, anyway; not in their current form. They were a different breed from the beets that came in cans.

"I like reading? I kind of like sci-fi, mysteries, stuff like that. And, um, worrying. I really like worrying," Elise tried. Eric offered her a conciliatory smile. She wasn't impressing him. She really wanted to impress him, give him the answer that would make her seem cool and punk or whatever. "My vibe is kind of like . . . doing shrooms in the woods. But also, sometimes, in the suburbs, but in the kinds of suburbs where, like, there's no sidewalks. You know what I mean?"

Eric nodded like she'd given the right answer. "The first time I ever did acid, my girlfriend put her purse on the ground and I was like, 'What the fuck. Why is the ground so good at holding things?'"

"You weren't wrong," Elise said. She stomped her foot in its too-tight boot on the pavement. "Look at that. Didn't go through even an inch."

A truck rolled up. Eric took the ticket from the driver; they didn't need to take a sample so he came back to Elise's side.

"How about you? What are you into?" Elise asked.

Eric had his answer right away. "I do a lot of shit. Right now I'm working at the Portland Bike Project," he said.

"Oh, that's cool," Elise said. "I love my bike."

Actually, she had not been terribly successful at translating her upstate wide-street comfort to Brooklyn's lawless shoulder-width bike lanes. She'd meant to save money on subway fare by riding her bike to work every day, but . . . fuck. Eric didn't need to know that.

"Oh yeah? What kind of bike you got?" Eric didn't give her a chance to answer, which was good because Elise did not know what kind of bike she had. It was a tall thin one with stickers over the branding on the bar thing under the seat. "I'm gonna use my money from this to buy this beautiful seventies Masi Gran Criterium. It's a sexy-ass steed, brazed top tube guides, new stem and skewers. A dream, I'm telling you."

"Wow, cool," Elise said. "I love vintage stuff."

It was a dumb response, and betrayed Elise's ignorance of bicycles in a way simply saying "Hell yeah, sounds great" wouldn't have. She stepped away as the truck in front of them lowered its bed so she could wave it around and return the dirt. *Return the dirt* played in her head again, piped in as though through an ancient transistor radio, broadcasting its sad and lonely message across the bleak concrete wasteland that was Elise's brain. Thoughts like that made Elise admire her self-loathing. It could be so creative.

Eric leaned in to yell something in her ear. She couldn't make it out over the thunder of beets dropping into the chute.

"What?" she yelled back.

"I'm taking a break," Eric said. "Then you can take yours."

That was fun, that Eric had decided on their break schedule all on his own. It was orientation, a four-hour shift; Elise didn't really feel like she needed a break. But whatever. She wasn't going to completely cave to her inner bootlicker. Elise kicked at a sugar beet, hitting it with the side of her foot the way she'd been taught to kick a soccer ball. She was garbage at soccer. At all sports, actually. She knew this because her parents had forced her to try all of them at one point or another. Part of an eternal quest to make Elise lose weight and gain friends. Shocking that routinely being the reason the team lost did not help Elise accomplish either goal.

While Eric was gone, Elise tried to make eye contact with the drivers, wanted to express some sort of camaraderie, but they were all aloof and cranky. She wondered how much they were making.

Struck, suddenly, by the knowledge that she'd be doing *this*, every night for *twelve hours*, for the next *three weeks*, that she'd *chosen* this, that she'd invested money in *doing* this, that she couldn't back out now, Elise turned her face up toward where Tom was working the controls in the operator box. She couldn't see him, blocked out by the lights and the dust and, somehow, the noise. Could he see her, though? She wanted, so badly, for him to notice her anguish, to come down and hug her and say, *We'll get through this together.*

Except they wouldn't, because he was up in the machine and she was down on the ground. She had to get through this alone.

10

THE SCALEHOUSE HAD NO SPLENDA AVAILABLE FOR THE coffee. Of course it didn't. There was only Salt of the Earth sugar.

It had been a very long time since Elise had real sugar in her coffee. Her mother carried packets of Splenda in her purse for situations where it wasn't available. Elise knew that, to all the people who didn't have to settle for the stuff, fake sugar tasted weird. But to her, sugar beet sugar tasted weird. Someday, the ugly, lumpy beets in the piles outside would be sugar in someone else's coffee, but not before some complicated human interference. Boiling, probably. Was the sugar a separate thing from the beet? Was a beet still a beet when broken down into its simplest starch? Elise was not a philosophy student anymore. She did not need to think about that shit.

"Going good out there?" Jeff asked, smiling as he sat at the table. His walkie-talkie stood silent beside his hand. Sydney was leaning out the window to talk to one of the truckers. A little radio with a wire antenna piped out a commercial for FarmersOnly.com. The jingle went: "You don't have to be lonely, at Farmers-Only-dot-com."

"Yup," Elise said, lingering a moment in case Jeff had anything else to say to her. He just nodded and looked down at the table, smiling, tapping his foot on the ground as though the radio were playing music instead of commercials. Elise had to fight the wind to get the door open.

She sat in the backseat of the car so she could stretch out a little, and kicked her boots half off: her toes uncurled, throbbing as feeling returned. Could she keep this up? Would she need to buy new boots? How much could she afford to spend—$20? $40 max— that would bring her account to $67. Doc Martens would be cool, though, after the harvest. Just a little treat for all her hard work. She really would do the right thing with the rest of the money. She could tell Tom she found them at Goodwill. Gotten lucky. But when had Elise ever been so lucky? Except, of course, that was only a story Elise told herself about herself. Elise had always been lucky. She'd never been poor, only broke. She'd never gone hungry except on purpose. Just because Tom was loaded didn't make Elise underprivileged. She was college-educated, and able-bodied, and white, and still couldn't get her fucking life together.

Elise had watched her red-collar parents slowly move from the working class to the middle class over the course of her life, and her understanding of how they did that revolved chiefly around not living on credit. They were also civil servants. And in unions. And had gotten their liberal arts degrees basically for free. At any rate, Elise had not inherited her parents' understanding of living within one's means. She had inherited, instead, an inviolable sense that living outside of one's means was a reprehensible personality flaw and that debt was something only idiots with no self-control accrued. Her parents had no idea what Elise's financial situation was, and she would die to keep it that way. She felt guilty for wasting the upward mobility they had worked for her to have. Tom literally invested the money he had to spare, taking tips from his dad on which actual fucking NASDAQ-ass stocks to put money in. Or ETFs, or mutual funds, or whatever it was that Tom talked about on the phone the first Sunday of the month. He told Elise he did this to appease his parents, and Elise did not challenge him on it. She did not say that investing in Wall Street was not punk, because Elise spent her spare change buying expensive sustainable toilet paper and compostable trash bags and basically any T-shirt that made her tits look good, and Tom never said that was stupid.

Sometimes Elise convinced herself that everything would be fine if she could just go back on her antidepressants. The generics made her intolerably ill, and her marketplace insurance would only really be worth anything if she got cancer or something. It certainly didn't cover the name-brand pills. Or even seeing a psychiatrist who'd prescribe them. When she'd first gone on them, junior year of college, it was like the world turned right side up. Even her reckless spending slowed down. When she had to get off them, the summer they moved to Brooklyn, the summer when Elise nearly drove Tom away for good, the withdrawals made her suicidal. Now, she operated at what felt like the lowest possible vibration, everything but bare minimum out of her reach. It was all she could do to keep her neurosis in check, get herself to work, stave off the anhedonia with external pleasures she couldn't afford.

Elise's break was up. Or it wasn't, because they hadn't decided how long breaks should be, but Elise decided it was up because she was bored and cold and thinking too much, feeling sorry for herself. She took a swig of coffee that had already gone cold because Elise's thermos was from the dollar store; undissolved sugar crunched between her teeth. A younger version of Elise had stopped herself from putting sugar in her coffee by imagining it was salt. If she tried hard enough, she could even taste it.

11

THERE WAS A LOT OF NIGHT LEFT WHEN THEY WERE cut loose. Everyone was considerably dirtier clocking out than they had been clocking in, but morale seemed high. Jeff, in a show of midwestern hospitality, gifted them a thirty-rack of Milwaukee's Best—to enjoy, he said, just as long as it didn't make them late the next night.

While they'd been working, the campground had filled up. They sat around the picnic table outside the Mainers' RV, drinking Jeff's gifted beer. Dogs approached their group, accepted affection, then drifted away. Arin held court outside his Jeep, drawing attention with the impressive timbre of his voice; a crowd outside one of the RVs included a guy playing something doleful on an accordion. Aya and Chet's friends had arrived, part of the larger group of train kids, all dreadlocks and high-laced boots and handkerchiefs.

"Just be careful about your stuff when you're not around. They're known to steal shit," Ryan said about the train kids. Elise thought that this was kind of rude—though likely true.

She held her beer in fingers beginning to freeze. She warmed them, kind of, with a cigarette. Elise sat down next to Cee on the picnic bench.

"Can I borrow one of those?" Cee asked. Elise proffered the pack. Elise already knew that she would give Cee anything she asked for.

"I think we're gonna run out of beer," Elise said. It was the first thing that popped into her head. It probably made her sound like she was worried about running out of beer, when she'd meant it only as a kind of half-humorous observation on the size of their group.

But Cee lifted her eyebrows and nodded vigorously. "Totally," she said. "Wanna make a run to get more? With me?"

"Oh, yeah, okay," Elise said.

"Cool," Cee grinned. "Let's go. I feel like walking."

Elise regretted offering herself up as companion for this chore—she was lazy and it was cold and she felt it would somehow be colder once they left the campground. But her excitement at feeling chosen by Cee outweighed the remorse. Elise and Tom's entire courtship had revolved around leaving parties together for beer runs, so the activity took on unnecessary romantic weight. Sam had gone to the bathroom, but Cee didn't seem to care that she was leaving without telling her partner. It really wasn't such a big deal. Sam was probably cooler than Elise.

They had to fight the wind on the uphill trek to town, dust blowing into Elise's eyes and blowing Cee's snapback off her head.

"Leave it, leave it!" Cee yelled when Elise turned back to chase it down—they watched as it disappeared into the night. It wasn't worth talking until they were on higher ground, walking the few blocks between the park entrance and the gas station.

"Fuck, it's cold," Elise said.

"This time tomorrow we'll still be at work," Cee mused.

"Yeah, but you'll be all sheltered and warm in your little operator box," she said. She hoped she didn't sound bitter about it. She wasn't. Why had she said anything at all?

"Oh, you mean my throne room," Cee said. "I feel like the queen of the fucking beets up there."

Elise thought that if anyone deserved to be the Beet Queen, it was Cee. She had a crush on Cee, didn't she? Shit. Having a crush was so embarrassing.

The gas station looked warm and inviting, a fluorescent cube illuming their horizon. Bells chimed overhead when they entered; underneath the country music playing, the slushy machine turned and the heat lamps crackled over rolling racks of hot dogs (151 calories). The fridges at the gas station ran all the time. Lights, too. Elise thought about how much energy was spent keeping cold drinks cold just in case someone might want one. The ambient noise of convenience, industrial-strength fridges across the country each contributing their own little hum. She'd read about how artificial lights at night killed bugs, less food for bats. More confused birds flying into windows. Noise pollution made it harder for owls to hunt and frogs to mate. Sometimes the things Elise knew about the world stacked too high and she had to stop thinking.

They settled on a thirty-rack of Genesee Cream Ale, mutually delighted in finding it so far from home. After driving a hard bargain with her mental image of her bank account, Elise offered to pay. Tom would have rolled his eyes and asked her why when they had "no money"—but there was no reason he ever had to know. After paying for the beer, she should still have, like, $83 in her account. Enough for another full tank of gas before payday, which was almost two weeks away.

There were three other people waiting to check out—surprising, given the late hour and the small population. She was glad. It gave her and Cee more time indoors before having to go back out into the cold. More time to talk, too. Though they weren't talking, actually. They were standing in silence as a man sang about taking a woman fishing on a date.

"Maybe don't involve live worms on your romantic outing,"

Elise said. "Though I guess that's just what a city girl like me would say."

"What?" Cee said, looking at something over Elise's shoulder. Elise was never going to tell a joke ever again.

"Nothing. Never mind," she said. "So, you gonna do anything cool with your harvest money?" Elise wasn't sure if that was a polite or proper question to ask. According to her parents' old-fashioned mores, talking about money was tacky. But then, of course, she knew that "talking about money is rude" was a classist norm. Cee didn't seem to mind.

"Well, I want to get my sleeve finished," Cee shrugged out of one side of her jacket, held her arm out and rolled up her sleeve, giving Elise the opportunity to study the tattoo on her forearm. Koi fish conjoined and curled around her wrist among the outline of rippling water; above them, on a shoreline among some reeds, a turtle basked, its head outstretched, almost reaching her elbow. It was impressive. And hot.

"I love that," Elise said. "Who's the artist? Maybe if I ever end up near Portland—"

Elise could never afford to go anywhere. She hoped Cee didn't think Elise was inviting herself to visit after they'd only known each other for ten hours. Elise wished that she could be the Beet Queen. The Beet Queen probably didn't worry over every word that left her mouth.

"I'll get you their handle." The line shuffled forward. "Jesus Christ, this is taking forever."

Cee was scowling. It hadn't seemed like that long to Elise. The cashier appeared to be a centenarian, a slight smile on her face as she chatted with the customers—locals, obviously. *I'm boring and Cee doesn't want to stand in line with me*, Elise decided.

"I've got a really dumb tramp stamp," Elise said. She was deeply embarrassed about the shitty dolphin tattoo on her lower back, but it always did the trick in terms of conversation. Cee's mouth opened and her eyes widened with delight. A payday loans commercial took over for the country music.

"You have to show me, what is it?"

"A dolphin. Not here," Elise said. Her brain conjured up the words *muffin top*. "Later."

"Holding you to that," Cee said. "What about you? I mean, with your harvest money?"

"Um." Elise thought about what she wanted to tell Cee. Tom had wanted to put their paychecks toward moving out of their shitty studio; the upside of living above a pizza parlor was not having to pay delivery fees for pizza, but the downside was that they had to coat every corner of the apartment with borax to keep out roaches. Elise had agreed that would be a good idea but she had not committed to it. She couldn't commit to it because she knew her harvest money had to go toward her credit card debt, and she hadn't told Tom because that would involve telling him about the debt in the first place.

Elise's credit card debt was from stupid bullshit: too many rounds at the bar that didn't card, too many concert tickets and camping trips, too many supplements that promised to finally make her all healthy and good, too many trips to Walmart, too many ringer tees. Elise hated her nineteen-year-old self, that little voice inside her that *still* said things like, *If you just pay the minimum this month, you can get that bus ticket home for Julie's birthday*, apparently still unaware that, considering the interest rate, paying the minimum was like paying nothing at all.

"Probably just, like, living," Elise finally said. "You know how it is. Rent and student loans."

"New York's expensive as fuck," Cee nodded, leaning down to pick up the beer and slide it onto the counter.

Elise brandished her debit card. Even when she definitely had enough money in her account, like now, she always found herself praying for mercy while swiping. A moment later, the machine bleated at her.

"Sorry, hon," the cashier said.

Elise first felt cold, then started burning up. She must have been wrong in her calculations. She must not have had $107. She must have had less than $107. How much less? How could she have been *that* off in her calculations? Was it the credit card payment? She'd budgeted for that—she'd budgeted for it! She had, she honestly fucking had.

"Try it again," Cee said, making uncomfortable eye contact with the cashier. "Machine's probably broken."

That probably wasn't it at all. Elise had probably done something wrong because she was always, always, always doing something wrong. If Tom were here, instead of Cee—

Elise swiped again, knowing it was a waste of time. The machine beeped, a short slip of receipt paper spat out on the register. Elise's stomach clenched, a sharp lump rolling up her throat.

"So weird," Cee said. "Let's see if mine goes through."

Elise stepped back, away. She stared at her card. There was a mistake, obviously. She just had to call and ask. It would be fine. It would be totally fine. $107. Cee smiled at her as though nothing had just happened, as though it had been the plan all along for Cee to pay. Elise pinched the bridge of her nose, her head throbbing, heartbeat erratic. This was so embarrassing. So scary. So annoying. So stupid. The country music singer was singing about dirt.

"Call your bank," Cee said. "They probably just need to verify it's you because, like, you're halfway across the country. It's happened to me a ton."

Elise reached for the beer, thinking that it wasn't fair for Cee to carry it since she paid for it.

"I'm good," Cee said. "I lift, bro."

Of course she did. Elise hadn't worked out since college. A flash of hateful jealousy split through her. Elise followed Cee out the door, dialing the number on the back of her card. With the wind, she had to press her phone to her ear so hard it hurt. An automated voice urged her, again and again, to seek out help from the bank's website instead of suffering through the hold music. Her fingers numbed around the phone—she switched it from hand to hand, warming the free hand in her pocket until she couldn't bear it and had to switch.

Finally, someone came on the line and, after verifying her identity, told her that she'd been charged $175 by the Lapeer Motor Inn.

"That can't be right," she said, thinking there must be a receipt somewhere in the car that showed she'd paid $45 the night they checked in. She tried to tell the customer service rep as much, but was told that she ought to call the motel, in that case, to verify the charge. Elise asked if she could dispute the charge—and the rep said that if she was confident the charge was fraudulent, they'd be happy to open an investigation. It could take up to sixty days, in that case, to get her money back. Elise asked how quickly they would process a refund if the motel refunded her. That, the representative said, could take five to seven business days—and there'd be no reimbursement for the overdraft fee, she was afraid. Elise ended the call without taking the optional customer support survey, though she knew it wasn't the representative's fault that the bank's policies were so cruel.

"Yikes," Cee said. "That didn't sound good." They were back at the hill, this time headed down.

"This fucking stupid-ass motel overcharged me!" Elise said. "Like, way way *way* more than they were supposed to. So now I'm overdrafted and it's, like, fully fucked."

"That sucks," Cee said. "But you'll be okay! You made it here, right? And you've got Tom. Stop scratching like that, it's just gonna make it worse."

Elise hadn't realized she'd been scratching her neck. She didn't know what Cee meant by making it worse. But that didn't matter. Fucking Tom. Now, he'd know she didn't have as much as she'd implied she had when they started this whole thing. She should have had enough to cover a surprise $175 bill. She should have had more than the bare minimum.

She would not tell him. She would simply not tell him. He would never know.

"Here," Cee said, stopping and turning toward Elise. She put the beer on the ground, ripped open the top of the case, and handed one over. "You can worry about it in the morning. Just chill. You'll call the motel and straighten it out. You're too pretty to be upset over money."

Elise took the beer with numb hands, poured it down her dry throat. They could see, now, a huge fire going in the center of the campground. That was just a nice thing Cee had said, right? She didn't mean it. Not really. God, Elise wanted Cee to have meant it. Elise would never have the guts to tell a pretty girl she was pretty like that. How was Cee so much better than Elise? How was that fair?

"Can you do me a favor?" Did it sound like Elise was about to ask for money? She hoped not. Cee just smiled and nodded. "Can you not mention this to, like, Tom, or whatever?"

"Why would I?" Cee said, cocking her head now. Elise didn't know why Cee would, she only knew that she needed Cee not to. "Secret's safe with me. But let's gooooo! They might have marshmallows."

Elise finished the beer in three greedy gulps. Cee was right; Elise couldn't do anything about the money that night. She'd have to wait—and in the meantime, she might as well let it go. She reached for another beer. Marshmallows had gelatin in them. They weren't vegetarian. If Cee were a man, Elise might have teased him for not knowing. Elise flirted with men by bullying them; she didn't know how to flirt with women.

The campground's disparate groups had come together around the bonfire. Sitting on stumps and lawn chairs and blankets and haunches, dogs weaving between conversations like furry exclamation points, the fire cracking and popping in the center. Tom was sitting between Ryan and Dan, talking about music.

It would be fine. She'd figure out it, get the money back into her account before Tom ever even guessed that something was up. She would do better for him. She would pay off her credit cards and start saving for school, the new apartment, the dog, all of it. She would take him up on his offer to help her "get into investing" so that they could build the future she knew he wanted: one where they lived independent of his family's money. She would start fresh when they got back to Brooklyn, only shop at dollar stores, no more organic apples, stop ordering takeout, cancel Netflix and Hulu, quit smoking. Maybe Tom would never ask her what she did with her harvest money. Maybe Tom would love her no matter what.

She passed him a beer over his shoulder, leaned down to kiss his cheek. Because she was tipsy from chugging two beers, the kiss felt heavy with meaning. Then she saw Cee watching from across the fire, and it felt light as air.

12

BAMBI AND MURPH WERE PASSING ONE OF THE WORMY puppies back and forth between them. Bambi had a neckful of ink, Murph had a split tongue, and they had traveled together from Seattle by freight train, waylaid briefly in Missoula when Murph was picked up on an outstanding warrant for spanging, forcing the girls to miss a ride with a friend who didn't have a phone. The girls were going to New Orleans next. The worst part of riding trains was the cold. It could get so, so cold. You could freeze to death, easy. Plus, people got beat up all the time. "Fuckers will steal your shit."

It was hard to imagine anything Elise could say about her own life that would be interesting for the train kids to hear, but Cee was good at keeping the conversation going—an easy, natural, charismatic conversational partner. Elise was careful with her questions, since asking too many or the wrong sort would mean that Elise was an uncultured normie who didn't even know what spanging was.

At some point Bambi and Murph angled themselves toward a guy whose name might have been Alien. He was using a flashlight to illuminate his face from below, punctuating the end of the campfire story he'd been telling. Elise only heard the last line: "That spring, they pulled a dozen bodies from the beet pile." The people listening laughed.

Empties were piling up all around everybody everywhere. Elise brought out the bottle of gin and she and Cee passed it back and forth, making puckered faces and coughing between chugs.

They were drinking like teenagers. It was fun. Cee told Elise to tip her head back, and poured gin into Elise's mouth. Too much, but Elise didn't mind. Cee was so hot and cool and she acted like she liked Elise and wanted to be Elise's friend. Elise didn't have to be jealous of Cee because Elise was cool, too. Sam had long since gone to bed, leaving with an exaggerated eye roll when Cee tried to get them to sit in her lap. Elise had some song stuck in her head, kept singing the chorus loudly and off-key, and Cee not only found this funny but also found the song on Spotify and played it. They were annoying everyone, but Elise was too drunk to notice or care.

"Isn't there supposed to be a river around here?" Elise asked when the night felt like it was circling around to an ending.

Someone whose name Elise couldn't remember pointed toward the dark distance, across the grassy field where some bushes obscured the view. Elise stood on shaky legs to go find it, and Cee went with her. Elise heard someone express concern, perhaps to Tom, that someone should go with them, drunk as they were, but no one followed and they set off in the dark with their phone flashlights guiding the way. They found a section of brush that had been cleared, a small wooden dock hanging over the edge of a thin and slowish body of water. In the dark, the water looked like nothing, a black space mimicking the sound of water lapping at shoreline.

"You and Tom been together for a while?" Cee asked when they were sitting at the end of the dock. She pulled two cans of beer from the kangaroo pocket of her oversized hoodie, handing one to Elise.

"Five years," Elise said. She was a little embarrassed at how quickly the number came to mind; counting anniversaries felt kind of basic. Like each completed year of coupledom earned them participation trophies.

"How'd you meet?"

"Dude, you're like, very cool, you know that?" Elise said, not meaning to evade the question but unwilling to let Cee feel that Elise wasn't appreciating how easy this was turning out to be. "You're just really nice to talk to. I'm, like, I just do not have people skills."

"What?" Cee laughed. "I think you're cool. You just have this"—Cee gestured around Elise's body as though she were making a chalk outline—"vibe."

"How about you and Sam?"

"Only about a year," Cee said. "For real, though, how'd you guys meet? Tell me a love story."

Elise was drunk enough to feel uncharacteristically generous with her personal history. "We met in class. Philosophy department was really small so everyone knew everyone. Four years of student loans and he's all I got to show for it."

"Fuck college," Cee said. "Like, for real."

A companionable silence filled the space between them, until Elise dipped her head back.

"Oh," she said. "The stars!"

Cee didn't seem impressed; Elise excused herself with New York City. Even in Albany, you had to do some driving to get a good view. Cee shook her beer, indicating its emptiness. Elise poured some of what was left of hers into Cee's.

"I don't know about me and Sam," Cee said. "I don't know."

"I didn't think we'd stay together this long. Not at first," Elise said, because that was a normal thing to say, a vague vote of confidence in the face of doubt.

What if Sam and Cee broke up during the harvest, and then Cee confessed her love for Elise and they drove off to the *other* Portland together and immediately found a huge group of friends who adored them and adopted two big dogs and one tiny one and spent the rest of their lives attached at the lips? When they died, the laminated cards handed out at the funeral would be a photo of them kissing, Elise's palm cupping Cee's cheek. That would be so cute.

"But do you feel like you and Tom are gonna make it?"

Elise heard something in Cee's voice, a desire for the love story. She wanted to give Cee what she wanted.

"I don't know why things would change," Elise said. "I love him. We love each other. We've talked about marriage. A little."

Their talks about marriage had been fraught, not romantic. Elise wanted marriage. Tom didn't explicitly not want marriage, but he didn't think highly of it as an institution, and had a tendency to roll his eyes when Elise suggested it as a possibility for their own future. Elise did agree that marriage was a conceptually bankrupt institution. State-sponsored monogamy. A series of rules regarding private property codified under the auspices of love.

Elise didn't know why she wanted marriage as much as she did. She probably didn't want children; she would never take a man's last name; divorce existed, so it wasn't like being married actually meant the other person would stay. She wasn't in it for Tom's money, because she would marry Tom even if he gave all the money in his trust fund to Food Not Bombs. At least she thought she would. Maybe she wouldn't. Maybe she was a gold digger, after all, and Tom didn't want to marry her because he could smell it on her, a sixth sense wound around in his blue-blood DNA.

"That sounds like a relief," Cee sighed. "No more looking."

"Yeah," Elise said, thinking about the motel, how he hadn't wanted to stay, her bank account in the red. If they did marry, and then did divorce, chances are that Tom would walk away with less than he came in with while Elise walked away with more. A bad deal for him. His parents would be pissed. "Tom's great. He knows more about music than, like, anyone I've ever met. And we just feel the same way about the shit that matters. I don't have to convince him to fucking recycle or whatever. And he's really talented. I mean, his band is whatever but he's talented. He's not weird about me being bi. Some guys are. I love him. I really fucking do."

She really fucking did. Talking about it made her want to go back to the bonfire, crawl into his lap, nuzzle his neck and be held. She did love him; he was good. Kind to others, and kind to her. His heart always in the right place. He told Elise she was pretty and smart. When they watched a movie together, he always had interesting things to say afterwards. He once told Elise that she was funnier than him, which she denied but secretly believed to be true, but more importantly was something a man had never said to her before. Tom had offered to pay for her antidepressants when she had to stop taking them, and he didn't press the issue when she refused, both important. He grabbed her ass in public in a way that told Elise he was not ashamed to be seen with her, perhaps even proud of it. Given the opportunity to nurture and care, he would.

But then, she'd also just casually mentioned being bi to Cee. Was it obvious? Desperate?

Cee was quiet. Had Elise brought the mood down? Fuck.

"What do you like about Sam?" Elise asked.

To her relief, Cee laughed.

"They're quiet and gentle and kind," she said. "And I haven't had a lot of that in my life."

"Yeah. I get that," Elise sighed, closing her eyes against the parade of people she shouldn't have fucked. Tom could be quieter, gentler. He had a temper, was prone to hitting inanimate objects that weren't working. He was impatient, visibly frustrated by every line he ever stood in. He'd crash at a friend's overnight without texting Elise to let her know, then just show up the next morning hungover with a bacon-egg-and-cheese only for himself. He wasn't perfect. He was good enough, though. Elise wasn't sure that the same could be said for herself. "Sometimes the best thing about someone is who they aren't."

She realized, after she said it, how sad a statement that was. But it still felt true. The water was black, and the stars were only impressive because Elise was used to seeing so few of them.

13

ELISE WOKE UP WITH A THIRST LIKE SHE WAS A RUS-
sian doll and each of the selves inside her needed their own gallon
of water to recover. She did not remember returning to the bonfire
after the river. She did not remember going to bed. She didn't see
the gin bottle anywhere; it seemed impossible that they'd drunk it
all, but maybe they had? Tom slept beside her; Elise guessed it was
early morning, before nine. Hangovers and insomnia were sister
cities in Elise's personal geography.

Immediately: panic. The money. The motel. Not telling Tom.
She had no money. He'd find out. Her credit card payment, due in
three days. What was going to happen now? Something bad? Was
something bad going to happen? Something bad was already happening! Something bad was always happening! Elise curled onto
her side, clenched one hand into a fist and hit herself in the side of
the head—not hard, just enough to shake her brain a little bit—
until the anxiety blurred down to a manageable level.

It would be okay. Maybe she'd get her money back from the
motel. Maybe the bank would be on her side. Payday was in twelve
days. The food was free. She had a carton of cigarettes. She'd be
too busy working to go anywhere, spend anything, anyway. If they
had to gas up at some point, she'd pretend she'd left her wallet
at home, she'd tell Tom that she'd just get him back on the trip
home. Or she could just fucking tell him, instead of lying. Maybe
it would be good to know, actually, how Tom would react. If he'd

give her shit over it, or if he'd just sympathize with how shitty it was. If he'd carry her, or let her fall.

She drank the last few inches from the Gatorade bottle she'd filled with the campsite's potable water the day before; it wasn't enough but the thirst was preferable to the prospect of navigating outside to refill it. Her phone was on the charger, which was good. She had, apparently, downloaded the latest season of *Pretty Little Liars*, which was pretty ingenious of drunk Elise. Giving sober Elise something to watch during breaks. She was surprised the campground's shitty Wi-Fi had been enough for the entire season. She hoped she had not told Cee that she liked *Pretty Little Liars*. It was not a cool edgy punk show. It was a show for teenagers.

She had a new email notification. The subject line read "Thanks for Staying at Lapeer Motor Inn!" and had a PDF attachment. A flash of memory came back to her: talking to someone, middle of the night, a slurring argument over whether Elise had made a call using the phone in the motel room. Elise remembered saying "No one does that anymore!" and someone, maybe Cee, laughing in her other ear. Elise went back to her calls list, but there were no outgoing calls from the night before. Maybe she'd used Cee's phone? But why? Had she even been coherent enough to give whoever she'd talked to her email address? She must have, because here it was: an email.

She opened the receipt attachment, which showed an inflated total for her stay. There was a "phone call" charge for $143. The second page of the PDF was a phone log, a single call made at 10:17 p.m., lasting until 12:32 a.m. The number was not familiar. Of course it wasn't—she hadn't made any calls. The area code didn't match any area code that had ever been relevant to her. She googled the area code and was shocked to see that it was for Ananite

County, Minnesota. Home to Robber's Bluff itself. Elise was scratching her neck. She stopped.

It still didn't make sense. Unless Elise had sleep-called someone. Was that possible? No. This was a mistake. The motel's mistake. Elise hadn't done anything wrong. All she'd done was check a message that wasn't even for her. She'd call as soon as she could handle doing more than lying in bed. Call the motel. Sober, this time. Also, call her mom. First she needed to sleep off the hangover and fortify herself for a twelve-hour shift. Fuck.

She was scratching her neck again. It didn't even feel itchy; she was just doing it. Her fingers came away damp, a clear, not-quite-oily serum that her first instinct was to smell. She refrained. She felt grimy. Maybe she would feel better after a shower.

Elise could hear, through the canvas, a lively day occurring on the other side. Chatter, banjo, dogs barking. She could hear someone laughing—her first instinct was maniacally egotistical: *laughing at me?*

Elise attracted little attention as she climbed out of the camper, towel over her shoulder. It was a guy named Pete who was playing the banjo. He and his girlfriend were in one of the silver Airstream trailers. Arin was outside his truck, holding an almost empty bottle of the same gin Elise had bought in Canada. Whatever. He was talking to one of the train kids Elise hadn't met, a girl in an oversized parka who stood hunched over and clutching herself tight, either in pain or against the cold, while Arin's dog sniffed her feet.

The campground bathroom was no worse than any institutional bathroom she'd ever been in, and significantly better than some dive bar bathrooms. Three stalls with functioning doors on one side of the room, a shower with a vinyl curtain on the other. In the bathroom stall, above the toilet paper dispenser, someone had written *I <3 infanticide*. On the back of the bathroom door, someone had written *solo blumpkin*.

In the dirty mirror, Elise's reflection frowned. Elise had a rash on her neck; it was what she'd been scratching. A significant portion of the side of her neck was red and puffy, small blistery bumps stretched from her neck to just under the collar of her shirt.

As a teen, she'd had eczema: summers spent scratching herself raw, the backs of her knees always either oozing or crisp with scabs, her armpits, open wounds, stinging from compulsory shaving and deodorant, her nipples sporadically breaking out in flakes, all of it a horror. But this seemed more like a bug bite than eczema. Either way, it was terribly unattractive. She leaned over the sink for a better look. Pulled gently at the skin. Underneath the red bumps, there appeared to be a bruise.

Did the camper perhaps have bedbugs? Or the motel? Some kind of mold, or allergies? She'd have to look it up. Elise patted her face with cold water. Cold water trickled down her shirt, making her shiver.

Trying the shower before undressing, Elise contorted herself around the angle of the faucet and stretched her arm as far as she could to keep from getting caught in the stream. The pressure sucked but the water ran hot. All that separated her nude and vulnerable body from other women who might see her was a flimsy, near-clear, mildew-spotted sheet. Not that anyone would want to ogle her. As a child, after watching *The Truman Show*, she was terrified that there were cameras in her bedroom, some way that everyone could watch her change and laugh at her fat body— disgusted. Quick costume changes in a communal dressing room were the most dreadful part of her high school drama club career even before she'd caught the director peeping—a memory that always struck her with a surprising stab in the gut, an overdramatic reaction to something she was pretty sure hadn't been that big of a deal. He hadn't, like, touched her.

Whatever relief Elise felt after showering was considerably diminished when she put on the same dirty clothes she'd been wearing before. Outside, the wind had picked up and it was cold; she jogged back to Burt, thinking of how her mother always told her going outside in the cold with wet hair would get her sick. The last thing she needed. She'd already forgotten about looking up the rash. She lay down beside Tom and continued to feel sick and bad and shitty until she fell asleep and dreamed about having to autopsy a pile of dead dogs even though she kept telling the people in charge that they hadn't taught her how to autopsy dogs in school.

"You're a vet tech," the people in charge in the dream kept saying, staring at her as though annoyed. "You have to do this or we'll take away all your money." Dream Elise had already spent all her money; she was panicked and confused and scared of the dead dogs piled up in the corner, how it just got bigger each time she looked at it.

"You got the pillow all wet," Tom said, shaking her awake sometime later. "What's wrong with your neck?"

14

TOM AND ELISE WERE ALREADY SEATED IN THE MISsion with their plates full—in Elise's case, full of boiled carrots and iceberg lettuce—when the Mainers entered in a gust of dead leaves. Elise's stomach dropped: now she'd have to interact with Cee, deal with the ramifications of being so drunk that she couldn't remember what dumb, awful things she must have said. How deeply she'd embarrassed herself. What if she'd tried to *kiss* her? It didn't have to be that intense, either—what if Elise had just been weird? She probably had been. She stared down at her plate and acted like she didn't even notice the Mainers were in the room until they'd taken seats at the table and she couldn't pretend anymore.

Cee took the seat beside Elise. Her arm brushed Elise's arm as she put her tray down. Elise, feeling like she might burst into tears from the tension, pretended she was listening to Tom so intently that she didn't even realize Cee was sitting next to her.

"Fuck," Cee said. "I'm so hungover, I wish I was dead."

She made a gun with her fingers and mimed shooting herself in the head. Elise laughed, loosening all over.

"Totally," Elise said. "Big same."

"Did you sleep all day? I couldn't."

"Oh, yeah, kinda. It was lucky, I never—"

"So jealous. At least I got to play with the puppies, though."

"Those puppies have worms," Elise blurted. "And possibly internal bleeding."

"I know, it's sad," Cee said. "They're still cute, though."

"So cute," Elise said. Why had she said that thing about the worms? What was wrong with her? That wasn't a good thing to say to someone. It wasn't normal or cool at all.

"Oh, by the way"—Cee leaned across Elise to talk to Tom—"Sam and I are going to Walmart tomorrow morning. After work. If you wanna come and get something for the zipper?"

Elise's gut twisted. When did Tom and Cee discuss Burt's zipper? Why was Cee only asking Tom? Elise knew she had to be cool; she had to be cool. Cee already had a partner. And Cee might not even like men. Elise was the one who'd spent the whole drunken night talking to Cee; she was the one who'd walked off into the darkness, alone, with Cee. Not Tom.

"Sick," Tom said. Then he turned to Elise, a smirk on his face that Elise recognized. She preemptively rolled her eyes. "Too bad Elise can't go. She's banned."

"Banned? From Walmart?" Cee asked. "What does that even mean? How would that even work?"

"It doesn't mean anything," Elise said. "He's kidding. I can go to Walmart."

Except should Elise go? What if she went and Tom asked her to pay for whatever he was getting to fix Burt? How often did she think she could get away with leaving her wallet at home? And if Elise insisted on going, would it make her look crazy? Like she needed to keep tabs on Tom? Elise's feet throbbed in her too-tight boots. A memory of unlocking Tom's phone while he was in the shower forced itself into her head. She scratched at her neck.

"Just as long as we enter five minutes apart," Tom went on. "You're not dragging me down with you, Pancho."

"Elise, is he serious?" Cee's eyes gleamed in amusement.

Elise felt like she'd say absolutely anything to keep that brightness on her.

"I got into some trouble in college," she said. "I got caught shoplifting."

"Twice," Tom said, holding up two fingers.

Elise grabbed his outstretched hand, pushed it away. Touching Tom felt like nothing sometimes. It was like grabbing her own hand. Elise only noticed because of how sharply she'd felt the brush of Cee's arm against hers. This was, of course, only natural. Very normal. Absolutely fine.

"Oh, you're a bad girl," Cee said. Her eyes darted over Elise's head, meeting Tom's. "No wonder you like her so much."

Cee winked at Tom. Elise's gaze met Sam's. She noted how they stiffened and scowled. Elise drew backward, struck by the feeling that she was looking into a mirror.

15

THE ELDRITCH NIGHT SHIFT CREW DECIDED TO CAR-
pool to work, taking two cars instead of three through the dark,
flat country. Ryan, who had long legs, sat in the front next to Tom,
while Cee, Sam, and Elise squeezed into the backseat. Sam sat in
the middle—perhaps by accident, perhaps by design.

A constant haze hung over the fields: dust, water vapor, pesticides. From inside the fog, yellow beams of light stared forward
from tractors or reapers or threshers or whatever machines were
churning across the horizon.

"Don't they look like will-o'-the-wisps?" Elise asked, pointing
out her window.

"That reminds me," Cee said, not answering the question. Elise
wondered if it had been a stupid question. "I heard that we're actually
far enough north that you can see the northern lights sometimes."

"That'd be cool," Elise said, not believing it—not because she
knew enough about the northern lights to say whether they'd be
visible from Minnesota, but because it seemed too good to be true.
This work was too hard, the experience too shitty, to be worth
anything but the paycheck at the end of it.

There was the Big Boy in his field, his eyes vacantly glowing blue.

Sam pointed to him, arm outstretched in front of Elise's nose.

"My husband," they said. Elise laughed and Sam smiled at her
and Elise thought maybe she and Sam could be friends even if
Elise had a crush on Sam's girlfriend.

The gravel parking lot was much fuller than it had been the

night before; the day crew, who worked 8 a.m. to 8 p.m., were waiting for the night crew to take their places. Elise did not know if she imagined the look she got from the guy at the piler who handed her the shovel he'd been holding.

"Keep 'er clean for us," he told her, which she thought might be a joke except his tone was firm, even a little suspicious.

"Sure," she said, smiling. He was probably just exhausted. The men ambled off together toward the scalehouse to clock out. A truck pulled in and the night started, loud and cold and idiotic.

It was their first real shift; the first time they were looking down the long barrel of night. Elise was still vaguely hungover. The ground got messier and messier with each truck. She would try to clear the ground of beet guts and mud before the next truck pulled in, but it was a losing battle. However, the bursts of work did serve to temporarily warm her body. Unfortunately, her boots' treads were so worn down that she was always slipping on the beet guts, nearly busting her ass on the cement. She could no longer feel her toes, whether from the cold or from the boots being half a size too small, she wasn't sure.

"When I get back, I'm gonna have a whole keg of beer waiting for me," Eric said. "I'm brewing it myself."

"Nice. I like beer," Elise offered. "Well, I like light beer. I don't really get how people like, *like* beer—hoppy stuff or stouts? What kinds of beer do you make?"

"You need to have a palate for bitterness," Eric said. "It doesn't come naturally to everyone."

"It just seems like, you can't even really get drunk off that heavy stuff because you can't have more than two. So why put yourself through the trouble? I mean, I'm saying for me. Obviously I get that some people like it. But I don't even like coffee, really. Or dark chocolate."

"You have to train yourself not to expect everything to instantly please you. Then you can learn to savor bitterness as its own experience," Eric said. He walked off to *return the dirt*. Elise wondered if she was allowed to be offended by Eric talking down to her like that. Elise's toes ached, curled tight like snail shells.

"Fuck, that was obnoxious, wasn't it?" Eric said when he returned to her side. "Sorry. I'm working on it. I just get nervous sometimes, around new people. And I don't know. I'm an asshole. It's like, I know I'm being an asshole. I can see myself being an asshole. But I can't stop it. It's a defense mechanism. I'm working on it."

"That's okay," Elise said. "I get it. I'm kind of the opposite. I'll just, like, agree with anything. 'Whatever it is, you're right! You know more than me!' Even if it's literally the only thing in the whole world that I'm totally certain about, I'll just let the other person think they're right. But I'm not working on it. No self-improvement for me. I plan on being exactly this terrible for the rest of my life."

They smiled at each other, perhaps the first genuine smile they'd shared. Elise felt like she could be friends with Eric. The question, of course, wasn't if Elise would like Eric; it was if Eric would like Elise. No matter how many years there were between the current Elise and the teenage Elise who'd had a ham sandwich pressed into her face by some popular kids, it still felt like most people *de facto* hated Elise. Which required its own brand of mental gymnastics to explain how, ever since high school, people rarely behaved as though they hated Elise. She even had friends. Elise herself had never felt compelled to spend her precious few years of youth and beauty with people she hated; either everyone who was nice to her was beatifically sacrificing their own comfort out of pity for her, or Elise was not intolerable. But perhaps the only thing keeping her tolerable was the knowledge of her own intolerability, without which she would evolve into mecha-Elise, an unbridled and monstrous beast of a woman, the missing link between humans as they currently existed and a new, doomed generation of people who were too unlovable to breed with each other. Elise: the beginning of the end of mankind, which was quite the honor to bestow upon herself. Maybe someday she would be in history textbooks: the worst person to never actually do anything that bad.

Ash scooted over in the skidsteer and got out to help Eric load the beet-filled sample bags into the shovel. Elise hefted a new pile of empty bags onto the machine. Ash lingered after they were done.

"They're ordering us pizzas," Ash said. "Jeff and them. They were like, 'How many pepperoni? How many meat lovers?' or whatever, so I said they needed to make sure they got a vegetarian pizza for you."

That was a very nice thing for Ash to do. She smiled at him.

"And Jeff goes, 'Vegetarian pizza? Now, that's about the most boring thing I can think of.'" Ash's fake midwestern accent was thick for comedy but also not terribly far from the real thing.

"The man lives in Minnesota," Elise snarked. "It's impossible for 'vegetarian pizza' to be the most boring thing he can think of."

She added, to no one, "No offense." She did feel bad laughing at Jeff; he hadn't done anything wrong. Buying pizza was a nice thing to do. Minnesota was fine. *Just look at it*, Elise told herself. She gave the flat, dark, featureless expanse a chance to impress her. All it did was make her think: This was the place where she was, and this was the job she was doing, and this was the body she was doing it in, and this was the only world she'd ever know, and this was the only life she'd ever have.

Which was not an unimpressive thing for a landscape to do.

16

ELISE FORCED HERSELF TO WAIT UNTIL HER SECOND break before eating. Saving lunch gave her something to look forward to, and also she would have a more equal distribution of energy throughout the night. Their breaks were as long as they wanted them to be, and they could take as many as they wanted. It was a one-person job. She and Eric could just trade off standing by the piler and sitting in the car all night long. One was not terribly better than the other.

She kept herself occupied watching *Pretty Little Liars* on her phone. The four protagonists were drinking while the secret antagonist called "A" dug up the grave of the liars' dead best friend and attempted to frame the gay liar. The liars' alibi was that they'd spent the night at the rich liar's family's lake house. All the liars were rich, but that one was super rich. That was part of the appeal of the show: living comfortably made for more interesting problems than being late for work because you had to retrace your steps from the subway to your apartment because you'd lost your unlimited monthly MetroCard on the eighth day of the month.

Now on her second break, Elise reached up to the front passenger seat, where she'd left her brown-bagged lunch. She'd investigated the pizza in the scalehouse and found it unworthy of its 235 calories: flat, chalky dough with a too-sweet sauce, black olives and raw green peppers and cheese that was mozzarella in name only. Jeff wasn't there, or she'd have had to take a slice just to prove she was grateful. She unwrapped layers of plastic wrap from the sandwich nestled in between an apple (95) and a banana (105) and a pair of granola bars (132). She put the banana back in the bag. She had not eaten bananas since she first imagined that when she was unpeeling one, she was actually tearing the flesh off her own finger, starting at the cuticle and ripping down to the knuckle. A potent starvation tactic.

The sandwich was almost entirely hoagie roll (260). She only knew there was peanut butter (188) on it because there was peanut butter on the plastic wrap. She took a bite. Gagged. Her first thought was that they'd used some sort of savory jelly—or perhaps the peanut butter was rancid? But when she peeled back the bread she found slices of American cheese (104) topping the thin layer of gummy peanut butter. This was what Mission Mike thought vegetarians ate: peanut butter and American cheese sandwiches.

The peanut butter, while barely there at all, could not be removed without compromising the integrity of the bread. The American cheese could be removed, but its flavor lingered. Now it tasted like the ghost of a peanut butter sandwich that contained within it the ghost of an American cheese sandwich. Elise hated American cheese. Not just the too-sweet chemical taste, but also the wastefulness of those individually wrapped slices.

She picked her way around the bread like a child, crumbs littering her lap. She would act grateful the next night, and the night after, when Mike handed over identical sandwiches with his jovial grace. She would not mention that peanut butter and American cheese did not belong together in a sandwich. She made a mental note to look up, back at camp, whether peanut butter and American cheese were a legit combo in the Midwest. She needed to look up the rash on her neck. That was more important. She needed to call the motel. That was most important.

There was a pamphlet on the floor. Elise picked it up, fighting a delusional paranoia: this pamphlet might somehow reveal Tom's secret life and secret girlfriend, someone he loved way more than he'd ever loved Elise. The pamphlet did not reveal anything. It was called *You Are a Sugar Beet* and the cover was an illustration of an unreasonably happy white family: mom and dad and big brother smiled down at little sister as she held a pile of white powder in her cupped hands. It was meant to be sugar, but it could have passed for other, equally profitable white powders. *You will become more resilient as you grow, but there are dangers yet: you may succumb to rhizomania, root madness. If you are infected, you will be compelled to grow thin, hairy, dead roots that can't draw water. Your leaves will shrivel and yellow while your sugar content, the very reason for your existence, plummets to near-useless levels. You will experience a living death, and then you will die.*

Ew. Elise couldn't watch another episode of *Pretty Little Liars*; if she watched one episode per break, she'd be done with the season by the end of the week, and the campground Wi-Fi was way too weak to download anything else.

She played some music, flicked through her photo album, watched an old video of Tom interviewing her in bed on Thanksgiving morning: "What are you thankful for?" "Slenderman hentai." The way they laughed, it must have had more context than she could now recall. In the video, she took the phone back and pointed it at Tom: "What are you thankful for?" They looked so young, but the video was only a couple years old. The crack in her phone screen ran right between them. Tom said "Worms" and the video ended. He had a point. Worms were very important. No worms, no soil, no farming, no sugar beets, no sugar beet harvest money.

When her boring hour was up, she shoved her poor toes into the boots and rolled out of the car, brushing stale hoagie crumbs off her jacket into the wind.

Tom took his break then, Eric taking over the piler for a while, leaving Elise on her own again. She could hear laughter from the other side of the piler, where Jai and Jack were working. She collected samples. She *returned the dirt*. She went to wipe her brow and hit her hard hat instead.

By one o'clock, Elise's muscles were tight and aching from clenching close to her body. She thought about the specifics of this pain. Run a stuck jar lid under hot water so the atoms expand and it loosens. In the cold, everything contracts. She'd known it would be cold but, like thinking about being ill when you are well, had been unable to truly conceptualize how it would feel to be *so* cold. It hurt to shiver.

Elise watched two figures approach from the scalehouse. She recognized one of them sooner than she recognized the other: it was Tom and Cee, walking back from their breaks. Together. They waved to Elise. A flash of memory, Elise texting Tom seven times in five minutes because he wasn't home when he said he'd be. Elise was NOT! jealous about Tom and Cee spending time together on their breaks. She couldn't afford to be. She couldn't afford anything. She had no money. Less than no money. Elise put a hand to her chest, pressed her feet against the ground, braced herself for a sweep of panic. It never came, because Elise was using her other hand to *return the dirt*, and the voice in her head overrode the anxiety. A surreal, addictive relief.

17

THE NIGHT ENDED IN THE MORNING, AS NIGHTS GEN-
erally did. Day shift arrived to take over, and Elise thought about
how it was surreal, somehow, that when she arrived back at the site
in twelve hours, they would still be there.

When Tom came down from the operator box, Elise found she
had nothing to say to him. It seemed that, somehow, he already
knew everything she could have told him about the shift. After
all, he'd been watching from up there. A new chill ran down her
spine at that thought; she was thrown back into her adolescent
bedroom, changing into pajamas while still wrapped in a towel
in case hidden cameras were broadcasting Elise's hideous body to
everyone who hated her.

Tired as she was, it was hard to fall asleep with the brightness
of a cloudless day filtering in through Burt's green canvas walls.
When she finally slept, she woke up so soon it was like blinking.
Elise's head throbbed. Her body ached like a flu. Her lips cracked.
She trudged up the hill to the bathroom to brush her teeth, too
bitter and emotionally blemished to stop and pet the dog that
bounded up to her, wagging its tail. She wasn't sure which dog,
whose dog. Did it matter? It didn't matter. She walked right past
it, then felt guilty about it. Dogs asked for so little.

In the mirror in the bathroom, she examined the rash on
her neck. Red bumps radiated around a thin, milky layer of skin
overlaying a darker discoloration. She touched it. She scratched at

some of the flaking skin and it came off in a neat strip, revealing a bruise underneath.

When she came out of the bathroom, Tom was leaning out the window of his car, waving at her from the bottom of the hill.

"Think of anything you need?" he yelled when she was close enough to hear.

She'd forgotten. Totally fucking forgotten. There was Cee in the seat beside him. Alarm bells rang; she hadn't said she didn't want to go to Walmart with them, had she? She hadn't said anything either way, because they hadn't talked about it after dinner. Plans made without her. Conversations had without her. Going to Walmart without her.

"No," she said, hoping her voice didn't crack. This was good, actually. Would be good, actually. Tom would see how unbothered she was by him going off on some shopping adventure with Cee. Unbothered, naturally, because she trusted him. He'd think: *Wow, I'm so grateful that Elise put all that work into herself so that our relationship could survive. I love her so much.* And Elise couldn't be on the hook for paying for anything if she wasn't there to pay for anything.

"Not even any cough syrup?" Tom asked, that smirk on his face. She really fucking hated him sometimes. But she just leaned in, smiling, refusing to give him even an eye roll of acknowledgment.

"Have fun," she said.

They kissed, perfunctorily, before the car pulled away. Gravel kicked up by the tires slapped into her shins. She waved them off, a gesture that probably went unnoticed. She imagined Tom joking about Elise's lifetime ban. She imagined Cee throwing her head back, neck long, laughing. Elise saw, out of the corner of her eye, Sam standing in the doorway of the RV, arms crossed, eyes puffy.

Before Elise could wave or acknowledge Sam's presence in any way, they'd turned around and gone back inside.

Elise lit a cigarette and sat at the picnic table outside Burt, listened to two train kids outside Arin's truck argue about someone who was, Elise guessed, missing. How could they even tell whether someone was missing when it seemed like being able to go missing at will was half the point of being a train kid? Arin's dog, Cake, bounced over to Elise, forced his head underneath Elise's free hand until she gave in and scratched his ears. Elise liked animals, always had. She wasn't good at science, but she was sure she could handle being a vet tech. That's why it was an option. She had no idea how much vet techs made. More than cashiers, and more than unemployed philosophy majors.

"You don't even fucking know her," one of the train kids said.

"Yeah, but I know you, and I heard what you did to Mason. From Chattanooga? So excuse me if I don't trust you. For all I know, she's running from your controlling ass."

"Oh my fucking god, not this shit again. He cheated on *me*, he gave *me* the clap, suddenly everyone thinks I'm the bad guy?"

Jesus Christ, Elise thought. She welcomed the distraction. Without it, she'd just keep imagining Tom making jokes about her. He wasn't wrong that it was funny that Elise was banned from Walmart for shoplifting Robitussin, twice. That even after being caught the first time, she'd still done it again. It *was* funny, but he didn't have to always make the same stupid jokes at her expense whenever the opportunity presented itself. In truth, that had been a rough time in Elise's life. Her first semester of college, after four years of bullying and two years of alternately starving herself and making herself throw up. The friends she made were just as messed up and confused as she was, self-destructive in ways that bonded them intensely. They'd steal Heineken mini kegs from the supermarket and browse Erowid for ways to get fucked up that didn't require access to a good drug dealer. Robotripping was a dissociative experience that made Elise feel incorporeal and the world seem incomprehensible in a way that couldn't quite be classified as "fun." But when she was robotripping, Elise could be both awkwardly entertained and made distant from her emotional reality of body shame, calorie counting, general anxiety, social anxiety, ambivalent bisexual yearning, upstate ennui, and derogatory self-talk.

The problem with robotripping, which would have been the problem with anything, was that it cost money that no one had. And Elise, desperate for clout and sick to the point of recklessness, volunteered again and again to take the bus to the Walmart and steal as many bottles of Robitussin as she could manage. The first time she was caught was hardly the first time she shoplifted, which was less of a pastime and more of a calculated risk. It didn't give her a rush. If she could get something without paying and she couldn't afford it otherwise, why not? She didn't feel guilty stealing from Walmart. Walmart was a bad company that did bad things, something she knew at seventeen even though she couldn't yet say, specifically, why. How could it possibly be a good thing for one store to be a community's only source of pet food and hammers, hold its only hair salon, be its main employer? She'd worked retail, she'd worked for minimum wage, she'd worked after school and summers for three years and only earned enough to cover part of her first-semester tuition at a state school—never mind paying rent, feeding a child. She knew what people meant when they talked about poverty wages.

Elise recognized, as an adult, that trying to shoplift a second time after being caught once was indicative of something "going on" with her. The second time she was caught was less than two weeks after the first time. Both times, she was escorted back through the sliding doors into the store, marched past the metal bins full of pastel plastic bouncy balls and the end caps of hot plates and picture frames, into the same back office, so cramped and dingy compared to the bright white consumer blare of the showroom. Both times, the cops came. Both times, she was finger-printed and mug-shotted, released immediately with a summons for petty theft because she was a white college girl.

Now, that was just another past self Elise was forced to lug around. Here in Robber's Bluff she was not a nervous college freshman. And maybe the problem with Tom's jokes was that they dragged her backward, forced her to recognize that the stupid freshman who genuinely thought chugging cough syrup was cool was still there, inside her, inextricably linked to who she was and who she was trying to be.

Who had Cee been before? Elise was convinced that it was impossible for any of Cee's past selves to bear a resemblance to her own. She allowed herself a brief fantasy of having been Cee in high school, which only made her feel sick. Elise and Cee were cut from diametrically different cloths; she could just tell. Anyone could. Tom could, couldn't he?

The dog had wormed its way underneath the table, was sitting between her knees, head on her thigh, playing a frustrating, prim-itive game where whenever she went to pet him, he'd rear his head back and around, just to put his head right back on her thigh and look up at her like he was begging to be pet.

18

ASH AND ELISE WERE SITTING AT THE PICNIC TABLE outside the Mainers' RV showing each other memes. Jai was playing a keyboard while Ryan played a ukulele, noodling around with an Animal Collective cover. Sam was sitting under a tree, sketching. Eric was off in the distance, talking on the phone in Korean. Ash tipped his phone to show Elise a picture of a chicken wearing rain boots with the caption "he boot too big for he gotdamn feet." She laughed and showed him a meme of John Lennon walking weirdly with the caption "fuck it. i'm just gonna say it. John Lennon deserved to die for walking like this." Ash showed her a starter-pack meme for "White couple walking down the shoulder of the highway." Elise showed him a meme of Marco Rubio drinking water. They started talking about politics, then Tom's car came down the dirt road. Elise, wanting to look like she was so cool with Tom and Cee spending time alone together, waved. Tom parked beside Burt, opened the driver's side door.

"Elise, c'mere," he yelled, waving.

Cee's head appeared on the other side of the car; Sam followed Elise across the campground.

"I got you something," Tom said when Elise approached. He sounded giddy. He had a limp plastic bag in one hand, a shoebox in the other.

"Hey, babe," Cee said, kissing Sam on the lips and throwing an arm over their shoulder. Did Sam seem relieved, or was Sam normal? Elise was relieved, but she was also still cloyingly paranoid about what Tom and Cee might have talked about or done on their trip to Walmart. She shoved the feelings down and stomped on them.

"Because your boots are so shitty," Tom said, resting the shoe-box on the picnic table and lifting the lid.

"Aww," Elise said, hand to her chest. See? He was rewarding her for being cool. She tipped the top of the box up and gasped. Inside, a pair of neon pink construction boots. So clean and smooth, with thick, dusty pink treads and stiff pink laces. A reward, or was he making up for something? *Stop being crazy*, she yelled at herself.

"I helped pick them out," Cee said. "Aren't they so sick?"

"They've got steel toes, so you can kick the shit out of some beets," Tom said.

Elise wondered how much they cost. Guilt settled like sediment in her heart. Would he have bought her boots if he knew that she was keeping a secret from him? If she just told him, he'd understand. It wasn't her fault. She couldn't tell him. He'd hate her. Ten days, now, until payday. He never had to know. Why couldn't she tell him? What was wrong with her?

"Oh my god," Elise said. Her eyes watered. "These are perfect." She should just tell him. She couldn't.

"So sweet," Cee cooed. And then, when Elise and Tom embraced, she started chanting: "Kiss! Kiss! Kiss!"

So they did, chapped lips against chapped lips, the familiar taste of each other's spit. Elise laid her head under his chin, the stubble he needed to shave scratching her scalp. She loved him. She *loved* him. She loved him enough to lie. She couldn't protect herself from herself, but she could protect him, and she would, for as long as he'd let her.

19

DINNER AT THE MISSION WAS WET SPAGHETTI (221) with runny tomato sauce (70)—or, for Elise, a cold pat of butter that wouldn't melt (102)—and two single-serve packets of Parmesan (15) each.

"Does anyone else feel like trash after they eat lunch?" Jack asked, making Elise blush and look over her shoulder as though Mike might be able to hear from all the way across the bustling room.

"It's the meat," Tom said. "That meat is fucking rancid."

"I feel fine," Cee said.

"Did you get the peanut butter cheese sandwich?" Elise asked. Cee gave her an odd look.

"No," Cee said. "Did you ask for that or something?"

"No! It's gnarly. What did you get?"

"Just peanut butter."

"I'm going to ask for vegetarian lunch," Jai said. "If I eat another of those sandwiches I'll shit myself."

"What kind of meat is it?" Elise asked.

"Probably technically *not* meat," Ryan said. "But I guess you could call it chicken."

"That's what they get," Cee said, in a low voice meant only for Elise. Sam had heard, though, and gave Cee a strange look. Cee didn't notice because Cee was looking at Elise. "I'd take peanut butter and—wait, what kind of cheese?"

"American cheese," Elise said.

"Gross."

Tom got up. When he returned he had two Styrofoam bowls on his tray. He put one in front of Elise. It held a fruit cocktail of some kind: she recognized cherries (25), pineapple (50), something green. All encased in a white fluff.

"Ambrosia," Tom said. "They just put it out."

"You know what this stuff is?" Elise said, silently estimating the calories. She settled on somewhere between 100 and 250, depending on whether the white fluff was low- or full-fat whipped cream (15–60), and whether there were other ingredients: she suspected, perhaps, marshmallow fluff (91). Tom did not know that this was what Elise did with food. As far as Tom knew, Elise's atypical relationship with food began and ended at being a vegetarian. If and when he noticed her occasionally skipping meals, he chalked it up to all women dieting all the time. She knew this was true because he had told her as much, offhandedly, in the way only someone who has never been on a diet could. She had never told Tom about her disordered eating because she had never told anyone, ever. It was Elise's most secret self. She didn't trust herself not to weaponize it, use it to beg for affection he might otherwise not be willing to give. She also didn't trust him to not see it as just more heft to the anchor that she was, always weighing him down: *Now I have to worry about her starving herself, too? Ugh.* Elise put far too much effort into being worthy of his love to risk it.

"Yeah," Tom said. "It's ambrosia."

"What's in it?" Eric asked, leaning across the table to peer into Elise's bowl.

Thus began a conversation about Miracle Whip (50), grandma recipes, and trailer park food. Elise put a spoonful of the stuff in her mouth. It tasted fine, but when she bit down on a cold cherry, pain shot through her jaw. She dropped the spoon, clutched her cheek. The food in her mouth stayed where it was as she processed the pain. There was something deeply uncomfortable about this: an aberration of the eating process, which, to Elise's understanding, was designed to keep you from thinking too much about it as a process at all. Food—external *things*—entered your body and you mushed them up with the help of your own bodily fluids, then the mushed spit bundles went even deeper into your body, where mysterious and uncontrollable things took place. The body breaking the mush down into sugars, proteins, acids, wastes. Turning sugars into fats. Layering the fats under the skin, adipose tissue taking form. All of it happening invisibly, subterfuge, only to express itself in highly visible physical changes.

"You okay?" Cee asked.

Elise nodded. The tooth pain did not feel like regular cold-food sensitivity, or like a brain freeze. She had never felt this pain before. Perhaps it was a cavity. She'd never had a cavity.

Elise did not have dental insurance. Obviously.

She ate the rest of the ambrosia, which tasted good in the sense that it was sweet and creamy, careful to only chew on the right side of her mouth.

On their way out, as they stopped to collect their bagged lunches, Mike's ever-earnest eyes grew troubled when they glanced below her chin. She instinctively covered her neck with her hand. Elise forced herself to smile as brightly as she could: "Thank you *so much*," she said, taking the brown bag with the hand not covering the rash that was continuing to exist, the bruise beneath it deepening and blooming.

Outside, she opened the *V*-marked bag Mike had handed her.

Peeled apart the hoagie roll: peanut butter and American cheese. She looked up, wanting to show Cee, prove that Elise wasn't making it up. But Cee was walking ahead, next to Sam, laughing. Because of course she was, because she was Sam's girlfriend, not Elise's. Elise had a boyfriend. Elise had Tom.

20

TOM LEANED OUT OF THE PILER OPERATOR BOX, WAVing his arms to get their attention. He made a motion with his hands like he was snapping a twig, the sign they made when someone needed a break. Eric left Elise on the ground, and Tom trotted down the steps, zipping up his jacket.

"Fuck, it's cold," he said, approaching her. There was a truck on the other side of the piler now, but none approaching Elise's side.

"No shit," she said. There was a beet next to her foot. There were always beets next to her feet. She went to kick that particular beet toward the pile, but right before her foot made contact the beet started throbbing. Usually that only happened when she was alone. She looked up at Tom. He was looking at the beet, too. But he spoke before she could ask if he also saw the circulatory pulsing.

"Did you hear about the other piler operator?" Tom said.

Elise shook her head. Her lips were chapped; she licked them, a mistake, inviting a new type of cold into her sensory experience. She and Tom stared off in the same direction, watching a truck turn off the highway and approach the scalehouse.

"She disappeared," Tom said. "Like, straight-up gone."

"What?" Elise said. It came out as a laugh for some reason.

"She never came back from her break. And she's nowhere on the site."

The truck pulled away from the scalehouse, onto the paved path leading toward the pilers. This was always a highly anticipatory moment: Would the truck turn toward Elise's piler, or the other one?

"I don't blame her," Elise sighed. The truck turned toward Elise. Now the question would be which side it would come through. "This shit fucking sucks."

"Here's the thing: She doesn't have a car. She gets a ride to the site. But Ash said that, like, no one came to get her, you know?" Tom went on. "Obviously she just walked down the highway or whatever. But it's still weird."

"It's ten times worse down here, too," Elise said, following her own conversational thread. "She didn't know how good she had it up there." Though maybe she did. Maybe she'd been a sample-taking grunt before. Elise knew nothing about Bless Up. She was so tired. She imagined Bless Up typing out an SOS on her phone, waiting for someone to pick her up from the side of the highway. But no one even saw her walking off the site? Elise frowned. Maybe Jeff was off doing whatever site supervisors have to do. Maybe they saw her walk up the gravel drive and assumed she was meeting someone and would come back. Or maybe Bless Up disappeared into thin air, walked straight ahead into the pile of beets and was swallowed alive, who fucking cared, it was so cold.

"You doing okay?" Tom asked, putting an ungloved hand on Elise's puffy coat sleeve.

She kicked a foot out and pointed to her boot, now almost completely caked in grayish muck.

"Look," she said, pouting. "They got all messed up."

"I know," Tom said. "Maybe we can get them cleaned afterwards."

"That'd be a good use of the money," Elise grinned at him.

He kissed her on the cheek. It felt like nothing: his lips stiff from cold, her face numb from it. She tried, with her tongue, to free a shred of apple pulp from between her teeth. The truck crossed the metal platform, the driver's side window rolled down, an anonymous arm already outstretched. Tom and Elise walked together toward the cab, but Tom kept walking when Elise stopped, waving goodbye before disappearing around the other side of the truck.

21

IT WAS ELISE AND ERIC'S FIRST TIME ON DIRT BOX duty. The dirt box filled up over the course of the night, and two people had to go in and scrape the dirt stuck to the walls onto the conveyer belt. Elise's lock hung heavy on her belt loop. The constant weight of it was making her pants loosen around the waist, tugging and tugging all night long. It was a relief, then, to pop it open and onto the scissor lock beside the others when they locked out the piler.

It took five minutes to coordinate this. Cleaning the dirt box took another ten to fifteen minutes, and then there were five more minutes of unlocking the locks. Twenty-five minutes, total, out of the 720 minutes of their shift. They'd already been at work for 425 minutes. Cold wind. Heavy shovelfuls of beets. Aching feet caked in mud and starch. Too much coffee, too much sugar in the coffee. Elise was bitter and raw.

She and Eric each took an oversized spade, climbed the metal staircase up to the machine, and crawled inside.

"Holy shit," Eric said, laughing a stuporous laugh. "This is . . . a lot."

It was the closest Elise had ever been to being in a grave. The walls didn't need to seem like they were closing in on them, because they literally were.

"Hell is a place on earth," Elise said.

The soil breathed wetly into the ambient warmth, the piler running hot like a car engine, the dirt box right at the heart of it.

Almost as soon as they began working, sweat was trickling down Elise's back. Elise had seen pictures of six-foot-long earthworms. That's what Elise felt like, squirming around in the dirt box.

Elise and Eric stood back-to-back and stabbed at the walls. The spades sank into the muck, loosening chunks of dirt that fell crumbly at their feet. Dirt got into Elise's new boots. Elise flashed back to a sensation: the feeling when a nice hefty chunk of food finally exited her body and splashed into the toilet bowl.

This was where the voice came from. Elise realized it with a jolt. *Return the dirt.* This is what said that. The dirt box said it. It wasn't saying it now—it wasn't saying anything, just exhaling silently with its loamy breath. Or perhaps the voice was always speaking, but Elise's earthworm-ears couldn't hear it—could only occasionally hear that one simple command: *Return the dirt.*

Elise was equal parts comforted to have an explanation for the mysterious voice and concerned about the existence of a voice at all. Up until this moment, Elise had held on to the possibility that it wasn't a voice, just her own mind. It would be *more* problematic if it was actually her own mind speaking to itself, as though it were a foreign entity. It was, in fact, crazier when she thought of the voice of her eating disorder as Ana instead of accepting it as her own internal monologue, her own venom burning through her own veins. Veins were a lot like worms.

The area underneath Elise's eyes grew irritated from sweat. She used to get eczema there, flaking red dry skin.

"I think that's good," Eric announced, stilling behind her. His voice in the small, dark space felt like it was disrupting something holy. Elise shook off the instinct to protect the sublime silence of her soil.

Eric and Elise emerged and retrieved their locks, the weight again tugging at Elise's belt loop, and Jeff flipped the switch to turn the piler back on. Tom, from up in the operator box, ran the dirt return, and all the detritus they'd loosened was vomited onto the concrete. Ash scooped it up in the shovel of the skidsteer and scooted it away. The other piler shut down for the same procedure, funneling all the trucks to Elise's piler until the line of beet-filled beds waiting to be dumped reached back to the scalehouse.

The truckers never looked at her when she came to collect their tickets. They, too, had to be exhausted. But they weren't windburned, like she was. And they weren't sore from shoveling, like she was. And they didn't have mud and beet guts forming a second heel under their boots, and they didn't have to listen to a voice telling them to *return the dirt*, and they hadn't had to morph into giant earthworms inside the dirt box. And they weren't so cold that their bodies ached from twining down into tighter and tighter knots in an attempt to conserve their body heat.

All the truckers were men. Impatient men, sticking their arms out the window with their sample tickets, the heat from the cabs radiating just out of reach. They tried so hard not to see her that she thought they'd rather run her over than acknowledge her. She wished one of them fucking would.

22

"WE WERE ON THE HIGHWAY COMING BACK FROM Coachella, I was with half the group in the van and the other half was ahead of us in the Jeep, and suddenly the Jeep swerves off the fucking road and bounces down this embankment and—shit, I really don't even like talking about it." Eric stubbed his cigarette out against the piler, leaving a black streak of ash.

A truck pulled up and Elise took the ticket from the trucker's hand, took the sample ticket back to the sample chute, put the ticket into the clear window on the vinyl bag, fitted the vinyl bag around the chute, waited for the Edison light to light, pushed the button when it lit, tensed against the tumble of beets falling heavy into the vinyl bag, cinched the top of the vinyl bag, looped the vinyl strap around the top of the vinyl bag, snapped the strap in place, and tossed the vinyl bag onto the pile of vinyl bags. Elise pressed the dirt return button and the voice in her head said *Return the dirt*. She turned back to Eric, put on her best Jeff voice.

"Now, that's just about the most boring thing I've ever heard." Eric laughed.

"But the thing is, right, that, like, everyone lived but some of my friends got really fucked up. I just thought, 'They're dead. They're all dead. All my friends just died.'"

"Shit, dude," Elise said. She really wished that had not happened to Eric. If she could, she would have made it not happen. She didn't like thinking of Eric in pain, because Eric was her friend. They stood outside for hours at a time with nothing to do but talk. If they hadn't become friends, they would have had to become enemies.

"So that's my first thought, right? But—and I've never told anyone this before—my tenth thought? Or, you know, whatever, it wasn't my first thought but it was pretty early. My friend Dani, I'd fronted her the money for her ticket. And she was gonna pay me back when she got paid the week after we got back. And it was a lot of money, and I needed it to pay rent. So I'm still convinced that she's dead, they're all dead, but I'm thinking about money and paying rent. I'm thinking that maybe it sucks that she died because then I'd never get the money back."

"But that makes sense, though," Elise said. "That's the point of trauma, right? Your brain isn't making sense. Maybe you just latched onto some stupid problem to not have to deal with the, you know, overwhelming grief."

"Yeah, I mean, I don't hate myself for it or whatever," Eric said. "I just, I don't know. I don't know why that story would make you feel better."

"It's not a feel-good story, bro," Elise said, tilting her lips in an approximation of a smile.

"I think you should tell him," Eric said, shrugging. "It's just money, right? But the anxiety is legit. There's a reason I thought about not being able to pay rent. Tom's a good guy, at least it seems like he's a good guy. He'll understand."

"Maybe," Elise said. She knew Eric was right. Tom wouldn't break up with her if she told him about the motel and the overdraft. He might be upset that Cee, and now Eric, knew before he did. Maybe they'd have to have a hard conversation. But it had to be better than what she was doing now—periodically fighting off anxiety attacks, which is how she wound up unloading the whole story onto Eric. He'd seen her, eyes closed, hand around her neck, panting. Elise didn't know why she was reacting like this. Maybe it was the mortifying thought that she might have to ask her parents for money. She knew how the conversation would go. The disappointment and agitation and some variation of "I told you so." They wouldn't say no, but they'd bring up the last time they loaned her money, for car repairs, back before she moved to Brooklyn.

They were so anxious about her ability to support herself, so confused by her inability to get a good job and save money like they had. Their concerns were never coercive or cruel—just annoying and, in Elise's opinion, based on an idealized world that no longer existed. They'd tried to set her up to get her degree without taking out loans by dutifully depositing half of every paycheck from her part-time jobs into a savings account. Whenever they visited Elise and Tom's apartment and looked in the fridge, they'd gently remind Elise that a world in which she was able to afford organic vegetables on a minimum-wage paycheck was a fantasy world.

Elise had failed, miserably, to learn every lesson, and she hated herself for it. She wanted to be the perfect person for everyone, and she'd never once gotten close. There were too many other fucked-up versions of herself hanging out inside her, no room for the one true and flawless Elise to be born.

"Thanks," Elise said. "For talking it out with me."

"What else are we gonna do out here? Got anything else you wanna unload? Weird fetish? Childhood trauma?"

"Childhood trauma actually is my weird fetish," Elise said. "I'm always begging Tom to tell me about the year he got a Game-Cube instead of a PlayStation for his birthday."

Eric snickered, but Elise knew she shouldn't have made that joke, implying that Tom's life had been charmed. He had his own issues and anxieties, shame and guilt. It seemed, to Elise, like she'd ended up with Tom and not with any of the other people she'd slept with or dated because the friction of their worst selves rubbing up against each other was tolerable. They'd had fights, bad ones, but never actually hurt each other. She'd never told Tom he was a spoiled little rich boy, and Tom had never told Elise that no one liked her. She looked up at the operator box, at the vague shadow of Tom inside it. Eric went to take a sample, Elise positioned herself to *return the dirt*.

"Hey," Eric yelled to her over the sound of the piler piling beets. He pointed with his chin toward the pile. "The moon."

There it was: orange and full, setting over the mountain of beets. Elise's breath caught in her throat. She knew that the moon was a cold gray rock tumbling through cold black space. That did not stop her from lifting her face toward it, eyes closed, expecting some warmth to reach her.

23

ELISE HATED FAST FOOD FOR MANY REASONS: ENVI-
ronmental, political, economic. But the main reason was, of
course, insipidly personal. Because to be seen ordering fast food
was to be judged fat and lazy and stupid. Even in a large group, she
felt singled out, like she was back in high school, caught standing
in front of the vending machine. *Cough TrimSpa cough.* But this
was not the only reason that Elise did not want to eat at Spaghett
About It. She also couldn't afford to eat at Spaghett About It, even
if she wanted to.

But everyone else wanted to eat at Spaghett About It, especially Sam, who was—according to Cee—"so gross, actually,"
because they mostly only ate fast food. Elise thought they were
pretty skinny for someone who mostly ate fast food. So, not
wanting to be a weirdo who demanded no one eat at Spaghett
About It because she didn't want to, Elise decided to do something she was pretty good at: pretending not to be hungry even
though she was starving.

Spaghett About It played up the Little Italy shtick, everything
done in red-and-white check, their mascot a chubby chef kissing his fingers. Grapevines and Italian words (*famiglia, grazie,
mangia, barbabietola*) snaked around each other on the walls. It
smelled strongly of garlic—too strongly for eight in the morning.
The lone cashier probably felt the same way, standing behind the
register with lidded eyes.

"Do you see anything we can eat?" Cee asked. Elise uncrossed her arms. *We*, Elise thought with a warm flush. She liked being a *we* with Cee. Elise noticed Sam, standing off to the side, arms crossed.

"Oh, I'm not hungry," Elise said.

Cee rolled her eyes and leaned in close.

"I got you," she whispered. Elise looked over Cee's shoulder toward Tom, heart kicking, wondering if he'd somehow heard, and if he'd somehow heard, then maybe he'd somehow figured out what Cee meant.

"It's really okay," Elise muttered back.

"It's totally not, though," Cee said, smiling easily, even nudging one elbow into Elise's side. "You're really gonna make me eat whatever veggie slop they're serving all by myself?"

Elise knew Cee was just being nice. But when she started to protest again, Cee rolled her eyes.

"How about cannolicakes? I guess those are like, pancakes?" Cee asked like the matter was settled. Elise had chosen "squished hamsters" as her pancake-avoidance imagery. It hadn't stuck. Elise looked up at the menu hanging above the cashier. There was a breakfast menu and a regular menu and a combo menu and an "al fresca" diet menu and a "ciao dolla" menu. She reflexively logged the calorie count listed under the prices. Cannolicakes: 650.

"I guess cannolicakes are the only thing on the breakfast menu without meat," Elise said. Still not committing to eating any of the food Cee was going to have to pay for. Elise scanned the rest of the breakfast menu: garlic bread breakfast sandwich (830 calories), spicy meatball breakfast burrito (700), breakfast ravioli (960).

"I'm never up for breakfast," Cee muttered. Elise nodded. "I'm not that into breakfast foods."

"I like oatmeal, but only on, like, snowy mornings," Elise said, stupidly, since oatmeal wasn't on the menu and it wasn't a snowy morning and no one had asked. "Are you gonna get the cannolicakes?"

"Maybe I'll just get a salad."

Smart. That's what Elise should do. She assumed that Cee had always had the perfect body, never had to memorize calories. Or just naturally ate well, craved salads the way Elise craved ice cream. Elise wished she was Cee. *Like* Cee, that is. Her aching arms begged for food with real nutritional value. She could tell, by the vacancy in her stomach, the headache forming at her temples, and the mathematics of how many calories she'd consumed versus how much work she'd done shoveling beets—surely that added a few hundred to her basic daily maintenance calories—that she was hungry. But she wasn't going to eat. She wasn't going to let Cee pay for her. Tom would notice, and he'd ask, and she'd just wind up fucked.

Everyone else had ordered and was waiting against the wall. One by one their orders appeared on red-and-white-checked trays.

"Shit, I can't decide," Cee groaned, wiping a dirty hand across her face.

"You should get the cannolicakes," Elise said, galvanized by the prospect of helping Cee make a decision.

"*We*," Cee said. "You're eating half. Don't say no again, babe, I don't want to hear it. You can just pay me back. I know you're good for it."

Nine days to payday. Elise wondered if Sam was paying attention, if Sam recognized that their girlfriend was buying another girl breakfast. Cee probably called everyone babe. What would she do if it was Tom buying Cee a meal? She wouldn't *do* anything; she couldn't do anything. Her whole life was one long tightrope walk over the sharp terrain of her frivolous, unmanageable emotions. Elise looked for Tom; he was sitting with his back to her, eating what appeared to be the breakfast lasagna (1,034). Tom didn't know it, but he had never seen Elise eat that many calories in one sitting.

Cee stepped up to the register, ordered cannolicakes and a Fanta. She turned and smiled at Elise with glossy, unchapped lips. Cee did not look like she'd just worked outside for twelve hours in the frigid Minnesota wind. "You want a drink?"

"I'm good," Elise said, neck burning. Cee swiped a black credit card and stepped back. They waited under the pickup sign. "Did you see what happened to the other girl? Bless Up?"

"No, I didn't. But whenever I'd go up to relieve her, she was just, like, *real* weird."

"Well, you know her birth name probably wasn't Bless Up," Elise deadpanned. She hoped that hadn't sounded racist, somehow. She didn't mean that Bless Up's name would have been something more South Asian-sounding, she meant that no one's birth name was Bless Up. Cee blew air out through her lips in a half-laugh.

"No, but for real, she'd linger when I went up to relieve her. Hang around over my shoulder for fifteen minutes like she was worried I'd fuck it up. Or like she didn't even want to go on break, she just wanted to stay and keep working. And it's like, 'Yo, chill, it's not actually *your* machine,' you know?"

"Totally," Elise said. "That's weird."

"Can I ask you something?" Cee was looking at her with narrowed eyes. It suddenly occurred to Elise that she should have chased down Cee's hat that night they went on the beer run, even after Cee said not to; she should have done something noble and chivalrous and cool. Or would it have seemed too eager, a Labrador returning a Frisbee?

"Sure," Elise said.

"What were you like in high school?"

A trickle of cortisol ran through Elise's blood. High school had been bad. The eczema. Her first kiss, a boy who'd told her afterwards it was just out of pity. A perpetual cold in tenth grade that turned her into a walking wad of used Kleenex. Greasy hair. She'd once written a love letter to some guy and slipped it into his locker, anonymously, but it took practically no time at all for him to figure out who it was. He never spoke to her again, though he hadn't spoken to her much beforehand, either. Period stains. Overzealous about PETA. That paradoxical need to be seen despite the attention always hurting her. Her body, so repulsive and flabby.

Of course everyone hated her, bullied her relentlessly, sometimes lured her into a friendly conversation only to laugh with their friends at whatever she'd said as soon as she looked away. Threw stuff from their cars if they drove past her on her bike. For a while, Elise fantasized about publicly killing herself. She wanted her bullies to see what they'd done to her.

Then there was the summer Elise and her only two friends got jobs at the mall, fell in with a group of emo kids. She found the pro-Ana forums and stopped eating. She adopted Myspace aesthetics, heavy eyeliner and chunky black studded belts pulled tighter and tighter around her waist as she shed the weight. She started smoking cigarettes. She slept around with the emo boys because it seemed like a very "Criminal"-era Fiona Apple thing to do. She had sex with one of the girls, too, "Bright Eyes" playing in the background as they lay on her bed in a haze of marijuana smoke. A secret she kept until coming out in college. When she went back to school, she wasn't fat anymore and had enough cool new vices to ward off the worst of the bullying, used those same vices to numb herself to what cruelty remained.

These girls—the pre- and post-anorexia Elise—were more dead

weight inside her, only ever emerging to force painful and embarrassing memories to the surface on nights when Elise couldn't sleep. But Elise couldn't tell Cee any of that without sounding like she was either begging for sympathy or still bitter over it.

"Well, I was in drama club all four years but never had more than one line, if that tells you anything," she said. She didn't mention the stuff with Creeps McGee, the director. Elise and her drama friends called him that because he was always standing too close, gazing too long; and then, of course, there was the time Elise caught him watching her change out of her costume. Cee didn't need to hear about that, or about Elise's grown-up fears that because she'd only ever told one person, and because that person hadn't believed her, Creeps McGee had continued to make teenage girls feel unsafe long after she'd graduated. Maybe he'd done it to other girls in her grade, even. Maybe she could have been the one to get him fired. Instead, she'd just forced herself to be flattered that a man wanted to see her gross, fat body.

"Funny," Cee said. "You remind me of this girl I knew back then who I didn't know I liked until, like, three years ago, you know? But she was a jock. I don't really know why you remind me of her."

Elise laughed, blood rising to her cheeks. What did *that* mean? "No, I was not a jock. And my inner emo child is offended, actually." This made Cee smile; making Cee smile was quickly becoming one of Elise's favorite things to do. "How about you? In high school?"

"Oh, you wouldn't recognize me," Cee said. She rolled her eyes. "I was a total prep. Cheerleader. Juicy Couture. Rhinestones on my phone. All that shit."

Cee was right; Elise would not have imagined her as a Paris Hilton–type popular girl. Cee was pretty enough, for sure; she had a very cup-in-your-hands-able face. But Elise had a hard time imagining any of the popular kids from *her* high school growing up to work the beet harvest. Elise wondered if Cee had been a bully. If Cee would have bullied her. Probably.

"What happened? To you?" Elise asked, immediately seeing how that could be interpreted as rude. But Cee just looked toward the ceiling and considered the question.

"Well, in college, I guess, my roommate was pretty crunchy," Cee said. "I thought college would be all pregaming and wearing sweatpants to class, but I somehow just didn't fall into a crowd like that. I started smoking a lot of pot and then I took some classes in, like, sociology. You know how that goes. Then I met this girl, and realized I didn't only like boys, so that was a whole new thing. Also, my parents died."

"What?" Elise said.

"Yeah, winter break of my freshman year," Cee said. "I should have taken the next semester off but I couldn't—I didn't have anywhere to really go. My parents were deep in debt. By then my older brother had already made like a shit-ton of money, so he paid for me to stay in college, but honestly, he's a dick. We had to sell the house and I wasn't going to live with him. So I went back to school. I guess that left me pretty, you know, shocked. Put shit in perspective."

It seemed to Elise that Cee had told the story out of order. It was quite clearly her parents' death that drove her away from the Juicy Couture and frat parties. But while Elise was still trying to think of something to say that wasn't that, their food arrived and they sat down with Sam and the boys, who were mostly already finished. The cannolicakes turned out to be deep-fried crepes with sweet ricotta filling, and were delicious but made Elise woozy and made her newly sensitive tooth throb. Sam ate what was left of both the salad and the cannolicakes. Then it was almost nine in the morning; no one had come into Spaghett About It the entire time they were there.

On their way out of the parking lot, Ryan pointed out the window. There were dozens of sugar beets lying on the side of the road: escapees from the trucks that drove constantly between the farms and the sites.

"Jeez," Elise said, thinking of what Robber's Bluff must look like by harvest's end: snowed in by beets, critters running amok, a scavenger's feast of human failure.

24

ELISE STARED AT HER NECK IN THE GRIMY MIRROR AS she combed through her just-washed hair. The rash was hardly red at all now. Just a bruise with blistering around the edges. It looked diseased. She worried that it was necrotic; she ran her fingers around and down the area. There was still sensation; almost too much sensation. It felt like someone else's lips and tongue brushing against her pulse points. Elise's heart pumped faster.

She crawled into bed next to Tom, pressed her clean body to his, wrapping her arms around him. Her wet hair held on to the cold, dampening her pillow. She kissed the back of his neck just under his hairline. His hair smelled like beets, his body warmer than hers but dirtier. He dropped his chin toward his chest, bending away from her lips. Elise swallowed a vision: Tom and Cee walking back from break together.

"Sorry," Tom muttered, putting his own hand on Elise's and bringing it to his chest, trapping her bicep under his.

"Everything okay?" Elise asked.

"Yeah, uh . . . I came already today," Tom admitted, turning his face toward her with a sly, almost-shameful smile.

"Oh," Elise said. "Just now?"

"No. In the piler."

"What?" Elise sat up on her elbows. "You jacked off up there?"

Tom shrugged. "I just felt like it, and I, you know, I could."

Elise tried to picture it. Tom with his zipper undone, fisting his dick in short jerks.

"Where did you . . . ?" Elise asked, imagining Tom wiping his hands on his overalls, or against the metal door. She also imagined Tom and Cee fucking. Maybe in the port-a-potty. Maybe in the dirt box, somehow. Tom could be lying about jacking off. He could always be lying, about anything and everything. But Elise was the one who was lying and keeping secrets. Cee playing with her ponytail.

"Lunch bag," he said, and now Elise imagined him positioning the empty, crinkly paper bag under his dick. Gloves off to the side. Or only one glove—he didn't need both hands free. But wouldn't his hands be dirty?

"Oh," Elise said.

Tom kept looking at her expectantly, clearly tickled by his own deviance, waiting for her to feed the feeling by exclaiming how gross and wrong it was. It was like he'd taken a bite of something disgusting and wanted her to taste it, too. But she couldn't stop thinking about his dirty hands, and then how close she'd come to letting his dick into her, now she'd just gotten clean. When she couldn't give him the response he wanted, he turned back away from her and closed his eyes.

"Maybe tonight," he said. "Can you turn off the heater? It's hot."

Elise did. But when she got back in bed, Tom was looking at her over his shoulder again, frowning.

"What's wrong?"

Tom blinked a few times, looking up toward the ceiling. Elise forced herself to be patient. She looked at the place where the zipper wouldn't zip. They hadn't fixed it yet. They really ought to.

"Nothing," he finally said, rolling onto his side to face the green canvas wall. "Good night."

But it wasn't night; it was full, birdsong morning.

25

ELISE COULDN'T SLEEP. SHE SAT ON THE BED BESIDE Tom and looked at her phone.

Are you having the most fun yet? Carly had texted her. Elise responded by sending a selfie she had taken the night before in her hard hat, duck-lipping and giving a peace sign in front of the piler. There were other texts from other friends, asking questions or sharing memes. Elise sent the same picture to everyone.

She sent herself back to her home screen. She put her phone down, sucked a whisper of glass out of her thumb. Tom snored. She picked up the zipper repair kit he'd gotten from Walmart. Elise could be pretty handy when she put her mind to it. She picked the phone up again, thinking she could find a YouTube video that would show her how to fix the zipper. Picking up her phone made her think of something else, though. She opened the email from the Lapeer Motor Inn. She studied the call log with the strange number. She tapped the number into her phone. She was curious. Maybe she would just get a voicemail, and the voicemail would tell her who the motel was claiming she'd called and talked to for over an hour.

"Burt?" the voice, frantic and hoarse, blurted at her.

"Um." Elise should just hang up. Burt? She knew this woman's voice, didn't she?

"Holy shit. You've got some fuckin' nerve," the woman said. "I heard you. I HEAR you! Homewrecking slut, are you with him right now? Are you *with* him *right* now? Burt? *Burt!?*"

Elise pulled the phone from her ear. Before she could hang up, she heard a man's voice come through the speakers.

"Linnie, I'm right here," the voice said. "Jesus, woman! I'm right *here*. Linnie, how could I be anywhere else?"

"You think I'm stupid, Burt? You think I'm an *idiot*? I know you're with her, I know you're with her right now. You hear that, bitch? You fucked the *wrong* man. You got the—"

Elise hung up. Tom rolled over, but he was still sleeping. Elise recognized the frantic, crazed voice not only because it was the voice she'd heard on the motel voicemail, but also because it carried the distinct flavor of the crazy girlfriend Elise had been that summer they'd moved to Brooklyn. It had only been for the summer, over a year ago now. She'd had no right or reason to peek at Tom's Facebook messages when he left himself logged on to the computer. But she'd seen it when a new message popped up, from his ex-coworker in Albany: "u feeling better?" She scrolled up to see the conversation preceding it.

Tom was saying things like "This was a mistake" and "I wanted to leave her in Albany" and "I can't figure out what I really want, but I don't want to break her heart" and "I always thought you were the cutest girl at the cafe" and "I wish I'd kissed you that night." According to the time stamps, this conversation had taken place two days after they moved into their studio. As she read these messages, she was sitting on the first thing they'd purchased together: a stained and saggy forest-green sofa from Housing Works.

How, Elise would wonder later, had they survived this? How had Tom convinced her to stay? She couldn't remember the fight they had when he finally came home, what he'd said or done. Elise must have been more scared of losing him this way than she was of losing him another way. Elise must have wanted to believe him more than she wanted other things—the truth, as abstract and vapid a concept as it was, so subjective and malleable with time and new information. She would have been desperate to hold on to this sole, sustainable thing in her life. She wouldn't have been able to afford to live on her own.

For two and a half horrible months, Elise's mind was constantly unspooling possible scenarios, visions of Tom actively seeking out her replacement. She was waiting for the night he'd come home with some girl on his arm and tell her that time was up: she needed to leave so he could start his new life. She was paranoid, felt completely out of control, incapable of stopping herself from doing all the things that crazy girlfriends did: looking at his phone, texting him nonstop, demanding reassurances, again and again.

She'd gotten better when he gave her the ultimatum. Or, at least, she'd gotten better at hiding her anxieties. Elise was capable of fixing shit that required fixing, even if she didn't always choose to fix things. She chose to fix this and had mostly succeeded, by simply pretending not to be paranoid, kicking the fear deeper and deeper under the bed. When she wanted to text him, she texted memes to the group chat of her mostly single college friends. When she wanted to call, she called Carly, or Jenna, who were also not single and could sympathize without enabling. She sought distractions: mindless games on her phone, new recipes, drinking as much water as she could as fast as she could.

Still, she worried that Tom still saw the old Elise when he looked at her. She was not convinced he had ever really forgiven her, which made it all the more likely he'd want to start fresh with someone else. She was so afraid to give him the last ounce of ammunition he'd need to dump her. Like, for example, if she'd lied about how much money she had or how much debt she was in or exactly how dystopian her financial future was.

Her phone buzzed. The number was calling her back. She

rejected the call and blocked the number. Clearly Burt had called this Linnie woman during his stay and somehow the call had made its way onto Elise's bill instead. She could call the motel and explain it and they'd refund her money and all would be well. Then she could even call her mom and wouldn't be lying when she said everything was great.

26

ELISE WOKE UP SWEATING, NUDE FROM THE WAIST down. She'd pulled her leggings off at some point. The space heater was on again. She combed her hair with her hand before unzipping Burt, the zipper still unfixed. She should fix it. Call her mom. Look up the rash. Call the motel. Call her bank. Be a normal, productive person. Be a good, normal, productive person.

The first thing Elise saw was Tom and Cee at the picnic table, heads bowed together in deep conversation. New sweat sprang to the surface of Elise's skin. Tom had his back to her, but Cee saw her and instantly changed her facial expression, brightening and smiling and waving Elise over. As though Elise needed an invitation to sit with her own fucking boyfriend at their own fucking campsite. Did Elise hate Cee, actually? It was unfair that Cee got to be everything Elise had ever wanted to be.

No, Cee was an orphan. Elise was the lucky one. Elise's problems were her own fault. She would not trade her parents being alive for Cee's charm or body. She clambered out of the camper and into her now-brown boots.

The camp was buzzing. The temperature had crested 55 degrees, threatening rot, so the day shift had been sent home. They saw Aya and Chet, someone was laughing inside a chrome-plated Airstream, two train kids were harmonizing on a ukulele and a flute, someone was rolling down the hill behind the church, walking back up the hill and rolling down it again, and Arin, with Cake, was sitting in a camp chair drinking from a thirty-rack.

"They sent the day shift home," Cee said, waggling her eyebrows. Elise looked for the rest of the Mainers, saw them sitting in a semicircle around Aya and Chet's van, holding puppies. Elise wondered how they were doing. Them, and the worms inside them.

"I see that," Elise said, straddling the bench beside Tom and lighting a cigarette.

"You guys know Sarah and Josh? Over there?" Cee pointed to a bright silver Airstream. Elise did, vaguely, though not well, since they were day-shifters. The bulk of their interaction had been Sarah telling Elise that she was a freebleeder because of a picture she'd seen once of a tampon with mold on it. "Sarah told me that someone at her site, something happened, I don't know what, and he went out to his car and got a rifle and started walking back to the site with it."

"Holy shit," Elise said. This was very high-caliber gossip, enough to override her petulance at seeing Tom and Cee talking so closely. "What happened?"

"They thought he was going to go after the foreman because I guess they'd had a fight or something. But some guys tackled him before he could do anything."

"Fuck, that's crazy," Elise said.

Two of the train girls came out of the back of Arin's truck, sleepy-eyed and dreaded, and accepted the beers he offered them. They were night-shifters, but it wasn't like you couldn't do the job perfectly well shit-faced. Elise would have envied them if she did not already feel so physically unwell: dehydrated from too much caffeine and muscle work, the food from the mission always on the cusp of spoiling, her toothache not improving, her boyfriend always secretly talking to the hot, charming, queer girl that Elise had a dumb, embarrassing crush on.

Mindy, a ginger who lived with Pete in an ugly brown RV, was walking toward them from the bathroom. Sarah, the freebleeder, was approaching from diagonally across the park. Elise and Tom and Cee were sitting right where their paths met.

"Find him?" Mindy asked.

Sarah shook her head.

"Have you guys seen E.T.?" Mindy approached the picnic bench, hands on her hips. She was wearing a folksy Dust Bowl-esque dress, a floor-length skirt of pale yellow and pink flowers with a ruffly white bib over her chest. Either Mindy or Sarah or both smelled like lavender and orange juice and weed, a smell Elise didn't like but still found comforting.

"Uh . . ." Tom stalled, and Elise wondered if he was trying to think about where he might have seen E.T. or if he was wondering who E.T. was. She knew who he was, kind of. She struggled to picture him clearly in her mind's eye but knew she'd recognize him if she saw him. He'd been one of the people fighting over the other person who'd run off. Or gone missing. "No?"

"I haven't," Cee offered.

Mindy looked at Elise.

"I just woke up."

"Well, we can't find him," Sarah said. "It's my fault. He usually rides with me, but for some reason I thought he was in the other car, but now we don't know which car he was in and we called the site but he's not there."

"Oh," Cee said. "That's scary, I'm sorry. I'll keep an eye out, for sure."

Mindy had already turned away, walking toward the Jeep parked beside the RV. Sarah made to follow her.

"We'll let you know if we hear anything," Tom said before they were out of earshot.

The train kids and crust punks operated on a scale of freedom incomprehensible to Elise. People parted ways, then met again in cities hundreds of miles away. People did whatever they wanted, and if that meant leaving without saying goodbye, then that was their prerogative. Surely that's how it was with Bless Up. They definitely didn't give a shit if they were overdrafted on their bank account, if they even had bank accounts. Imagining herself abandoning all her debts, all her responsibilities, changing her number so no one could call her asking for money, shedding all the traceable parts of her identity, starting fresh—it brought her a moment of immeasurable relief. But she knew she never could, or would. Tom would certainly never go for it.

Elise excused herself to the bathroom to brush her teeth. She would miss her friends if she disappeared herself. She was supposed to have called the motel. She was supposed to have looked up what kinds of rashes or bug bites could leave bruises. She kept forgetting everything. Her mind was perpetually foggy. She'd call the motel as soon as she got back to Burt. She'd remember this time. She texted her mom: working hard but will make time to talk soon. In the group chat, Lydia had told a story about forgetting her old OkCupid password and starting a new profile, and then winding up with her own profile suggested to her, but only being a 92 percent match. We call that self-growth, Elise wrote. Elise imagined stumbling upon her own OkCupid profile, so old now that she couldn't even remember what pictures she'd used: how she would look at this younger, pre-Tom version of herself. Hotter and skinnier and much more fun, but that hadn't stopped her from waking up, hungover, and fantasizing about the same thing as now: packing up and leaving, starting fresh someplace where no one's current perception of Elise could be tainted by things her previous selves had said or done. It felt almost like a compromise with the people around her: they could make a final decision about who

Elise was based on their memories, and she could leave behind all those versions of herself that only kept existing because other people remembered them.

Coming out of the bathroom, Elise saw Tom and Cee still sitting together, heads close again, expressions vivid. She forgot the motel. Her phone vibrated again, and again, and again.

27

"MY WIFE LIKES THIN SOUPS. SHE LIKES BROTHS. Chicken soup. I like thick soups . . . chowders, I like chowders, and, well, I like thin soups, too, if I have a cold or, you know, thin soups are alright. I like the . . . what is it . . . the blue can, they have a beef stew, and now, that's almost like a thin and a thick soup all in one."

Jeff stopped talking about soups to take a bite of his sandwich. Elise was waiting for Sydney to finish refilling the coffee urn.

"She likes barley soup," Jeff started speaking again. "Mushroom and barley. We both like tomato soup. She doesn't like cream-of-anything, celery, nothing. I like that. Now, here's the funny thing, is she likes crackers, what you want to call them, salty crackers. Oysters. I can't stand that. I could do . . . well, I don't mind bread, you know, a piece of white bread, whole wheat, she's got me eating the whole wheat bread now. I got used to it. She bought some last month that was hard. Not stale-like, but harder than what I like. Now she's back to buying the regular bread. Regular whole wheat, tastes almost like white bread. Or the same texture, anyway."

"She ever buy the bread with the seeds?" Sydney asked before patting the coffee urn and smiling at Elise. "All good, honey."

Sydney was younger than Elise. Sydney was still in college. The degree she was getting was probably practical.

Elise refilled her thermos. It was warm in the scalehouse, but it was no place to spend a whole hour. She emptied three packets of Salt of the Earth sugar into her coffee—it took more sugar than Splenda to make her coffee as sweet as she liked it. Maybe this was the cause of her toothache? She wondered if she'd gained any weight from switching from the artificial stuff. She was probably having six packets a day in her coffees—that was about 75 calories, but sugar calories were special, they were digested differently, somehow, Elise guessed. That's what everyone said, anyway. Everyone meaning everyone who wrote the diet books her mother read, then parroted back to Elise.

"Seeds?" Jeff asked. "No. Bread with seeds. Now what's that like?"

Except she'd been doing hard manual labor the whole time, so no. The sugar wasn't hurting Elise. Except, perhaps, her teeth. And perhaps because she was now gaining a taste for the real thing, and it would be annoying to have to transition back to aspartame. *And because the sugar is actually worm eggs,* Elise thought. A strange thought, kind of funny. But it was her own thought. Weird thoughts happened to people all the time.

"Feels funny when you bite it," Sydney said, sitting back at the window. "And I wouldn't recommend it for toast."

And what if she couldn't make the transition back? What if she got really fat again because of sugar?

"No, I don't think I'd like that," Jeff said. "Don't go telling my wife it's good for me. She'll start buying it."

Elise needed to stop thinking about sugar. She wondered if Sydney was talking about Ezekiel bread, like the kind they sold at the health food store. Way back at the health food store, a lifetime ago.

"That's what a wife's for," Sydney said. She swirled her stool around to lean through the window and hand a trucker a slip of paper. Someday Sydney would be somebody's wife. Elise might be a wife someday. Tom's wife. She thought about someday saying, *Hi, I'm Tom's wife.* She thought, in Tom's voice, *This is Elise, my wife.*

Sometimes Elise thought that being a wife would be like a rebirth. Maybe once you were something else entirely, the way a wife was something entirely different from a girlfriend, you got to abandon all the previous versions of yourself. At last, empty as a stomach.

Or was she just thinking of money, again? Tom's family's money erasing her debt. She felt queasy with guilt, swallowed against the anxiety. She didn't want that because he didn't want that. Tom wanted to divorce himself from his inheritance, ease his own guilt over coasting on unearned wealth. He wanted to do it on his own, even though, obviously, he very much had already benefited from that unearned wealth. And Elise wouldn't take Tom's money even if he begged her to let him pay it all off. That kind of deal could only lead to one person having eternal leverage over the other. And Elise wanted to be the kind of person her parents would approve of, and her parents did not approve of people who took the easy way out of problems they'd gotten their own selves into.

"Going okay out there?" Jeff asked Elise.

"Yeah, it's all good," Elise said.

"Okey-dokey, you just radio if you need me," Jeff said, smiling.

Elise did not have a radio. Only the piler operators had radios.

"Okay." Elise pushed the door open at the same moment a truck rolled up to the station window. She fought the wind to get the door closed. She headed toward the pilers, sharp yellow lights in the dark illuminating the grayish wall of beets. She only had fifteen minutes left in her break. She might as well visit Tom.

"Hey," she said as she entered. Then had to add, "Oh! Ha-ha. Hey!"

Cee was in there, standing next to Tom, one hand resting beside his on the operating panel. Resting so close to his that the sides of their hands were touching and Cee's pinkie was almost overlapping Tom's pinkie. For a brief, insane moment, Elise's own pinkie itched.

The box was only just big enough for three people, the floor covered in rubber mats, the windows smudgy with dead bugs and ash and age. There was a metal stool in the corner, a little radio standing on it, tuned to the local classic rock station; Bob Seger was singing about Mainstreet. A small heater blew warm air at their ankles. There was no wind in the operator box. But there was Cee, whipping her hand away like Elise was never meant to see it there.

"Hey! I was just leaving," Cee said, turning around, crossing her arms and leaning against the panel. "I came up to ask about something weird my baby girl is doing over there"—Cee pointed toward the other piler. "He was showing me how to fix it."

"Oh," Elise said. "Word."

Tom was not looking at Elise, or at Cee. He was looking out the window at the beets. For a second they just stood there, triangulated in silence. Then Cee walked to the door, a movement requiring her and Elise to shrug past each other. Cee laughed a little bit, at nothing.

"Peace!" Cee said, letting the wind slam the door shut behind her.

Elise watched her kick her way down the metal stairs, making the operator box shake. Elise's heart was beating very hard and she was kind of nauseated. She knew she had no right to be. She hadn't caught Tom and Cee doing anything that she herself and Cee hadn't done: they were just talking. Touching, probably accidentally. Actually, they hadn't even been talking. They'd been silently staring out the window.

"What's up?" Tom asked.

Elise thought it sounded less like a friendly question and more like a weary concession: *Well, you're here now.* She shook it off. She had to lean *away* from the crazy girlfriend inside her. Down on the ground, she watched Eric stand facing the beet pile, hands on his hips. On the other side of the piler a truck was depositing beets into the machine. Jai and Ryan kicked a beet back and forth between them.

"Nothing," she said. "Just figured you could use the company. I mean, I guess you already had company."

"Hmm," Tom said.

Was that a bad thing for Elise to say? Did it sound accusatory? She cleared her throat, as though she could cough out any hint of jealousy.

"Wanna teach me?" Elise watched his hands on the panel: there were surprisingly few buttons and switches, and in truth she already knew basically what he did. There were only so many actions to perform: lift and lower the gates, signal the trucks to raise or lower their beds, turn the conveyor belt on or off.

"Um."

A truck pulled up on the other side and Elise watched Tom press buttons and flip switches. Bob Seger turned into Billy Idol.

"I loved this song in high school but I only knew it from VH1," Elise said. "*I Love the 80's.* I loved that show. It made me think I loved the eighties, though, which I fucking don't."

"Yeah," Tom said. "Michael Ian Black."

"Yeah." It seemed impossible that she and Tom would not have already had this conversation, but she couldn't remember ever having it.

"Then I acted like I was this huge Billy Idol fan but I only knew this song and like two others," Elise said. She was talking just to talk, as though the talking could settle her stomach or convince Tom that she wasn't paranoid about him and Cee, wasn't trying to control who he talked to. "The eighties were stupid."

"Reagan," Tom said with something like agreement. He hadn't turned his eyes in either direction for the entire time she'd been in the box with him. When she'd first come up, there'd been no jerky movements, no rattle of belts or zippers. They had not been breathing hard. Their cheeks had not been red. Tom was not acting like this because he was annoyed at being interrupted in the middle of fucking a hot chick. They had not been doing that. It made perfect sense for Cee to be in the box asking Tom a question about the piler. She had to stop thinking about it. This exact shit had almost broken them up once before. After day-drinking sangria with her coworker, she'd demanded he come home at midnight, and when he didn't, and didn't respond to her calls, she'd shown up at the bar wild-eyed, greasy hair held back in a ponytail. The night ended with Tom screaming, Elise sobbing, doors slamming, a late-night subway ride to sleep on her friend's floor, convinced it was over, almost relieved to be done with it.

Billy Idol stopped singing about weddings. An advertisement for a credit union played. Tom wasn't fucking Cee.

"Okay, if you were an eighties song, what would it be?" Elise asked, hearing a malicious avoidance in her own voice.

"Dunno," Tom said. He looked straight ahead again. "They wouldn't play it on this station. This station sucks."

"Well, you don't have to listen to it," Elise said.

"What should I listen to, then, Elise? Maybe some fucking MGMT, or, or, Radiohead? Bon Iver?"

"Fuck, dude! What's your problem?"

"You know what? Nothing. I don't have a problem. No problem at all. Everything is just so, so great."

This motherfucker. Didn't he see how she wasn't saying a god-damn thing about him always talking to Cee when she wasn't around? How she was being *so* cool about everything? Every-fucking-thing? Elise opened her mouth but Tom spoke first.

"You know what, Elise? Maybe you're my problem. Maybe it's you, and it's always been you. Maybe all of this fucking shit has been a waste of fucking time, just trying to figure out how to deal with you when you're such a fucking *burden*. You hold me down, and you do it on purpose. You want me to fail so I don't—"

Elise's mouth split open. Tom jerked back from the controls.

"Shit!" Tom cried out. He looked at her, finally. He looked like someone who'd just woken up.

"Don't what?" Elise choked. "Why would I want you to fail? And, like, at what? Fail at what? Why?"

"Shit," Tom said again, quieter. "I didn't mean it to come out like that."

"You're fucking crazy," Elise crowed, her voice too high, crack-ing. A lump in her throat and tears at the edges of her eyes. "You're crazy if you think I'm going to let you talk to me like that. Out of nowhere? Nuh-uh."

The radio was just making noise now. No commercial, no chatty late-night DJ, no the Romantics singing "I hear the secrets that you keep." It was like the radio was listening to them, dead air picking up the strained vibrations of their hearts, their love doing all it could to hold back the things that would hurt it.

"Elise, just . . ." Tom stepped away from the controls, turned toward her, color seeming to leach back into his cheeks where they had been sallow and pale before. "I have a reason that I'm upset, okay? But we can't do this now. I can't do it now. I have to . . . work."

He was trying to de-escalate it. He was trying to end the fight.

But Elise kept hearing: *You're my problem, you fat crazy bitch.* And why? Because she'd come into the operator box at the wrong time? Because she'd walked in on something Tom didn't want her to see? Because he wanted to leave Elise in Brooklyn, because he thought Cee was the cutest girl at the harvest, because he wanted to kiss her while he had the fucking chance?

"Oh, you can't do it now. You can't do it, now. With me, you mean." *Oh god, no. No, no, no.* Elise begged herself not to do it. Not to say it. Not to let the sharp-clawed thing make its way up her throat and out of her mouth. *Don't do it. Please stop. It's not too—* "Because you could do it with *her*, couldn't you? You could do it just fine with *her*."

The piler groaned between them. Tom turned around, put his hands back on the controls. Plucked at a lever; pushed a button. Elise's ears rang, her stomach a clenched fist. Her heart entirely absent. Why was this happening? What had happened between Tom driving them to the site and Elise walking into the operator box?

What had she done?

"Tom," she said. "I'm sorry. I don't know why I—"

"Elise," Tom said, low and measured. "Don't do this again. Don't do this to me again. I don't need it. I can do better than this. Than you."

The radio blasted on again. Everything lurched and spun. Elise wanted to puke right into Tom's face; but he wasn't looking at her. He was looking out the window. Below them, through the glass smudged with dead bugs and dust, Eric turned around, lifted his face toward the operator box, and waved his arms back and forth. Elise pointed out the window, where the boom was getting close to the pile. If Tom didn't pull the piler back a few feet, the boom could get stuck in the pile and it would be a whole thing trying to get it out.

"Shit," Tom said. "Hold on."

But Elise left, the machine sputtering as Tom powered down the conveyors. Driving the piler backwards required lifting the two wings off the ground. Elise stood back and watched, for once letting the cold envelop her and feeling glad enough for the misery of it.

She picked up a beet. She thought about cracking it against her head, busting them both open. But it would only hit her hard hat. In her hand, the beet started to pulse.

28

ELISE STAYED IN THE CAR WHEN EVERYONE ELSE WENT to Spaghett About It for fettuccine fries and garlic bread breakfast sandwiches. She got two phone calls in a row from a familiar number, one she'd saved in her phone long ago as DO NOT ANSWER: her credit card company. Her payment was due yesterday. She was past due. She picked up *You Are a Sugar Beet* from the floor, the treads of someone's boots tattooed across the family's smiling faces. *You will emerge from the dark, triumphant and ravenous. Your seed leaves will unfurl, expand, bring you food from the sun. These seed leaves are only temporary. When you are strong enough, you will replace them. They will fall off unceremoniously. They will no longer be a part of you, you will no longer need them, and in time you will forget them altogether. It is better this way, for you. Enviable, even. Humans need to carry all of themselves at once, forever. We do not shed anything, hard as we try.*

She watched her breath go cloudy as the car's heat succumbed to chill, watched through the window as Tom and Cee conferred with bent heads and Sam and Ryan placed orders. Tom kept glancing up, looking back at Elise. In his expression she saw remorse without sadness. Back in the car, loaded down with the smells of basil and cream, Cee offered Elise some of her cannolicake (650). Tom ate his breakfast sandwich as he drove, one hand on the wheel, grease accumulating on his lips.

At camp, Tom and Elise sat in the car listening to the engine click. Elise's stomach growled. Tom should have brought her something, even though she'd said she didn't want anything. She'd said that because she was mad at him and didn't want him to think getting her food would fix it. He always did that: acted like getting her a gift would erase the need for a conversation about whatever fight they'd had. He, in turn, complained that Elise wanted too much talk, these long discussions that would extend indefinitely, widening gyres that began as pinpoint moments of disappointment and turned into a universe of failure.

"Hey," Tom finally said. "We fucked up, huh?"

Elise, against her natural inclination to stay mad at all costs, felt her anger ebb. It was a sort of relief, not having to convince Tom that whatever offhanded thing he'd said was offensive. But, of course, this had not been so offhanded, and it had not been something he could blame on her misunderstanding or intentionally failing to give him the benefit of the doubt.

"I don't understand what happened. I was just trying to have a conversation with you. We literally never have conversations anymore."

"We have conversations all the time," Tom said.

"Not, like, one-on-one," Elise said. "When we get home it's straight to sleep, and every other minute of the day we spend with other people. I don't think we've been alone together long enough to talk since we got here."

"You're so dramatic," Tom said, all hint of regret gone.

Elise knew she was doing it again, the thing he hated, blowing up the one incident he'd already apologized for into a grandiose opera of all their problems. He was probably thinking, *How dare she give me shit after what she put me through that summer? Embarrassing me in front of my friends, looking at my phone, constantly demanding reassurance? And she's still a crazy bitch.* Elise felt herself shrinking as she thought of Tom's many possible reasons to resent her. And he didn't even know the most recent one. She was being so high-and-mighty while also keeping him completely in the dark about her own fucked-up irresponsible issues. There was only so much he'd put up with, and she'd burned through a lot of that credit already. She didn't know how else to pay it off; all she could think to do was tolerate things she didn't want to tolerate. She needed to apologize, too.

No you don't, a voice inside her said. It was that newer voice. It wasn't very loud yet, easy to drown out. It was scary, thinking about the new voice, and what it would mean if she started listening to it. Who she would become; who it meant she already was. *What he said was unforgivable. He thinks he can do better? Let him try.*

"I just want to know why that happened," she said, tearing up despite her best efforts. Tom *really* hated when Elise cried. It tended to derail the conversation. "You got mad at me for literally no reason. All I wanted to do was keep you company. Why did you say all that stuff? Do you really think I want you to fail? Why would you even think that? What have I ever done—"

"No," Tom said.

Elise was glad he'd cut her off, and she was grateful he didn't continue listing all the ways she'd messed up in their relationship. It felt pathetic to be grateful.

"Then what?"

"It's not—Elise. I just know—" Tom sighed. He rolled his head back on his neck, rolled it from shoulder to shoulder. "Can't I just be tired? Aren't you tired? It's cold and boring and hard, being here. You know what, Elise? Fuck it. I know about the fucking, whatever, the thing. The money? You having no money? And you know what? It's fine. It's fine! It's fine. But you can't expect me to treat you like a fucking princess when you can't even *tell me* shit! You were just keeping it from me? Why? That's so fucking weird, man. So fucking weird. You act like I can't be trusted, but you're the one lying and shit. You think I care that you're always broke? You think I don't *know* that about you? You think I haven't already made my fucking peace with the fact that I'll *never* get to do the things I want to do because you'll never be able to—fuck!"

Tom went silent. He moved his fists around the steering wheel.

She'd told him? Cee, she'd told him? After promising Elise that she wouldn't? Elise could not have expected this new, seething pain to rupture in her chest. Why would Cee tell him? And then she'd just offered Elise *cannolicakes*?

"How did you find out?" Elise asked, even though she knew how he'd found out. Some weird part of Elise wondered if it hadn't been Cee at all—maybe Elise had told him. Maybe there wasn't even a Cee.

"Does that matter? Really, does it matter? It was an accident, okay?"

Was it? How? What had the accident looked like? Elise stared out the windshield. She could see Cee and Sam sitting side by side at a picnic table, backs to Elise, hands in each other's back pockets.

"I—I—" Elise couldn't put her thoughts in order. Maybe it was all Elise; Elise sitting with Tom on the picnic bench, Elise and Tom walking off for their breaks together, Elise in the piler operator box with her hand pressed against Tom's hand. Maybe Elise had turned into Cee at some point, or maybe Elise was going crazy. She was not Cee. Cee was right there.

"We really don't have to do this," Tom sighed, releasing the steering wheel to splay his fingers in front of him as though the thing he was trying to say was a physical object in the air in front of his chest and he was grabbing it, metabolizing it through his fingers, making it something that could be said and understood.

"And I *can't* do this now. Not right now. Later. We can talk later. Okay? You don't have to say anything now."

"Okay. Okay. I mean, I'm sorry. I am. I don't know what to say. I fucked up. I know I fucked up. I wish I could explain. I don't know why I . . . I don't know why I do the things I do. Sometimes I just make these decisions. I just do shit. I don't know, I get confused, I do these stupid things, I can't think straight, I'm just so anxious and scared and I just want it to go away."

Tom finally looked at her, relaxing his hands into his lap. The car reeked of garlic, and the cold was seeping in through the frosting glass. Elise remembered sleeping in the Walmart parking lot, a foot away from Tom and still too far to share his body heat. She'd been so cold.

"I know that. But you drive me fucking crazy, Elise," Tom said. "I love you. I don't care if you're crazy sometimes. You don't trust me but I love you. But sometimes . . . sometimes it's too much."

"Are you breaking up with me?" What had Tom ever even liked about Elise? His answers always so generic: funny, smart, cute. The same reasons she loved Tom, but Tom actually was all those things. Elise was just . . . not Cee. Elise was just Elise.

"Oh my god," Tom said. "No. You always take it to the most extreme. I'm allowed to just be hurt right now, okay? Can you just let me be hurt?"

"Okay, okay, of course. I'm sorry. I'm so sorry. I love you so much," Elise choked out. "I'm scared to lose you. I think, I have to do everything right—because I *know* I fucked up, okay? But I didn't want you to have to, you know, use your money to help me. It felt like, it was me? It was my problem? Not yours. I was scared to tell you. I don't want to be a burden, Tom. That's the last thing I want. Am I a burden? Did you mean that?"

Even in Tom's hesitation she felt the capacity for hurt.

"No," he finally said. A lie emerging sturdy as the cloud of breath that carried it. Or perhaps not; what did Elise know? What did Elise know about Tom, or his ability to love Elise? There was so much Elise and Tom had already decided about themselves and each other, and so much space between those decisions and whatever could be called the truth.

"Okay," she said. "I'm sorry. I'm sorry. Please, I'm sorry."

"I love you, Elise," he said. "Okay? Can we be done now?"

She thought he might kiss her then, but he just opened the driver's side door, letting in all that waiting, pressing cold.

~ 29 ~

ELISE WOKE UP ALONE, WITH A TOOTHACHE. NO alarm; her phone was off. She didn't want to turn it on, face more calls from her credit card company. She lay still in her sleeping bag, tired and ravenous. She thought about her mother making English muffins for her before school, and about the hundreds of mornings when she'd woken up tired and just lay in bed for as long as she could to keep from facing the cold outside the covers. How so much of life was the same thing under different circumstances. Then she remembered the fight: the things they'd said to each other. Awful things. *With her* and *do better than you.*

Elise went to peer out onto the campground and found that the zipper was fixed. The plastic bag the zipper repair kit had come in lay on the opposite bed, torn open. Elise felt warmth running down her spine. Maybe he'd done it for her.

Maybe not. Maybe he'd done it just to have something to do.

She didn't see Tom sitting at the picnic table. She saw Jack and Ash in front of the RV, and Cake tethered to Arin's truck, wagging his tail. The day shift was there, again. It was warm, the usually crisp air thickened with the hope of rain. Aya was talking to Mindy in front of Sarah's Airstream; Sarah appeared, opening the door halfway. One of the wormy puppies bumbled its small, bloated body out of the doorway. Elise thought that Sarah and Josh seemed to have their shit together enough to pay for whatever deworming medicine the puppy needed.

The last thing she saw before ducking her head back in was

that the car was gone. Tom had gone to get something. Maybe he was getting her a gift to make up for yesterday. He had said such awful things, even more awful because there was some truth to them. But Elise had said some awful things, too. Things that had no truth to them. If anyone was cheating on anyone, it was Elise with her big stupid crush on Cee. And she *had* lied. She should have just told him; why hadn't she just told him? Better yet, why hadn't she been more honest about how much money she had before they started the trip? Why hadn't she saved more money? He'd even bought her those boots, just on a whim. The guilt was thick and bubbling inside her stomach. Elise imagined her bank account languishing in the app she was afraid to open, a skeletal, starving animal. She turned her phone on, tried to call Tom but it went straight to voicemail. The girls in the group chat were lmaoing about something. About her? She was too scared to scroll up and check. Lydia had texted at some point while she slept: my mom wants you to bring home a sugar beet. For science. Lol. Elise couldn't think of anything funny to say back, so she didn't say anything at all.

Maybe Tom would leave her now. Maybe that was the last straw. Maybe his attempt to defuse the conversation that morning had been just deflection, saying anything he needed to say to get her to shut up so he could start planning his escape. Maybe he wasn't getting her a gift at all: maybe he was driving back to New York, abandoning her at the harvest, something he'd consider a kindness because how else would Elise manage to make up for the money she'd wasted on that fucking motel? Tom didn't need to work the harvest; he didn't need the money. She was the one who needed the money. It was her fault they'd come in the first place. Tom *could* do better. He could get someone hotter, more confident, less insecure and needy, better with money, more responsible. He could have Cee. Who'd told him. Who'd promised Elise that she'd keep the secret, then turned around and told the only person it had to be a secret from. Elise really thought Cee had liked her. Maybe Cee had seen through Elise all along: the pitiful way Elise envied Cee, her desires for and of her entwined in a messy, ugly knot. Tom was gone, she was alone.

Elise collapsed onto the bed on her stomach, pressed her face into her pillow, bit the cotton. Her tooth hurt. It *hurt*. Her heart hurt, her body hurt, she pushed her palm against the bruise on her neck so that would hurt. She drew her knees up against her stomach, kneeling now, rolled her head until her scalp was pressed against the pillow and she was looking at her thighs. Curled up like a roly-poly bug. She punched herself in the stomach, but in a weak and pathetic way, not in a way that would really hurt. She grabbed her tits and mashed them around, like a fucking weirdo. What if Tom came back while she was doing this? What if he unzipped the camper and came in and saw her rolled up, ass in the air, writhing in distress? Would he call her dramatic, too emotional? Or maybe he'd fuck her, finally. However long it'd been—since the motel—it felt like forever. Well, why would he fuck her with Cee around? Who would? She imagined Tom and Cee in Tom's car. Making each other come like four million times.

She pressed her face into the pillow again. She shoved her hand down the front of her leggings. Tom and Cee and Tom and Elise and Elise and Cee. Leaning up against a boulder. Fingers, dicks, not a boulder, a pile. The pile. Warmth spread, knees digging into the vinyl mattress, knees digging into the pile, two hands gripping a chest and using it as a support. Being watched. Elise's teeth around the pillow, wetted by her tongue—she could hear moaning in her mind, begging. Feel so much. The dirt and the hard bodies.

Everyone kissing with beets between their mouths. Elise worked herself harder, squeezing her breast with her other hand. The free fall, sweet and unstoppable. Tom disappeared, Cee disappeared, leaving only Elise, still straddling, still riding the pile. Beet dirt under her fingernails, and she was coming.

30

TOM WASN'T BACK YET WHEN ELISE WENT TO DINNER.
She worried that he'd be late coming home to pick her up for work.
Because he probably *was* coming back. That fight hadn't even been
the worst fight they'd ever had. She'd just been catastrophizing
earlier. She'd even begun to think that maybe Cee hadn't told
him on purpose; maybe it'd just slipped out. Maybe Cee had good
intentions and, like Elise, just sometimes did things. Maybe Eric
had told Tom. She tried calling again; voicemail. Maybe he'd text
her halfway through dinner to tell her he'd gotten her a grilled
Swiss cheese sandwich (450) and fries (365) from that diner near
the gas station. The only new text on her phone, though, was: bet
ur fat ass ugly ass bitch, hope you get hit and run over.

That was probably not from Tom. She blocked the number.

Elise was the only person in the buffet line by the time she got
there, everyone else already sitting and eating. Dinner was soggy
white rice with a mix of soggy peas and corn (126), and meatloaf
with the usual watery salad and white bread (79) on the side.

"How's the harvest going?" Mike asked. "Feeling okay? Doing
okay? Feeling good?"

"Sure," Elise said. "Everything's okay. Thanks, again, for doing
all this."

"Oh jeez, you all work so hard, you deserve it. You just let me
know if I can do anything for you," Mike said, and she tracked his
eyes as they landed on her neck. Elise felt guilty, almost: as though
she'd painted the bruise on herself to make it seem like Tom was

abusing her. Like she was making some kind of sympathetic profit off it.

"Weird rash, right?" she said, touching the bruise with two fingertips. Which just sounded like a bad excuse.

Mike forced a smile.

"Well, you have a good meal," he said. "Holler if you need me."

There were three empty chairs at the Mainers' table.

"Where's Cee?" Elise sat in the seat next to Ash, an empty chair between her and Sam. Her question was met with a heavy silence. Jai covered his mouth to cough.

"I don't know," Sam said, voice sharp as a scythe. "Where's Tom?"

31

"THEY COULD'VE HAD AN ACCIDENT," ELISE SAID.

Sam closed their eyes and kept them closed. Elise did not know what she was supposed to do about her missing boyfriend. It seemed to her that it was still likely that Tom had gone out for some benign reason, and brought Cee along for a reason just as benign. Likely, or at least possible. She couldn't have been right during her little freak-out. Elise turned to the rest of the group—strangers, still. If there'd been an accident, there was protocol to follow. She stared at her phone. Should she call his mother? Had he told his mother something—anything? Was his mother in on it? In on what? He wasn't missing yet. He just wasn't there right then.

But she didn't have Tom's mother's number. How could she not have Mrs. Henry's number? What did it mean—this lack of knowledge, this bridge unbuilt? She'd never been told to call Tom's mother anything but Mrs. Henry. Had Tom failed to give her his mother's number, or had she failed to ask? Did Mrs. Henry have Elise's number? She and Tom had been together for five years but Elise didn't have his parents' phone numbers. What did that mean? Where was he? Where had he gone? Should she call *her* mother?

Her phone went off! It was the credit card company. She pressed the ignore button very hard.

"Cee and I had a fight," Sam suddenly offered. "Before bed last night."

Elise stared. "So?"

"So? So they're obviously together."

"That doesn't mean they, like, *left.*"

"What else could it mean?"

Everyone but Sam and Elise focused on eating, looking down at their trays.

"Maybe they went to pick up something special to make up for fighting," Elise said, sticking to this story. Voice quavering slightly as the pitifulness of the statement washed over her. She didn't want to tell Sam that she and Tom had fought, too. She could hear an echo of her mother's voice in the back of her head: *fantasy world.* "Tom wouldn't leave me. Not like this."

He wouldn't, of course. How could he? Leave her with no car and no money? And Burt? Leave her, at all, period? She wasn't that bad. He'd fixed the zipper! That fight had been bad, but *she* wasn't bad, right?

Of course not, of course you're not, something inside Elise said, soothing but soft. She thought it might be that newer voice, the one with a little more spine to it. But that didn't feel right. It couldn't be the piler, could it? She was far too far away.

"I mean, he left all his stuff behind," she said, which seemed true—she hadn't noticed anything missing, anyway. "How about Cee? Is her stuff gone?"

Sam didn't respond. Elise hated them. Sam's chair scraped on the ground as they got up; Elise pictured them picking up their tray and hurtling it across the room like a Frisbee, ketchupy meatloaf splattering on the wall. Elise then imagined herself doing the same thing, allowing, for a moment, her anger and anxiety to breach the surface. But Sam just stalked out, leaving the tray behind.

Elise smashed peas under her fork. The corn kernels mixed in with her mushed-up peas were rotten yellow teeth. *I have to make sure to get Tom's lunch,* she thought. He'd be at work, eventually.

He'd come to work when the tire got fixed. The grilled cheese he'd gone to get her would be cold, the fries starchy and stiff. The best way to reheat fries was in a frying pan, her mind told her. One of her stupid former selves had learned that little trick and was offering it up now. She didn't have a fucking frying pan. She was in goddamn Minnesota.

"I'm sure everything is fine," Eric said. "But if you need to, like, miss work or whatever, I can cover for you if you want."

The fact that Eric was proposing the possibility of Elise not coming to work meant that even though he *said* everything was fine, he did not *think* everything was fine. Elise probably should not show up for her shift. She probably should stay by the phone and wait for the call to come in. But she could do that and go to work. In fact, that was probably the thing she ought to do—because nothing was wrong, and Tom had just gotten into a fender bender and was talking to his insurance agent and would show up soon enough, maybe rush into the cafeteria the very next second, ready to drive everyone to work. Maybe just a blown tire, Tom and Cee waiting by the side of the road since Tom didn't have a spare in the trunk—at least Elise didn't think he did. How was she supposed to know? And if she didn't go to work, she wouldn't get paid. Tom would have wanted her to make money. Why should she waste that financial opportunity just because Tom was running late? Why? Why should she? Why?

"I'm going," she said. *Good girl*, said the voice. An exciting shiver ran down Elise's back, a kinky, abject pleasure.

"Cool," Ryan said. Elise stared at her uneaten food. She didn't think she could eat even if she wanted to eat what was in front of her, which she didn't. She blinked; the rice turned into maggots; she blinked again; it was just rice. It was good she hadn't eaten the rice, or there'd be maggots in her stomach at that very moment.

Elise closed her eyes so she wouldn't have to blink anymore. They were a week from payday.

"You can ride with us," Ash said. Because Tom's car was gone. Elise rubbed her temples, which she'd seen people do in movies and migraine commercials. It didn't help. "We can squeeze you in. You're small."

"Or we could just take my car," Jai said.

Ash laughed, said something about how dumb he was, but Elise was hanging back in the unstable galaxy of bliss that *you're small* had thrust her into. Small like a maggot, small like a tooth. Obviously, she wasn't small enough. If she were smaller, Tom would still be here. Her phone buzzed on the table. It wasn't Tom. Ash was just being nice. Ash was talking about Elise's height.

Somewhere deep inside Elise, something woke up. She stabbed a corn kernel with the tines of her fork, infected pulp oozing from the skin.

32

ELISE STILL DID NOT KNOW WHETHER THE STEADY haze over the fields was dust or pesticides or water. The Big Boy's eyes were closer to the center than they'd ever been before. They were maybe even listing a bit to the left. The clouds looked properly apocalyptic and the wind was spiced with storm. Her mother, as though sensing across the states between them that something was wrong, texted: Daddy put on the Phil Ochs album you bought for hs birthDay last year, that was such a thoughtful GIFT. HOPE YOU ARE STAYing warm. - Mom. Elise pressed on the crack in her screen with her thumb; the pixels warped and bruised. Elise did not know how phone screens worked.

Tom and Cee were not waiting for them at the work site, as Elise, a sane and generous girlfriend, had dutifully allowed herself to hope. According to Jeff, neither of them had called in to say they'd be late or would miss their shift. Elise had no-call-no-show'd several jobs throughout her life, the conflict-averse alternative to properly quitting. But Tom wasn't like that. Was he?

Eric would take over as piler operator on their machine until Tom showed up with whatever perfectly legitimate excuse was keeping him away, but Elise was completely zoned out when Jeff asked who wanted to be trained in operating the piler so that they could relieve Eric. She was surprised, then, when Eric volunteered her for the job: an act of true thoughtfulness.

Jeff handed Eric one of the walkie-talkies, transferring to him the power to summon Jeff to the piler in the event of a problem. *Just until Tom shows up*, Elise thought, again, stupidly, so stupidly, like a stupid stupid moron.

"We're gonna have to get some more people out here," Jeff said, frowning down at his flip phone.

Behind him, Sydney rotated in slow half-circles on her stool by the window, an open textbook in front of her. Elise felt a stab of envy. She wished she'd majored in something practical. Then she wouldn't be in this position. They'd never have come to the harvest at all.

Jeff looked up with a smile and a shrug. "But we'll make it, right, gang?"

Jeff would make it, Elise thought, even if the "gang" did not. If every last one of Jeff's crew abandoned ship, the company would just send more people to the site to replace them, and it wouldn't make a difference to Jeff, who had never once said her name. The letters Elise had Sharpie'd onto her hard hat were faded. She didn't have a name. No one did. The workers were beets, forever tumbling into whatever empty spaces required filling.

A muffled scream came from Elise's jacket pocket. Her phone! Tom! Except, obviously, not. Elise's sore tooth throbbed. It was Carly, asking if Elise wanted to see Animal Collective in May. Elise felt the sudden surety that she would not live to see May. She told herself to stop being so dramatic.

The day shift was down a man, too. The guy who left the operator box was not the usual piler operator. The man Elise was replacing on the ground said nothing to her—just shoved a shovel into her hands.

"My boyfriend is gone," she wanted to scream, grabbing him by his dirty vest and shaking his bigger body until he acknowledged her. "I don't know where he is! I don't know where he went! He's gone!"

But before this fantasy even finished, she was standing alone on her side of the piler watching a truck make the turn around the scalehouse, the cloud of dust in the dark like a Midwest answer to a desert mirage: shimmering, shifting, nothing.

33

THE WORK WAS CONSTANT AND LABORIOUS BUT
required nothing in the way of thought, so Elise had endless mental energy to devote to wondering where Tom (and Cee) was.

Should Elise call the police? Elise was exactly the sort of person the cops were there to help: a white girl, concerned for her white boyfriend and his familial wealth. Had no one called the cops for Bless Up? Should they have? The cops almost certainly would not have cared. How would Sam fare, if Sam cared enough to call the cops? They were white but trans, looking for their gay girlfriend.

At any rate, Sam and Elise couldn't both call the cops. If they both reported that both their partners had left in the same car, the cops wouldn't take them seriously at all, no matter how white they were.

What about the area hospitals? She couldn't look up any of their numbers until she got back to camp, but she could borrow someone's phone. She didn't want to look crazy when Tom breezed back with an explanation. But she was worried. It made the moments she freaked out over money pale in comparison. Panic manifested in brief but painful periods of rapid heart rate and troubled breathing. The world would spin, the ground sink away from the gut-clogged treads of her boots, and all the beets around her would start to throb, inflating and deflating in time to her own heart.

But whenever Elise pushed the gray button that *returned the dirt*, the voice in her head made the anxiety scatter, roach-like, back into the corners of her mind.

Eric stepped out of the piler box and waved his arms to get Elise's attention, signaling for a break. Elise gave a thumbs-up, then walked around the piler to the other side, which was kind of like another world. On this side of the piler you could see the other piler across the yard, the fluorescent yellow vests of the crew. Not close enough to wave, but close enough to know they were there. Elise's side of the piler looked out on a blank, unpeopled plane. She found Ryan and Jack laughing, which she hated them for. Were they laughing at her? Even if they weren't, which they probably weren't, probably, they couldn't know how lucky they were to have someone to laugh with through all the night's long, cold, unbearable hours. She took a perverse pleasure in separating them, as Jack went to take her spot so she could cover Eric.

"Hey," Eric said, shrugging himself into his heavy brown jacket. "You good?"

Elise didn't know what he meant by the question: Was she ready to operate the piler? Was she having a good night? Was she still deluding herself into thinking Tom would show up sometime soon? Was she going to leap from the piler operator box into the piler, allow herself to be churned and pulped and broken down amid the beets? Finally make herself useful as sugar in someone's coffee? What was Elise's caloric content? Elise did something humans did: she pinched the bridge of her nose, between her eyes, and rubbed. Elise was a human, and humans survived all sorts of things.

"Uh-huh," she said. Bob Seger sang about Mainstreet. Eric showed her the different mechanisms on the control panel. Elise had watched Tom operate the piler enough to get the gist, but now she really tried to focus. There was a kind of calm in the operator box, a reprieve from the wind. She felt like she could think clearly for the first time all night. Elise was not so special that the general rule of being able to survive things did not apply to her. This, whatever it wound up being, would not kill her. Not without her permission, anyway. There were green buttons to start the different conveyors, red buttons to stop them, a button to sound the horn, buttons to run the dirt return, and switches to signal the drivers to lift or lower their beds. Labeled levers with billiard-ball-sized knobs controlled the wings on each side of the piler, sides lowering to let trucks through, then rising to contain the beets.

"The only thing you got to watch out for is making sure you don't clog the belt," Jeff said once he arrived, after showing her all the same things Eric had just shown her. "She'll shut down on ya if you overload her. Gotta pay attention. S'easy to lose yourself in this work."

Jeff demonstrated how to mete out the flow of beets by turning off the arterial conveyor belts at strategic intervals. He had her watch him work for a pair of trucks, then left her alone without waiting to see if she'd do it right. His faith in her was funny. She loved it.

Elise centered herself at the control panel. She looked out the window, down at the ground and the truck idling behind the raised wings of the platform. Waiting for her to let it in, for her to tell it what to do. She pushed down on the lever to flatten the wings. Everything went still, then her stuck-sugar heart dissolved.

34

THIS IS WHAT I WAS MADE FOR, ELISE THOUGHT.

There was a sweet consistency to the work. The hypnotic stupor of the beets' procession up the conveyor belt toward the boom, the metronome sweeping back and forth along the pile. The pleasure in watching the dirt-blackened beets first resist gravity, clumped together in the truck beds, then finally give in and release, a flood of relief, pooling into the wings.

Oh, the power of telling the truckers what to do: raise, stop, raise, stop, lower, lower, go. She could see everything happening outside but no one could see her. She was home there in the halogen lights and Billy Joel songs and the constant, companionable beets. She looked down upon an orgy of irregularly shaped bodies. Elise's own bulbous body fit right in. Her body had always been in the way of Elise's pleasures, the infinite embarrassments of allowing another to view and hold her lumps. The piler took the beets without judgment, with pure desire, shamelessly asking for more.

Elise, the beets said as they bounced and bumped along the conveyor belt.

Elise, the pneumatic tubes said as they lifted and lowered the truck beds.

Elise, the boom said as it clanked and creaked along its arc.

"Elise," Eric said. "I'm back. Go on break."

Eric was holding the door open; the wind pushed itself in, carrying with it the smell of Tom still being gone.

35

ELISE TOOK BOTH *V*-MARKED LUNCHES OUT OF THE trunk. The sandwich in the first brown bag she opened had peanut butter and cheese; the second bag only had peanut butter. Which made no sense: if it was down to a coin flip, random chance that one of the vegetarian lunches would have a peanut butter sandwich and the other a peanut-butter-and-cheese sandwich, then shouldn't, statistically, Cee have wound up with the peanut-butter-and-cheese sandwich at least once? Had Cee perhaps checked the lunches every night and made sure she got the regular sandwich? Elise felt betrayed by the idea, but only in a far-off and dull way. All her feelings felt far-off and dull, like the soggy, stale end of a full day spent smoking weed and watching *Love Island*. She put both sandwiches back into their bags. She only ate the apples (95). They were freezing cold and hard and sent sharp pains radiating down the root of Elise's fucked-up tooth.

She rewatched an early episode from the current season of *Pretty Little Liars*, in which someone put a necklace in the gay liar's bag, letter beads that spelled out DEAD GIRLS CAN'T SMILE with teeth—possibly human teeth—between the words. The liars flushed the necklace down the toilet. By episode three, the rich liar's mom was defending the killer cop and it was revealed that a character who was supposed to be blind could see.

It was all so empty, meaningless. The consequences were huge but imaginary. On the show, the characters were rich. Some characters who disappeared, you knew they'd come back. When the girls and their partners broke up over some dumb thing or another, you knew it wouldn't last—they'd be back together in an episode, or maybe next season. Nothing was forever, except for love.

It was not real, the world on the screen. It was a fantasy world. The girls were not friends. The boys and girls were not boyfriends and girlfriends. The girls and the partners did not exist. The danger existed, though. Elise felt sure of that, however sure she could be of anything. Her fears were warranted. Break it down as far as it could be broken down and you still had danger, heaps of it, piles and piles and piles.

36

THE DAY CREW ARRIVED, GRUNTING AND GRIPING. Tom had never shown up. *Maybe he's waiting for me in Burt*, Elise thought, and choked back a laugh.

No one spoke on the drive back, because Elise was speaking on the phone. She'd called the Robber's Bluff police department after Ryan looked up the number for her. She was told that there had been no cars matching Tom's or people who looked like Tom involved in any accidents or otherwise brought to their attention; and that she was welcome to file a report if she wanted but that they suggested, since Tom was an adult who'd left in his own car, that she not file a report yet, if at all.

"He'll either turn up or you'll hear from him, ma'am," the disembodied voice on the phone told her. "That's almost always how it goes."

Her credit card company called in the middle of talking to the dispatcher, beeping in the background throughout the conversation.

Elise tried the hospitals once they got back to camp, sitting alone and chain-smoking at the picnic table out in front of Burt. Elise was lucky they'd stopped in Canada before staying at the motel, and that she'd specifically budgeted for two cartons, since not only was she smoking more than usual, but also Cee was constantly bumming off her, and the other Mainers were intermittently bumming off her. Elise never said no, although she rarely, if ever, bummed smokes off anyone else.

Cee was gone, though. Elise would give Cee every last one of her remaining cigarettes if only she'd roll back into camp, laughing, with a great story and a grease-spotted bag of cold grilled cheese and fries. Elise had a headache.

"I'm not surprised," Sam said, making Elise jump. The wind ruffled Sam's short hair as they stood over the picnic table, casting a shadow in the opposite direction. "Her mom hated me. She said she didn't, but she hated me and we were never going to get past that. She thought I'd made Cee gay, somehow. She wouldn't stop using 'she,' either. I don't expect most people to respect me, anyway. I expect about a third of people to want to kill me. But Cee told me to get over it. Like it was hard enough for her mom to process that Cee might like eating pussy, why press it?"

Elise nodded, putting her useless phone down. That sucked. Sam sat without being invited to do so. Their presence threatened Elise's steadily faltering faith in things still being able to turn out alright. Did Tom's mother hate her? Maybe Tom's mother—a woman bursting with opinions on everything from Chris Christie's weight to the quality of service at Ruth's Chris Steak House—was actually very anti-Elise and had spent the better part of their relationship whispering slander into her son's ears. But then—

"Cee told me her parents were dead." Elise's headache throbbed against her temples.

Sam lifted their eyebrows. "Well, they're not. They're loaded and they retired wicked early and they live in Scottsdale and pay for Cee's rent. What did she tell you?"

A knot like a peach pit stuck in Elise's throat. Pressure built behind her eyes. All these physical symptoms and yet she felt nothing but mild curiosity. And there it was again, familiar as a fever: jealousy. Elise wished someone would pay her fucking rent.

"She just said—she said her parents died when she was in college," Elise said, though perhaps that was not quite right. There was something—what had she said? It seemed like being able to recall the conversation perfectly would be something Elise could do to elevate the situation beyond two pathetic dumped people trying and failing to commiserate over being dumped. But she couldn't remember exactly, only the gist of it. "She was talking about how she was really popular in high school but then in college she changed because her parents died."

Sam had their head in their hands. After a minute, they lifted their head but kept their hands cupped over their nose and mouth, eyes staring out into the middle distance. It was cold. Elise wondered, abruptly, if Sam thought that Elise was hot. She wanted them to; she wanted everyone to, all the time. She wanted to be wanted like the piler wanted the beets. For everyone in the world to want to fuck Elise into oblivion.

"She wasn't a fucking vegetarian, either," Sam said. Then they started crying. Little sobs filtered through their still-cupped hands.

Elise thought about the feeling of crying: the snot running from your nose, the painful shudders, the gluey afterbirth of tears on your lashes, sticking them together, easing you shut-eyed into sleep. Tears, she had read once, contained stress chemicals. Crying was a way for your body to calm itself down by purging excess cortisol. Elise had once watched someone weep on a subway, this person sitting alone under the subway map, and Elise had thought she ought to go ask if everything was okay (which it certainly wasn't), but there were other people—other women—on the train and none of them were getting up, and Elise didn't want to upset the person further or get wrapped up in the person's anguish and miss her stop. If the person responded well, leaned into Elise's proffered arms, Elise would not be able to extricate herself from the situation. She had to get to work. So Elise, like everyone else on the train, had pretended the sobbing person wasn't there. Elise wondered if, in the history of people weeping on the subway, anyone had ever actually helped. Of course the answer was yes. There were better people than Elise everywhere she looked.

With Sam, though, Elise was already, inexorably, involved. Whatever Cee's lie meant to Elise, it meant something else to Sam. Elise pictured herself rubbing Sam's back and saying "There, there," which was what she would have done in a movie, but it didn't seem right in this situation. Maybe she ought to start crying, too, in solidarity? But she couldn't, the pressure behind her eyes gone, the lump in her throat dissolved, as though Sam was crying for the both of them. Which, Elise guessed, they were.

"You can lean on me if you want," Elise said, instead. "Or, you know, whatever. You need. I'm here."

Sam shook their head, still cupping their hands around their nose and mouth, their sobs gone soundless now. Crying sometimes felt like choking, Elise thought, remembering. She had cried so much as a child, in fights with her parents or, shamefully, in front of bullies at school. Why was she still only thinking of herself while Sam cried right next to her, practically alone for all the good Elise was doing? "There, there," Elise could be saying, rubbing a circle on Sam's back, between their shoulder blades. "I know how you feel," she could be saying, which was about as true as that statement could ever possibly be. "You're not alone," she could be saying, which was not true at all. "He left me, too," she could be saying.

Instead, she lit a cigarette and held it out to Sam, noticing the shake of her own fingers. Sam finally took a hand away from their face to take the cigarette, but they didn't smoke it, just held it out in front of them, their other hand now covering their eyes, their shoulders slowly going still, the brutally human sound of them trying to sniff back their running nose turning Elise's stomach.

Her pediatrician had once said the phrase *postnasal drip*, which did not refer to snot running down the throat into the stomach, but that's what Elise's child brain envisioned and understood and the image had been making her sick ever since.

Elise had the very good idea, then, to get up and reach into Burt for the toilet paper roll that sat on top of all the shit piled on the second bed. But when she got back with it, the picnic table was empty and Sam was gone, the cigarette perched on the tabletop, extinguished, then rolling off into the dirt on the next hard, cold gust of wind.

37

ELISE STARED AT THE SIDE OF THE BED WHERE TOM'S body should have been, eyes under his elbow. The sunlight irradiated itself green through the canvas. Tom needed deep darkness to sleep. She should have brought that weighted sleep mask that sat in the drawer of their bedside table. It would have been the thoughtful thing to do. When she closed her eyes, she saw that bedside table and the bed next to it: too small for the two of them, they'd said, "We'll get a queen-size mattress." Now Tom's cousin was sleeping in their bed. Would Tom go to Maine, with Cee? She called Tom again. She called again. Her outgoing calls were Tom all the way down. Her phone buzzed, her heart jumped; but it was just the credit card company. Elise pressed ignore and they called back immediately. Then again. She put her phone on the charger. Outside, a dog was barking.

Maybe he'll be waiting for me when I get home, she thought. Then, *ha ha*.

Was she going home at all? What was she going to do with Burt when this was over? Did Tom expect her to buy a car with her earnings from the harvest? Why hadn't he thought about how she'd be alone to deal with this fucking piece of shit? Why had he fixed the zipper? What would happen if she just left Burt at the campsite? Maybe she could sell it to someone?

Maybe Tom would come back and she wouldn't have to worry about it.

"Sorry," he'd say. "I don't know what I was thinking. How can I make it up to you?"

But you wouldn't take him back, would you? said the newish voice.

Of course you would, dumbass, said Elise's more familiar voice, reinforcing that well-trod neural pathway.

Or, Cee would come back and say, "I got him out of the picture for us," like in a movie, as Elise flashed back to all the moments they'd shared, and understood that Cee was actually in love with her and thought that this was what Elise wanted. Or even: Cee and Tom returned and said they wanted to be together but they both also wanted to be with Elise and they'd make it work somehow.

Elise clenched her teeth. She turned over, away from where Tom wasn't sleeping. Now she faced the other bed, where all Tom's stuff still was. Didn't that mean he hadn't left her, actually? There were still things for Elise to do. She hadn't texted any of their friends, knowing even in her deepest denial that it'd be an exercise in shame. No way to frame it casually enough not to tip everyone off that she'd lost Tom in Minnesota. That he'd left her—maybe it was "finally." Maybe some of their friends would shake their heads, staring at her text, thinking, *Wow, he finally did it. Kind of a shitty way to go about it, but good for him.* Elise was making herself nauseous. She gripped her phone in both hands. Outside, the dog was still barking.

Hey! Just wondering if you've heard from Tom recently? He's gone AWOL from the harvest lol.

Before she could change her mind she sent the text to Tom's best friend. Then she turned her phone off, knowing that if she didn't, she'd just sit there staring at it, riddled with anxiety, then be too scared to look at the texts coming in.

She felt just as guilty not being scared for Tom as she felt stupid being scared for him. He wasn't gone. He couldn't be gone. That was an un-metabolizable idea.

The dog was *still* barking. Her thoughts finally stumbled away from Tom. It had to have been ten minutes straight. She slipped on her thermals and jacket and poked her head out of the camper. Ash and Ryan were standing by Arin's truck. Cake was facing the truck, barking at the closed doors.

"What's going on?" Elise asked, walking toward them, arms crossed.

"Dunno," Ash said.

"Arin's not in there?" Elise asked. "Passed out, maybe?"

"Well, we knocked . . ."

"Shut that dog up," someone yelled from across the camp. It was one of the train kids—seeing him made Elise think about how many more there had been at the start of the harvest. Those first few shifts, she'd seen them at dinner, their carpools leaving the site a little bit sooner than the Eldritch crew because their work sites were further away. She didn't see as many anymore. But maybe it was just her imagination. Or maybe they didn't eat at the mission because the food made them sick.

"You know where Arin is?" she called.

"He didn't come back with us this morning," the guy said after a moment, rubbing his eyes. Resigned to dealing with the problem, he hopped out of the van and made his way over. "Said he was gonna follow us."

"You're friends with him?" Ryan asked the train kid, whose name Elise thought might be Ty. He had a neck tattoo of a panther. Maybe-Ty shrugged.

"More or less," he said. "Maybe it needs some food?"

Everyone kept referring to Cake as "it," which perturbed

Elise. She stepped forward, tried the back door of the truck, found it locked.

"I've got this," she said, retreating to Burt. She came back with a bowl of tuna—Tom's contribution to their food stash. The three guys were still standing around watching the dog bark. Elise crouched, offering the bowl. He ate it in three gulps. Licked his chops. Elise was happy that a dog was eating Tom's food. No she wasn't. She was miserable.

Cake did not resume barking. Elise patted herself on the back. She knew that dogs had to eat food; she was practically a vet tech already.

"Okay then," Maybe-Ty said, and walked away.

"Good night," Ryan said, following Ash back to their campsite. Elise stood alone, making eye contact with Cake, who wagged his tail slowly. She felt weird leaving him outside alone, even though that's where he spent most of his time. He didn't smell that bad, as far as Elise could tell. His ears flopped in a triangle against the sides of his blocky head. He had caramel-colored fur speckled with white, like a fawn. He looked up at her with sudden adoration. He pawed at the air between them and wagged his tail.

Elise moved toward Burt. The dog followed. Elise stepped up into the camper. Cake whined. While she was thinking about whether it'd be weird for her to let Cake in, he coiled himself up on his back legs and sprang forward. Elise watched him duti-fully sniff at everything, then, satisfied, jump onto the bed. She sat down beside him, petting the silky place behind his ears until she began to feel blessedly, blissfully tired. At some point she lay down, and then Ash was calling her name. Elise had overslept; her phone was off. Cake was sprawled on Tom's side of the bed, grin-ning as Elise jolted up.

Outside, there was still no sign of Arin. Elise gave the dog another bowl of tuna, filled it with water when he was done, and left Burt's zipper open enough for the dog to come or go as he wanted. An irony, since the zipper was fixed now, because Tom had fixed it at some point when Elise was sleeping, before driving away from her without a word or warning. Like a goddamn weirdo.

There was no time for her to eat or even brush her teeth, and she piled into Jai's car hoping the cigarette she smoked out the cracked window would mask her bad breath. No one asked her how she felt.

Elise was hungry. All she'd eaten was those apples the night before. She liked it.

38

ELISE HAD THREE TEXTS FROM TOM'S BEST FRIEND.

Um what lol. No? He left or ????

Text me back when you can I asked his mom sorry if that's weird. But she said she hasn't heard from him yet. Is he back yet?

I asked Steve too sorry but I'm like this is weird. Just text me back.

She just wrote: No he's not back yet. Its ok you told people ig but idk.

Elise did not want to mention Cee; not yet, possibly not ever. If Tom and Cee had run off together, then soon enough everyone would know. He'd show up in Brooklyn with her and get his bandmates and cousin to help him get his shit out of their apartment and—

Elise gagged, put a hand over her mouth to try to hide it from the guys, who were talking about some drama back home. Her phone buzzed:

OK yeah idk weird. His mom said she wanted to talk to you but didn't have your # so I gave it to her.

It hurt Elise in her heart to know that Mrs. Henry did not have her phone number. It also made her kind of mad. Elise's mom had Tom's number. It was normal for your boyfriend's mother to have a way to contact you. She sent back:

You can tell her that I called around to all the hospitals and the police and stuff and no one was in an accident or anything and the police did not seem concerned but she's welcome to call them herself.

A moment later:

Ok will do

Are you ok?

There were new texts in the group chat. There were new texts from Carly and Lydia. A text from her friend Megan that was just an emoji. A beet. Elise didn't even know that was an emoji they had. She ignored them. Her friends hated her. It felt cruel to believe that—cruel to herself, and to them. Elise just wanted to be alone. Or something. She wanted something. Or she wanted nothing, lots of it, enough to carry her through this.

Elise put her phone on airplane mode so no more texts would come in and the credit card company couldn't call. She was fine. She was on her way to work. She had plenty of cigarettes. Payday was in six days. She was fine, she would be fine. No she wasn't and she never would be. Was Tom dead? Elise's heart hammered, and she dropped her cigarette butt out the window, then leaned toward it to gulp fresh air. Her blood hurt as it hummed through her temples, a monster just below her flesh, pulsing in an effort to rip her open. She thought she could vomit, and thought that the vomit might turn out to be blood. If Tom was dead, she'd die too. She needed to open the car door and throw herself out onto the asphalt. She realized she was making a soft keening noise, and Eric was looking at her from the other side of the car. When he reached for her, putting his hand over her hand, she croaked.

"Are you okay?" Eric asked.

The whole car had gone quiet. It was awkward, now, a discomfort circulating between these near strangers who were suddenly tasked with caring for her. The discomfort was a terrible thing, and Elise used that discomfort to propel herself into stoicism. Elise didn't make scenes, not anymore. They passed the Big Boy, his blue eyes definitely creeping leftward. He smiled so wide.

"It's okay if you're not," Ryan said from the front seat. "I wouldn't be. This situation is like, fucked or whatever."

It was the first time any of the guys had acknowledged "this situation." Elise had forced him to acknowledge it by making weird noises in the backseat. She could control herself, her dramatic inclinations, her oversized reactions, her tendency to pitch herself into the center of any catastrophe. No one could bully her so long as she controlled herself, her appetites and attitudes. She could be in charge of how people saw her. Beets were hard all the way through, flesh to center. Elise could be like that too. One of them.

One of us, said the beet guts caked underneath Elise's boots.

She breathed deep and said: "I'm fine." She took her hand away from Eric's and hid it under her big fat fucking thigh.

39

THE PILER BEEPED LIKE A TRUCK AS ELISE BACKED IT up. Down on the ground, Ash motioned with open palms for her to keep going. Two or three times a night they had to drive the piler backwards so that the boom would not get stuck on the pile. It was evidence of growth, which made Elise happy and proud. Ash closed his hand into a fist. Elise stopped backing up and lowered the wings so they could get back to work. Beautiful, beautiful, beautiful work.

Operating the piler was the best job Elise had ever had. It beat the shit out of working at the natural food store, acting as therapist for waif-y white Upper West Siders who needed her assurance that this brand of spirulina extract would not send them into an orthorexic crisis. And the dental receptionist job she'd held after college, where she was constantly fielding calls for the stoner dentist who hated responding to his clients' increasingly desperate pleas for answers about their post-surgical bleeding gums, and where she was constantly doing the wrong thing no matter how hard she tried. The campus gig as sandwich maker she'd held for the better part of four years, a position with no benefits or upward mobility. And her two part-time jobs in high school: delivering pizzas on the weekend, which required her to use her own car, so it always smelled like grease and garlic, made all the worse by the fact that she was so fucking hungry; and washing dogs at a groomer's after school during the week, where she'd have to turn the industrial-strength blow-dryer on her own skin, blasting at her inner elbows to get rid of the tiny dog hairs that would accumulate there. Her summer as a camp counselor: $500 for the whole summer, working every weekday from seven to three, with a small bonus offered only if she never missed a single day's work, an enterprise allowed only because she was fourteen and below the legal age threshold for an actual job.

In the piler, singing along under her breath to "Mainstreet" for the second time that night, beholding the floodlit and luminescent beety world below, wielding the power to command trucks and the men who drove them, the steady rhythms of the machine like part of her own organic processes, she was happy and she was not hungry. She was at peace with herself in a way she most associated with painkillers, a whole-body lightness and inner bliss. The part of her brain that restricted and judged itself turned off. She was allowed to just be: no repulsion, no loathing, no ridiculous ping-ponging between hyperaware self-control and morally illiterate wildness.

If, for instance, she was struck by a visual of herself sucking one of the levers into her mouth, accompanied by a surge of desire, she would not feel disgusted or aghast. She'd just observe the thought and its attached eroticism with a reserved pleasure. That the piler was sexy felt factual. So much of Elise's sexual history was a push-and-pull of wondering if the other person actually wanted her or was just horny enough to settle for her, so distracted by the question of being wanted that she rarely considered whether she wanted the other person. The confusing way her sexuality expressed itself, unevenly, easy enough to pretend that she was only attracted to men, convincing herself she only called herself bi for attention. Or that she just wanted to be close to bodies she liked because she was trapped in one that she hated. The piler, her desire when she was in it and of it and it itself, was a sexuality unmoored by bodies, firm and mechanical and pure. The air itself had nerve endings to tease and tongue.

In the piler, she rarely thought of Tom, and when she did, it was with a cool head: she might reflect on how she now understood exactly why Tom had jerked off in the piler. In the piler operator box, Elise felt no shame and no impatience and, certainly, no rush for the night to end. When Eric would return from his break, Elise felt a sense of loss that ran parallel to her grief over Tom's disappearance. At that dog groomer job, they called high-strung, snappy, dangerous dogs "reactive." That's how Elise felt when she wasn't operating the piler. Pure reactivity.

"I can keep going," she'd offer. "If you want to stay on break."

Eric would shake his head and give her a smile she read as fake—something in his eyes, an impatience to resume control— and she'd experience a fleeting rush of anger. But she couldn't afford to lose favor with the Mainers, who she could only hope actually liked her, or felt sorry enough for her to continue giving her rides and perhaps helping her solve the problem of how she was going to get back to the East Coast and what to do with Burt. That was how it was, always, when she had to take her hands off the knobs. The problems rushing back in with the wind. She would cede her place at the control panel and all her weight, all her selves would slam back into her body. The hunger would return.

40

THERE WERE SEVERAL EXTRA BROWN PAPER BAGS
with days-old hoagies scrunched carelessly among Jai's spare tire
and bottles of antifreeze and busted-up old boots and a pair of
dirty jeans: some were Tom's and Cee's from the last two days, and
some were there because the protein wasn't worth the gastrointes-
tinal cost everyone seemed to be paying after eating the chicken
sandwiches. Elise grabbed one of the unmarked bags. *This one
would have been Tom's,* she told herself.

She pulled up *Pretty Little Liars* and reclined, head against
glass, handle digging into her back. She dug into the paper bag for
the apple. She was so cold. All the time, cold. And hungry. All the
time, hungry. This wasn't true, but in the moment it was. She was
hungry in the moment, and the moment might as well have been
all the time. Her eating disorder was creeping back in. Elise was
stupid but she wasn't an idiot. She could feel it, a foreign presence
pressing her up against the walls of her own skin. The hot blonde
liar's backstory was that she used to be fat until she had bulimia
for a week, then decided to "take better care of herself." The hot
blonde liar was very skinny but she also liked cheese fries. Elise
pulled her hand out of the bag. Her hand wasn't holding the apple;
it was holding the sandwich, wrapped in greasy wax paper.

Elise peeled back the top of the hoagie bun: American cheese,
layered over a meat cutlet encased in some sort of gelatinous rind.
Elise touched the meat. She'd stopped eating meat as a preteen,
had only strayed a handful of times, usually during times of emo-

tional distress when she'd burn the roof of her mouth with Hot Pockets (360) that tasted like licking the bottom of a dumpster. After catching Creeps McGee watching her change, she'd eaten the ham steaks (203) her parents had in the freezer. The night she'd found the messages between Tom and his coworker, Elise had eaten the gallon of ice cream (285) in their freezer, spoonfuls of it chased by spoonfuls of peanut butter (188). Vomit and toilet water splashed back against her face when she threw it up. She blew her nose into scratchy toilet paper, her fingers coated in slime and saliva, the tips pruned like she'd gone swimming. When there was nothing else worth eating in the fridge, she ate Tom's leftover buffalo wings (441). Throwing those up hurt so bad she could no longer tolerate the smell of buffalo sauce. Tom had not mentioned the missing wings, which was, really, the barest mercy he could have provided her, all things considered. Tom wasn't such a great fucking guy, was he?

Elise's mind simply blinked off.

She put the sandwich in her mouth and bit down. The meat required a kind of chewing she wasn't used to, a different way of tearing. It tasted salty and fatty, sweetish and thick. She ate it faster. She ate it with both sides of her mouth, letting her cavity-bound tooth ache over it. Her canines dug into the flesh. She had to gnaw down with her front teeth to separate each mouthful from the next. Crumbs from the stale bread snowed into her lap like dandruff. She licked a scrunge of jelly from the corner of her mouth. Tiny sinews stuck in the gap between her molars. Her tooth hurt. She'd dropped her phone. She leaned forward, her head pressed against the back of the driver's seat, doubled over, feeding herself Tom's lunch bite by awful, painful bite. And then it was gone, all done. Just her lap full of crumbs and fingers slick with grease and a throb in her jaw. She was not full. She wanted more.

She tried watching the episode again. She started it over from the beginning. She waited for the stomachache to hit her so she could stop thinking about the lunches still back in the trunk. She ate a granola bar instead, congealed and crisped kitty litter. The artsy liar's adult-teacher-boyfriend was unemployed and broke and the rich liar told the artsy liar that she was emasculating him by buying him groceries. The hot blonde liar had to help out at the church rummage sale. All the girls were so skinny. Elise hit herself in the stomach. She scratched at her neck. She peeled the sticker off an apple and stuck the sticker in her mouth. The jacket the gay liar was wearing the night she'd blacked out was at the rummage sale. Elise waited for the stomachache. The rich liar was making out with her boyfriend and Elise's fucking boyfriend had run off with a superhot and chill girl that Elise was pathetic enough to think liked her.

Back at the piler, shivering, mind sharp with unexpected caloric energy, Elise's phone screamed at her. She rolled her eyes.

It's showing you things that aren't real, said Lydia. She didn't know what that fucking meant. But when she put her phone back in her pocket, she did see something on the ground: a beet, throbbing like a heart. She knew that wasn't real. Beets didn't throb. Just because she was seeing it didn't mean anything. She needed to figure out how a text could have come through when her phone was on airplane mode. She needed to figure out what was on her neck. She needed to call the motel. She needed to puke. Not because of the meat. If she could hork up her stomach, the whole stinking steaming bag of wet flesh and muscle, all her problems would be solved. She imagined her stomach on the ground, mixing in with the beets, her belly finally the cavity she'd always craved.

A truck pulled up and Elise took the ticket from the driver's hand and wrote the piler number and handed it back to him and went to wait by the conveyer belt for him to be done dumping his beets so she could *return the dirt*. At least that was still there; that had not abandoned her. That voice still wanted her. It wasn't as good as the piler, but it did temporarily mellow everything inside her head. Above her, the boom swung along its slow and brutalist course. She'd grown so used to the noise of the beets dropping from the conveyor into the funnel, but now she listened: like rain, like white noise, like a lullaby.

She pushed the button to *return the dirt*. Soil dribbled down, unfelt but heard, onto her hard hat. Then, a significant thud. Elise frowned, looked down at her feet where the dirt had fallen. It wasn't dirt. It was a ball of braided worms, struggling against each entwined other. The worms had nothing to say to Elise, though she listened close just to see.

Worms can't talk, said the beets.

～ 41 ～

IN THE CAR, ERIC TOLD THEM THAT THE DAYTIME piler operator, upon arriving to relieve him, had said: "Another day of cleaning up your shit."

"Fuck him," Ryan said, forehead pressed to the window. "Bootlicking dicks."

Elise's stomach hurt. A clawing, twisting, cold pain. She was afraid that she was going to fart in front of everyone. The pink boots Tom had given her were dark brown now, and stank of the same organic mineral tang as everything else in the world.

"Elise," Ryan said, twisting in his seat to hand her the aux cord. "Play it."

She plugged her phone in and played the Smiths song they'd started listening to on trips to and from the site, all screaming the line: "I was looking for a job, and then I found a job."

Except Elise did not scream with them this time. Sweat beaded her forehead. She lifted a hand to her brow but only hit her hard hat. She thought she'd taken that off.

Elise did not run to the bathroom when they got back to camp. She walked normally, like a normal person who was not about to shit her pants.

After, her stomach still hurt.

There was a note safety-pinned to Burt's green canvas:

Hey the dog keeps going into your camper didn't want to intrude but I looked in and he didn't seem to have gotten into anything any-

way if you want to take care of him for now that's fine if you need help let us know Aya fed him this morning we think Arin might have found a ride south so Z can take the dog down there after the harvest call if you need—S

Elise thought *S* must stand for Sarah. She didn't have Sarah's number but she did know which mobile home was hers. Was it weird that Arin was gone? How many people, now, were gone: Bless Up, E.T., Arin? Tom and Cee? Where was everyone going? Maybe it wasn't actually that many people, statistically. Most of them were gone because going was their *modus operandi*. Still, she felt uneasy: or, perhaps, it was hopeful relief she felt. If there was something going on, some conspiracy disappearing people, then maybe it meant—

It didn't matter. Hope was not going to help her. Elise had to help Elise now; this had not, historically, been her strong suit.

Cake woke up when Elise entered the camper, wagging his tail. Did he get heartworm pills? The family calendar, when she was growing up, always had little red heart stickers on the day when the dog was due for his pill. What about rabies vaccines? He was neutered, which was good. His short fur wasn't matted and he didn't smell any worse than a dog should smell, in Elise's opinion. He let her sit down beside him and even put his head in her lap, nose sniffing at the space where her thighs met before settling on one of her knees.

"That's what we call a thigh gap, bubba," Elise told the dog, manually pulling the meat of her thighs apart to mimic thinness. He yawned, and when he closed his mouth the tip of his tongue was still nestled between his front teeth, peeking out between his lips. Cake was a good dog, and to be left the way Arin left him was so cruel. Maybe she could be a vet tech and take Cake to work with her so he'd never be left alone again. She lay back, across the bed, her head where Tom's hips had lain so many nights, hair fanned out and greasy. Cake, probably thinking it was a game, crawled on top of her, a welcome weight. Tail wagging, he licked the tears and the snot from her face as she sobbed.

42

SHE WOKE UP TO A GRAY SKY AND THREE TEXTS FROM an unknown number. In all three texts, Linnie had called her fat. Linnie had never met Elise, never seen Elise, never heard Elise's voice, didn't know Elise's name. Linnie had no perception whatsoever of Elise. And yet she still knew she was dealing with a fat girl. Elise hadn't eaten since nibbling Italian bread at the mission. Elise thought about this stranger finding ways to text Elise even though Elise kept blocking her. Elise didn't bother blocking this time; she saved it in her phone as "pure id."

Tom's best friend had texted again:

Getting worried over here.

Tom's mom really wants to talk to you. She said she called but you didn't pick up. You should call her.

Sorry I'm sure this is upsetting for you too. Get back to me when you can.

There were five new voice messages, which must have been from Mrs. Henry because none of Elise's friends would have left a voice message. Maybe there was a voice message from the bank, though. Or the motel. Maybe Tom had actually driven all the way back to Michigan, backtracked all the way to that fucking fleabag motel, stormed into the lobby to fight for Elise's money. A grand romantic gesture. And he'd dropped Cee off at a bus station somewhere along the way as a favor to her, because she actually *was* leaving Sam. Cee had told that lie about her parents because she wanted Elise to like her. Cee did care what Elise thought of her. Cee was jealous of Elise. Cee wanted to be Elise.

Elise forced herself to laugh. She had been holding the phone over her face, and now she let it drop. It hit her nose, her cheek, slid onto the pillow. It vibrated; Tom? Finally, Tom?

Obviously not. It was the credit card company calling again. They'd never stop. Elise knew that they'd never stop. The point was to drive you crazy. Couldn't she just pick up, explain the situation, beg for mercy? Elise rolled herself up, the sleeping bag slipping down to her lap, her neck sore and her hair stuck to her cheek and the space heater blowing that hot air around, making her sinuses ache. Her mouth was very dry. The camper was very empty. She could not pick up the call. Her phone stopped vibrating. She would never pick up. She unzipped the camper; it was drizzling, the world taking on the flat, atonal sheen of a commercial for an antidepressant.

At dinner that night, after shitting her brains out again and feeding Cake another bowl of tuna—the last of the packets—and brushing a few humming sugar beets off her seat so she could sit down, Elise told the Mainers about the note. All of them except Sam, who was eating dinner by themselves back at camp.

"It doesn't make sense for him to leave his truck and dog," Elise said. "He wouldn't need a ride if he, you know, could drive himself there. I just think it's, like, weird." Elise was hungrier than she should have been. Probably from all the shitting. And because she'd only slept fitfully, the splitting pains of her tooth keeping her up. It was spaghetti again at the mission. Elise let Mike ladle slippery-slick noodles onto her paper plate. She did not intend to eat any. Spaghetti was tapeworms.

"I mean, it *is* weird," Ryan said. "But that guy drank like a motherfucker and definitely was a junkie."

Elise picked at the Italian bread, its topography torn up by cold pats of butter, crust hard enough to hurt the roof of her mouth when she took her single bite. When she was a kid, on pasta night, Elise would make little sandwiches out of spaghetti and Italian bread. She called them spaghetti sandwiches, and they disgusted her parents, even her father, who was usually less concerned about Elise's eating habits than her mother.

"I just think it's weird that people, like, leave," Elise muttered. "There's a lot of people gone now."

Discomfort rippled around the table. No one wanted to talk about people leaving with a person who had been left. Elise felt opaque, blurred from the rest of the world. No one could see her, even if they were looking straight at her.

"You're right," Jai said, sounding kindly disingenuous. "It is weird."

Everyone but Eric nodded down at their plates.

"Are you gonna take care of the dog?" Eric asked, boldly making eye contact. Implying that perhaps he *did* see her. An unexpected, almost unwelcome comfort.

Elise's head didn't quite hurt, but it didn't feel good. Her nails were heavy with all the black mud under them. Her skin smelled starchy. Her pores were clogged with beet debris, and that felt somehow tied to her non-headache.

"Um," she finally said, not completely able to comprehend what it would mean to "take care of the dog." She didn't have any food left to feed the dog. She supposed she could feed the dog sandwiches. The dog had eaten once today; she could feed it again later, she guessed. There was the shift between now and then: there was only ever the shift. It was not five days until payday because the shift would last forever, and there would be nothing after. There was barely even anything before. This was all barely happening. "Yeah. Yeah, I will."

"Cool," Eric nodded. As though he actually believed Elise was capable of taking care of the dog.

Elise endured a flash of heat, thinking about how Eric was her friend, was maybe interested in being more than a friend. Followed by shame at having even entertained the thought of anyone wanting her ever again.

We want you, said the beets on the floor beneath the table.

You are not hearing beets talking to you, said the newish voice. So confidently wrong. Elise wanted to stomp it down to pulp. The conversation had continued elsewhere, without her.

"She's, like, nice or whatever," Ryan was saying, about Sydney. "But she kept fighting me about big ag and, you know, overproduction and shit. I said, 'You get big strawberries but they have no taste,' and she goes, 'That's 'cause they're big so the flavor is more spread out.'"

"I don't think that's how that works," Eric laughed.

"I believe the children are our future," Elise sang. The guys laughed, but Elise felt weird. There were so many people to feed. What a luxury to complain about strawberries. She was jealous of Sydney. Sydney was getting a good degree; she would have a career. Sydney would never have her life ruined over $143.

Outside, the drizzle turned into rain, and all the phones at the table went off at once: the same number, an automated voice telling them not to show up at the site; work was canceled due to weather. Their first night off. Elise was surprised at how poorly she took the news. What was she going to do for a whole night? She'd go crazy, all that free time. She needed to work, she needed to be *at* work. She needed her piler, needed to *return the dirt*.

43

THE MAINERS DISCUSSED GOING TO THE LAUNDROMAT. Elise knew she should go with them. But she had no money. As though reading her mind, Ash turned to her. Elise guessed he knew, now, about her being penniless. Probably everyone knew. She shrank down in her seat.

"I can spot you, if you need," he said. She shook her head. "Really? You sure? It's totally cool. I know you're good for it."

"I'm sure," Elise said. Eric frowned. "Thanks, though."

She would just wash her stinky clothes one-by-one in the bathroom sink. Foam them up with pink industrial hand soap. It didn't matter. Nothing mattered.

Cake was underneath the picnic table, sheltering from the rain. He rushed to her, his hips and butt wiggling so hard his back feet left the ground. Elise reminded herself that Arin could return at any time and reclaim him. She was merely a temporary caretaker. If anyone was doing anyone a favor, it was the dog keeping her from sleeping alone. She toweled Cake down with Tom's towel.

She had to get her dirty clothes together. She had to get her shit together. She ran her tongue over her tooth, wished the pain would simply go away. She found a bottle of aspirin Tom had brought and took some. She took her phone off airplane mode, just in case.

The best she and Tom had come up with to maintain a semblance of organization in the tiny camper consisted of balling up clothes that were too dirty to wear again—a standard that had stretched to its most disgraceful limits—and throwing them into the far corner, folding clothes that were dirty but wearable in separate piles on the spare bed, and keeping clean clothes in their packs. Elise's pack was empty now. She grabbed Tom's pack, sat on the bed with it standing between her knees, staring down into its long and spacious interior as though there might be an answer inside—something Tom had stowed away from her, something that would explain it all. She'd avoided touching any of his stuff. She'd avoided making so many logical choices, because the more logical the choice, the more blatant the betrayal. If Elise made illogical choices—ignoring the situation entirely, not telling people, concocting fantasies about people being eaten by the beet pile—she could sustain whatever delusion was keeping her afloat.

All that was in Tom's pack was a pair of waffled long johns, a pair of gray sweatpants, and a plain black T-shirt with a hole in the armpit. All the rest of his clothes were on the bed. Dirty. God, why'd he leave it all? Because he wanted to move quickly and quietly, undetected. Because it was useless, stinky clothes and Cee would buy him a whole new wardrobe, and why *not* leave Elise with his dirty laundry? His wallet was gone. His phone, too. It was wishful thinking: *He might have left me, but he'd never have left his bleach-stained boxers.*

But he'd fixed the zipper.

Elise picked up the nearest of his dirty stuff: the thick flannel he'd gotten at a thrift store in Poughkeepsie. Actually, she had found it. She saw it on the overstuffed rack, thought it was Tom's style. She held it up to him and was delighted at his approval. It was so nice to really know someone.

The flannel smelled like him. Of course it did. It smelled, too, like beet starch. Elise let it fall onto her lap and picked up his old work shirt from when he worked at Orgrounds Coffee.

A T-shirt of a band Elise had never listened to, although she recognized the name—but did she actually recognize the name, or did she just recognize the shirt? She shook out a pair of crusty jeans, freeing a beet. It thudded to the floor and rolled up against the storage trunk.

Elise, said the beet.

She picked up one sock, then another. Cake stood on his hind legs, front paws on Elise's thighs, sniffing everything she picked up. Getting in the way. Elise piled Tom's clothes onto her lap until they threatened to fall over.

Then she gathered them all up and threw them through Burt's unzipped entrance into the rain. Then she stripped herself down, threw her dirty clothes into the pile of the rest of her dirty clothes, and put on the clean sweatpants and clean shirt from Tom's backpack. It felt disgustingly lush and cozy, wearing these clean, oversized, brand-name-soft clothes that smelled more like laundry detergent than they smelled liked Tom, in the camper while the rain pattered against the canvas, kept company by the dog who smelled like wet dog, which was a smell that Elise actually quite liked. Cake curled up beside her with his nose under his tail, a perfect circle, very much unlike a beet.

44

U sure u wanna sit out laundry?

I'm sure! TY tho.

we're going to movie after. we can get ur ticket np.

Elise was annoyed and touched by Eric's insistence on their friendship. He had no business shoving his kindness in her face.

sounds fun but i'm tired, just gonna nap.

She waited until she heard the guys' voices, the slamming car doors, the tires rolling over wet gravel. In the bathroom, she did her best to wash her clothes in the sinks, using the biodegradable laundry pods she'd brought from home. Regular laundry soap was toxic and didn't get completely filtered when the water went through the sewage system, dumped back into rivers and streams. Elise, who did most of the laundry because she liked doing laundry, ponied up for the good stuff: no phosphates, brighteners, chlorine bleach. Elise wanted so badly to be good. Tom just got whatever was cheapest, stuff that smelled "good" in a way the eco-friendly stuff didn't, and then Elise would refuse to use it and he'd roll his eyes, and she'd say to just let her buy the laundry detergent from then on, and then a month later she'd put *laundry detergent* on the whiteboard on the fridge to remind herself, and then Tom would see it written there and buy the cheap scented stuff from Duane Reade, and Elise would say she wasn't going to use it out of principle, and she also wouldn't use the fabric softener he bought, partly on principle but also because she didn't know how to use fabric softener and didn't want to learn, and Tom would complain about his clothes not smelling good or feeling right, and Elise guessed they'd just have kept doing that forever and ever if Tom hadn't disappeared. Elise, wasting money as if her little purchases actually made a fucking difference. How much had she spent on laundry pods over her lifetime: Enough to have kept her account in the black after the motel overcharged her? Enough to have made it so that Tom never had to find out because it never would have happened? Maybe Elise had been fucking herself over in five-dollar increments. Would Tom have left if she'd learned to use fabric softener? If she'd respected it when he said he didn't like how the laundry smelled, instead of rolling her eyes because the laundry smelled fine, just not like Fresh Linen?

Elise's fingers pruned as she twisted and sloshed the fabric around. Her clothes turned the water brackish, the nontoxic soap draining away, as worthless as the mud and sweat it took with it.

It had stopped raining when she left the bathroom; camp was quiet, everyone still sheltering inside. She held Tom's sweatpants up to keep the bottoms from dragging through the mud. Back in the camper, she laid her and Tom's towels on the spare bed and laid her clothes out on the towels and angled the space heater toward the clothes.

Her phone buzzed again; and again. It was Mrs. Henry. Elise faltered, then accepted the call.

"Hello?"

"Elise?"

Mrs. Henry's voice over the phone sounded deeper and more throaty than Elise remembered—had they ever even spoken on the phone before?

"Hi, Mrs. Henry," Elise said, marveling at how innocuous that sounded. How strange this conversation was about to get, although it began the way every conversation ever began. The camper felt, suddenly, too small. She rolled Tom's sweatpants halfway up her shins and went outside, leaving the flap unzipped for Cake.

"I'm glad I got through to you," Mrs. Henry said, voice clipped. "I suppose you've been busy?"

She said this with a hint of sarcasm, as though Elise couldn't possibly have been busy. Mrs. Henry had been supportive of them going to the harvest inasmuch as she thought it would inspire Tom to get his ass in gear in regard to grad school—his words, not hers. Something like scaring him straight, show him that the wealth he was so ashamed of was a good thing, actually. Anyway, Mrs. Henry hadn't been worried about Tom losing his job at the cafe, the way Elise's mother had been worried about Elise losing her job at the natural foods store. Maybe Elise was just going to have a headache for the rest of her life, and the only difference would be when it was worse versus better. She walked toward the river, where she and Cee had sat that first night.

"Um."

"You haven't heard from my son, I'm guessing, or *I* would have heard from him," Mrs. Henry went on.

Elise closed her eyes. Elise got the feeling that Tom's mother saw Elise as incapable of properly addressing the situation. She wasn't wrong.

"Well, I woke up and he was gone," she said. "The car was gone. I thought he'd come back but he never did."

Was that it, actually? Was that the story? It was missing a detail, of course: the most crucial one, by some accounts. But still, that brief and fragmentary statement was the whole story. In essence. The river was bloated and rushing. It had been too dark that night to really see it. It was thinner than Elise remembered, the opposite bank a stone's throw away. Was it a river, then, or a stream?

"Yes, dear, I understand that," Mrs. Henry said. "What can you tell me about his mood? Had you been quarreling?"

Quarreling? Mrs. Henry spoke like she wanted to be British. Mrs. Henry nurtured the fantasy of propriety the way Elise nurtured the fantasy of thinness. Tom's family was established, old New England stock transplanted to upstate New York. Not *Forbes* amounts of money but more than enough, trust funds and real estate investments and lots of little acreages scattered across the East Coast.

Elise walked to the short dock, stood at its edge, tried to remember how that night had ended. When had she and Cee decided to call it? Had Cee had to help Elise back to camp? Or had they leaned on each other, skin on drunken skin? Had Elise been alone, actually, and only fantasized about sitting here with Cee?

"Only a little, I guess. But the last things we said were, like, good things."

In fact, Elise had no idea what their last words to each other had been. She hadn't known, at the time, that the words would be important. And perhaps they weren't. They were just words. They didn't mean anything. Elise thought of the fight, and it felt like turning on the radio in the middle of a song: like the memory was constantly playing on a loop somewhere in the back of her mind even if she only sometimes tuned in. *With her. Do better. Holding me down. With me.*

"Hmm," Mrs. Henry said.

Elise had the irrational fear that Mrs. Henry didn't believe her. That Tom's mother was imagining a fight even worse than the one they'd had: a full-on brawl. Fisticuffs, even. That it was this that chased her son off—something Elise had done, or didn't do, or how Elise had responded to some perfectly valid complaint.

Which was maybe true. Elise fought an impulse to lie to Mrs. Henry that the last thing Tom had said to her was "Fuck me, you little whore." That was a sexy thing to think about.

"I don't—"

"I don't suppose you know what he was wearing. Just in case we'll need to actually file a missing person's."

"Um." Elise tried to think about what had been missing from Tom's clothes as she'd chucked them out of the camper. She couldn't think of what should have been among them but wasn't. If Elise went missing, her mother would have filed immediately. But the cops there would have said the same thing as the cops here, she was sure. Adult men with all their cognitive faculties who leave in their own cars are not missing people. Maybe Cee was a serial killer, though. Luring men from their girlfriends and murdering them and hiding their bodies in piles of beets. Maybe she'd hid his whole damn car in the pile. Maybe that was what that alarm was.

Elise wondered how Mrs. Henry saw her. She had always believed Mrs. Henry was passively accepting of Elise, willing to forgo her desire for a socialite or upper-crust daughter-in-law if it meant her only son would be happy, while also believing that Elise could not possibly make Tom happy in the long run because Tom would grow out of his grimy Brooklyn social scene. Elise as Tom's working-class-clout girlfriend. Cee as Elise, but better. Elise scratched her armpit through the hole in Tom's shirt. Had Mrs. Henry bought this shirt, these sweatpants? Judging by the labels, probably. How many times a minute did Elise think about Tom? Was Tom thinking about her at all? He was probably balls-deep in Cee at that very moment, her hair a spray of dark vines against crisp white hotel linens, or flipped upward, over her head and across his belly as he lay on his back and she blew him. There was a big rock in the middle of the river, water parting around it. By the time the water came together again on the other side of the rock, it was different water. Never the same river twice and all that.

"Well," Mrs. Henry said when Elise failed to produce anything of value. "We both know this is not exactly out of character for Tommy."

Elise had no idea what Mrs. Henry meant by that. Really, all rivers were one river.

"I don't follow," Elise finally said. She wondered what kind of detergent Mrs. Henry used.

"You do know that Tommy's done this before," Mrs. Henry said, her voice clipped again—and perhaps it was Elise's imagination, but she sounded slightly gleeful to be in possession of information that Elise lacked. "Three times."

"I didn't know—"

"Yes, dear, the first time he was sixteen and he was missing for three days. Worst three days of my life! The cops said a boy that age—well, they weren't going to send out search parties, exactly. But he turned up with poison ivy. He'd been camping. He'd hitchhiked all the way to Vermont and back. His father—anyway, we considered sending him to reform school. I'd hoped never to feel *that* kind of fear again, but then when he was eighteen—a week, this time, he took his car and drove to Miami to meet some girl he met on the internet!"

A beet bobbed down the river. Then another, and another.

"And I just said, 'Tommy, why can't you just tell us when you're going to do these crazy things?' Of course he promised he would, but you can guess what happened a year later. He was supposed to be spending spring break at home but he went to Montreal instead, to some, some music festival. By then, you can imagine,

I was quite worn out by it all and I just thought, 'Perhaps this is how Tommy is.' Never mind his poor father. You wouldn't know it, but Paul—well."

Elise didn't know what to say or think about this. Tom had never mentioned any of it to her. These, she realized, were his secrets. What had ever made her think she was the only one who'd hidden things? Although, in comparison, Elise's stupid little secrets looked even stupider and littler. This felt like some defining characteristic, Tom's omission of these stories more like a lie. More beets flowed along the current. Had Tom spent the entire five years controlling the way Elise saw him? Had he told Cee? Elise must have looked like a fucking idiot, giving him all the information he'd ever need to see her as her true, pathetic self while he wisely hoarded this *foundational* information. The things Mrs. Henry was telling her were not only news to her, they did not fit into her idea of who Tom was. Tom was many things that weren't great, but she'd never thought he was *that* selfish or thoughtless. How could he have let his mother worry that way? Mrs. Henry sucked but she was his mother. Elise needed to call her mother. Tom was a bad son. Elise was a good daughter. The beets agreed as they flowed past her, encouraging whispers in the ear not pressed to the phone.

"Elise? Are you there?"

"I'm here," Elise said. She wondered where all the beets were coming from, because there really were quite a lot. One came close to the dock, rotating mindlessly as the water took it wherever the water was going.

"It's become something of an embarrassment that the gentlemen down at the precinct know me so well. And I think—perhaps—oh, you know how men are. They need to express their wildness somehow. We should be happy that Tommy expresses it the way he does, instead of—I don't even want to imagine something worse than disappearing on your poor mother every year, but I'm quite sure there are worse things."

Then again, fuck Mrs. Henry. Maybe if she had Mrs. Henry as a mother, always henning around like someone in a Jane Austen novel, she'd want to inflict a little psychological torture, too. Elise's mom had her faults, but she wasn't an insufferable stuck-up WASP. A beet hit the big rock, was immediately carried around it.

"Anyway, he hasn't used his credit card yet," Mrs. Henry said. "Though I suppose that doesn't mean anything, does it? He probably has plenty of savings."

"You can access his credit card?" Elise said. She'd never give her parents access to any of her financial records; sometimes she was scared to die not because of dying itself, but because her parents would find out everything.

"Well, of course," Mrs. Henry said. "We're the ones paying it."

What did that mean? Elise was pretty sure Tom only had one credit card. She saw him use it a few times a month. Her debit card and his credit card were both linked to her Grubhub account. Sometimes he put that card down at a bar. She'd always assumed that he paid it off himself. No wonder Tom always had money to invest, with his parents bankrolling his pleasure purchases. How often had she gotten the next round or the next takeout order because he'd paid for it the time before?

"Elise, is the connection bad? Are you hearing me alright?"

"No," Elise said. Was Elise annoyed because she was hungry? Hungry, but not. Never hungry, always hungry, there was no difference. Why should Elise care where Tom's money came from, who paid his credit card? Wasn't the whole point—wasn't her whole *thing* not caring about his parents' money, never wanting it to save her from herself? "I'm just thinking."

"I understand this must be terribly hard on you. But I know my Tommy—he may have these frivolous sprees on occasion, but he will not leave you stranded there in Minnesota. I raised him better than that."

Tom was fucking spoiled. Elise should never have let him forget it. And she shouldn't let Mrs. Henry think that she'd raised her son "better than that," because she clearly hadn't.

"There was a girl," Elise blurted out. There it was. The final detail that brought the story into focus. Now she'd told the whole story: he was gone, the car was gone, the girl was gone. Elise closed her eyes. She wondered if she was shaking. She felt like she was shaking. She opened her eyes. The whole river was nothing but beets. She gasped.

"Oh," Mrs. Henry said, voice lowered now.

"Is he going to come back?" Elise asked, her voice cracking, eyes boiling over so that everything dissolved into one multitoned mist. "Is he coming back for me?"

Mrs. Henry did not respond. Elise used the heel of her free hand to wipe her eyes. The flood of beets had passed. She turned her head downriver, but more tears blurred her vision.

"Just let me know when you hear from him," Elise said. Then she hung up. Slipped the phone into Tom's sweatpants pockets and wiped her eyes clear; the beets were too far downriver now for her to see them. But she saw something else, barely poking out of the brown reedy riverside vegetation. Elise picked her way toward it.

Elise's phone buzzed in her hand—Tom's mother calling again. She let it vibrate in her palm. Tom had once made a joke about using a phone as a vibrator. Tom's mother called him Tommy. If Elise and Tom had ever actually had a chance at a future together, Mrs. Henry would be Alice, not Mrs. Henry. Elise pushed through a wall of dying bluejoints. Cee's snapback, the one the wind had blown off her head, was hanging from a branch, weighed down by water, the brim hovering over a current that would have whipped it away if it had been just an inch lower. It was soaking wet, but Elise put it on anyway. The beets must have brought it to her.

45

HER HANDS AND FEET WERE LEADEN, HER SHOULDERS wilted and her hips heavy. She wanted to lie down and be rid of herself, all her selves, for a long, long time. She wanted to go to her childhood bedroom, where her mother always put fresh linens on the bed and flowers on the nightstand, clipped from the garden during warm months or bought from the grocery store during cold months, where the color palette was a comforting buttery yellow and there was always almond milk and hummus in the fridge. Elise's parents hadn't even liked hummus until they started buying it for her. She wanted to go there and be sleepy, and sleep. If she'd had a cavity when she was a child, her parents' insurance would have covered it. She wanted dental insurance so she could go to a dentist.

You aiight, bitch? Carly texted. Elise texted back a smiley face and a worm. In the group chat, her least favorite friend had written: come home, lady! Elise scrolled up to find the context, and couldn't. It didn't matter. She assumed that it was not meant for her. What kind of person even had a least favorite friend? Elise should have been thanking her lucky stars that she had any friends at all, that any percentage of the population was born without the otherwise-universal gene that made people dislike Elise. It was hard to tell whether it was more exhausting having the bad thoughts, or knowing how dumb the bad thoughts were.

The rain started up again. A comforting pedal on the canvas. Cee's hat was drying on the bed with all Elise's just-washed clothes. Tom's black T-shirt had white dog hairs on it.

It occurred to her that she could ask Mrs. Henry for help—she could likely be guilted into it. The thought turned Elise's empty stomach. It was pathetic, and also felt like some odd permutation of blackmail. Besides, wasn't it still technically possible that Tom was dead? Wasn't it still technically possible that something had *happened* to him, that he and Cee and Bless Up and E.T. and Arin were all victims of something? No, no, that was stupid. She had to stop being so fucking stupid all the fucking time.

If she needed help, she should call her mother. She should call her mother, anyway. She thought about lying: she could call her mom and not mention Tom leaving. How long could she maintain the illusion, though? Only until she couldn't pay the rent. Actually, she *could* pay the rent—with her harvest money. It'd buy her almost two months of not having to tell her mother that she'd been dumped. Emotionally, that felt like a good deal.

There were daughters in the world who'd tell their moms first if something like this happened. Elise pictured Cee telling her still-living mom about Tom: Had Cee finally found someone with sufficient wealth and an appropriate gender expression to make her mother happy? Tom's mother would be happier with Cee as a daughter-in-law. Elise knew her own mother would be supportive and compassionate if and when she finally told her. She also knew that her mother might somehow, in some way, make Elise feel that she was at fault. There was a possibility that Elise's mother would mention, in a well-meaning way, Elise's weight. That had been her solution when Elise was being bullied: "Let's try low-carb together."

She rubbed her neck, which meant rubbing the bruise. Her

tooth still hurt, she took more aspirin. Probably she'd gotten the cavity from suddenly drinking so much real sugar in her coffee. What if Salt of the Earth Sugar was putting *something* in the scale-house sugar packets? Like worm eggs? And her stomach was full of worms, like the puppies.

"Do you have worms?" Elise baby-voiced Cake, rolling him over to scratch his belly. "Are you my wormy boy? Are you my low-carb wormy boy?"

Elise's phone buzzed.

This movie is just about the most boring thing I can think of. Meet us at American Legion after? Elise put her phone down. She'd respond later. She stank, stinking up Tom's clean clothes. She needed a shower. Soon the credit card company would call again. She turned her phone to airplane mode.

Elise noticed some dried blood on her pillow. She couldn't think what it was from: probably a nosebleed, or a crack in her lips. Elise picked up Tom's pillow but she did not bring it to her face to smell. She just sat with it on her lap, staring down at the hands she folded on top of it. She wasn't sure what cuticles were, exactly, but she could see how her skin flaked all around the nail bed, the lines where blood collected at the place where the nail met flesh. She'd always had very soft hands. Her one real girlfriend had liked that about her. Now they felt tough and dry. *I should look up what kind of bug bite leaves bruising. I should do that before I forget. I should call the motel. I should call.*

You should return, said a beet from the corner.

Dirt plinked down on Elise's hard hat in a steady trickle. It dribbled off the conveyor belt that returned the dirt to the trucks and onto her as she stood holding the button. It was wet dirt. It was falling all over her. She looked down. She was barefoot. It wasn't dirt. It was water. She was holding the knob of the shower in her gloved hand while water fell down on her. She was naked except for the gloves and the hard hat. She turned her face up to see where the water was coming from. It was coming from the showerhead. She was taking a shower. She was getting clean.

46

CAKE WOKE HER UP AT NOON, WHINING AND NUDGING at her arm with his wet nose. The wind billowed the canvas walls like sails. She had a missed text from the night before, Eric asking her, again, if she wanted to meet up. Elise couldn't remember what time she'd gone to bed, but she knew she hadn't ultimately gotten much sleep. The cold fever of pain in her gums had her tossing and turning, taking too much aspirin. Her pillow was wet. None of her clothes had fully dried.

Elise unzipped the door to let Cake out. Eric was standing there, holding a plastic bag. He jumped out of the way as Cake launched himself into the wind, bouncing off one of Tom's T-shirts. The rain had left puddles, rivulets of muddy water between them like a stream system. The wind moved the water in the puddles, an ecosystem of running currents polluted by cigarette butts and fast-food wrappers. The wind was overwhelming and even Cake paused, his floppy ears lifting, one blown over the top of his blocky head and exposing the soft pink flesh inside. Then he bounded off, ecstatic to exist.

Eric stepped toward the camper.

"Hey," Eric's cheeks grew redder. Elise thought that this might be the coldest it had been yet—a dubious and depressing distinction. She stepped back, made room for him to enter, then zipped the door closed again.

"What's up? How was the movie?" Elise asked, acting normal. Eric looked around the camper. Only Tom and Elise had ever been in here. Elise briefly entertained the idea that he was going to make a move on her. His eyes would narrow and he'd lunge forward and push her against the bed and they'd fuck like drunk teenagers. Eric was hot but Elise didn't know if she even really wanted that. And, she told herself, it was stupid to assume he'd want it. Why would he want her? Why would anyone? Tom didn't.

We do, said the corner beet.

"Shit," he said. "But we got you some dog food. For the dog."

He handed her the plastic bag. Purina. Elise's capacity for gratitude felt dusty and insufficient. She just wanted to be sad and mad.

"Thank you," she said, opening the bag and pouring an indiscriminate amount into the bowl on the floor. The bowl still smelled like tuna. The whole camper smelled a little like tuna, now that she noticed it. This was embarrassing.

"Um. This is weird, but Sam's, like, gone," Eric said after a moment.

"Gone, like . . . how?" Elise didn't like that Eric was looking at her before she'd had a chance to look at herself. She wondered how her bruise was doing. Was Eric her friend? Did he like her? Did she like him? Did he just feel bad for her? Did it matter?

"They left. They wrote a note, said they were giving up. Not, like, a suicide note. At least it didn't *seem* like a suicide note. I mean, they weren't really one of our friends, before this, they kind of came with Cee and we don't really know them, so—" Eric faltered.

Elise wished she could leave. But also, she didn't want to leave before the job was done. She wanted to be there when the pile reached its most full self. But also:

"That's weird," Elise said. "Right? It's weird? That they just left?"

"I guess," Eric said. "But, like I said, they came with Cee. This is kind of embarrassing, but none of us even have their number.

They were really shy. Or, I don't know. It didn't really seem like they liked us."

"Yeah, but, like, that's so many people who're just gone or whatever—should we be worried? Are you worried?"

"The last thing they said was that they wanted to leave. They were really upset last night, and they kept saying they'd given up and they didn't want to be here anymore and it was all too much and shit like that. Then they asked for a ride, but no one could take them 'cause we were all drinking. You got my texts? They probably walked or got a ride after we all fell asleep. Their note basically said good riddance. It was like, 'I don't know you, you don't know me, I just want to forget any of this ever happened.' Basically."

Elise stared at Eric. He didn't see it. Only she saw it. Bless Up walking off into the night. Cee and Tom driving away, never to be heard from again. E.T. and Arin not making it home. Sam, somewhere. Her head hurt. When had she last eaten? The Mainers had been drinking without her. They were the cool kids. They'd invited her. She'd ignored them. Had anything ever not been Elise's fault? She sat down hard on the bed. She cradled her face in both hands, thumbs down her jawline and index fingers framing her cheeks. Why was everyone leaving? Where was everyone going? The beet pile, the car alarm, the voice in the dirt box. Looking up at Tom's silhouette in the piler box. It could be anyone's silhouette. It could be hers. She had to go home before whatever had happened to Tom happened to her. Nothing had happened to Tom. No one wanted her. She wasn't supposed to be thinking about this. It was stupid. People left because it was a shit job. She couldn't leave. She had no money.

"Hey, hey, you don't need to worry about it," Eric said. "They're definitely fine. I didn't come over here to stress you out. I wanted to tell you that I'm gonna move to the other piler, just making sure that you're gonna be down to work the piler full-time. Is that gonna be okay? Because we can get someone else, train Jai or something."

Was she gonna *be down*? Was it gonna *be okay*? What the fuck did that mean? *Obviously* she could do it. She was perfectly fucking capable of operating the piler. What, did Eric think that she was incompetent? Too stupid? Too emotional? Too *weak*?

"Uh, yeah," she laughed. "I can do that. I'm not a fucking imbecile." She dropped her hands, glared up at him. Eric looked hurt. She felt guilty but she liked the way the guilt felt. Her heart was boiling now, a red filter bleeding into the corners of her vision. Men. These fucking men. None of them thought to get Sam's phone number? They thought Sam didn't like them, maybe Sam had every right not to like them. What if she punched Eric in his stupid hot face? How good would that feel? It would feel awful, terrible, it would feel so awfully terribly good. She'd hate herself and it would be good. She was a monster.

As though he could sense this, Eric stepped back. All Elise had going for her was self-control. All she'd ever really been good at was starving. She wished Eric would put his hands around her throat and bite her lip until it bled, and she was embarrassed to want him and she hated him for not wanting her the way she fantasized he would and how that made her embarrassed, forced her to be ashamed, angry and turned on and viscerally alive, aware, red-blooded and burning.

"Okay, okay," he said. "Sorry. Listen, uh."

But Elise didn't feel like listening, and anyway she doubted Eric had anything to say. It was just something men said when they were biding time to think of the next shitty thing to say. She didn't want to be told what she should and shouldn't care about. She didn't want to be told to fucking *listen*. If she wanted to worry about Sam being gone, she could. She'd worry so fucking hard. She'd worry her eyeballs out of her fucking head, she'd worry all the flesh off her fingers, she'd worry until she dropped to her knees and licked Eric's vegan-leather Doc Martens, or until she puked worms all over Eric's vegan-leather Doc Martens, or did whatever the fuck she wanted to do.

"Elise, you know that we're friends, right?" Eric said.

"Sure," Elise answered through gritted teeth. *Were* they friends, though? Were they, really? Did Eric pity her? Did Eric hate her? Was Elise angry, or was she having a panic attack?

"Oh fuck," Eric said, laughing a little bit. He dug into the kangaroo pocket of his tie-dye hoodie. "Duh. I also came to give you this. She—they—left it for you."

Eric held out a folded piece of paper. Elise read her name printed military-neat along one corner. She took it from him. Eric pulled at the zipper, inviting a gust of wind into the camper, icy and hard. She grabbed the canvas flap, holding it open. He left, his head down. She hated everything she saw out there. Somewhere, someone's trash had been knocked over. Empty beer cans bounced like tumbleweeds down the gravel road. A bloody tampon lay wedged under one leg of Elise's site's picnic table. Someone had made a cairn of beets in the middle of the road; it was somehow still standing despite the wind's best efforts. At the RV, Eric wrestled the screen door open, though he lost his grip and it ricocheted off the side with an aluminum slap, and then he was inside and gone, out of sight.

Elise unfolded the paper; it was a sketch of her and Tom, the tender graphite curves of their cheeks close together. Both smiling. Elise wondered when Sam had done it. And why. Just to be nice? Except that Sam had written over most of Tom's face, x-ing out his eyes.

FUCKBOY, they'd written across his forehead. And, almost obscuring his smile: *BETTER OFF WITHOUT HIM.* The letters were hard to read, though, and Elise couldn't tell if it was *HIM* or *THEM.* Did it matter? Why had they left this unhinged drawing for Elise? Had Sam been her friend? Or, at least, her ally? Had Elise failed them? Did they need help? Should Elise follow them, wherever they went? Elise didn't actually want to fuck Eric, she decided. What she wanted was to be held very tightly as she cried. She wanted to be the human she was. She wanted the beets to hug her in a burial shroud. She folded up the sketch again and put it under her pillow, then stepped out of the camper to smoke.

At first Elise did not recognize the thick brown thing that two of the campsite dogs were using as a toy, tugging in different directions, but then she realized it was a pair of Tom's thermal underwear. The rest of his clothes still lay in front of Burt, a grotesque monument to being abandoned. Elise looked around for Cake; he was on the hill near the bathrooms, rolling on his back.

Cake was rolling, getting up, sniffing, rolling again. He looked like he was having a great time. But as Elise got closer, she saw white things on Cake's fur and dotting the ground around him. And a rotten smell radiating. She walked faster, breathing hard as she started up the hill. Cake was so focused on whatever he was doing that he didn't notice her at all. She called his name. He was rolling in something. Something that stank. Little white things. Little white worms. Maggots. Elise jogged, barking his name. The smell of something dead. A bloated batch of fur. Maggots on the dog. Maggots on the corpse. Maggots on the grass. Maggots on her dog. Elise ran.

"Cake!" she yelled, and finally he heard and stopped, jumping to his feet and grinning at her, tongue out, while the maggots burrowed into his fur, crawled all over him, burst from the dead thing like triumphant confetti—

—except, they weren't maggots. And it wasn't a corpse. It was a rancid sugar beet, trampled and squashed and rolled-in. Harmless, wormless, little shreds of starch blending into Cake's coat like the white speckles of his own fur.

You need to eat something, Elise told herself, that new adult voice sounding weary but proud, as though it had been fighting for its life to get to the front of her head and be heard over all the others. It said it again: *You need to eat something*. But Elise didn't.

47

MISSION MIKE WASN'T AT THE MISSION THAT NIGHT, so someone else scooped tater tots (230) onto her plate and no one offered to make her a cheese sandwich to make up for the hamburger she couldn't eat. Elise told herself the tater tots would have the mouthfeel of cockroaches. She ate undressed iceberg lettuce (1) forkful by careful forkful. No one mentioned that Elise was wearing Cee's hat.

She wasn't even hungry anymore. She remembered, now, how it went: once she got through the worst of it, she moved into a quieter, sharper place. Back in high school the bad hours always lined up with drama practice. She spent so much of her self-control on her hunger that she didn't have much left over for anything else. Sometimes she'd storm off the stage in the middle of rehearsing the same song and dance for the third time that afternoon, go out to the strip of grass across the street from the school, listen to angry music and chain-smoke. In retrospect, Elise wondered if this had been "a cry for help," but if it was, it hadn't been a very good one because no one gave a shit. Everyone just thought she was being dramatic. Which was fine. No one owed Elise any concern. She had been being dramatic. Her life had been easy, always clothed and fed and loved and believed in. A world where Elise needed help was just another of her fantasy worlds. Maybe it was why Creeps McGee knew he could get away with watching her change. He knew she was too weak and spoiled to do anything about it.

On the ride to the site, she smoked two cigarettes in a row. Her wet thermal undershirt irritated her skin under Tom's black T-shirt. Her wet jeans trapped the cold against her flesh. Her wet socks made her feet itch. The sides of the road were like sidewalks made of beets instead of cement. They didn't talk about Sam, though it seemed like everyone was on edge because of it. One less person made the job a little harder, and everyone was getting tired of people leaving without saying goodbye. Goodbyes weren't great, but without them, it was like little pieces of the social order eroding from their makeshift labor-based society. Elise would slit her wrists for a goodbye note from Tom. The Big Boy welcomed her back. She'd missed this so much.

Jeff rubbed his chin as Eric explained how he was going to take over Sam's piler. Ryan would get trained to operate the piler to relieve Elise. Ash would spot-cover as needed for breaks. Elise had to take Cee's snapback off her head to put her hard hat on.

"I'm gonna get us some more workers out here soon's I can," Jeff promised as the crew clocked in. "Gotta say, this happens just about every year. People can't hack it. Or they don't wanna. They get worms inside of them. You guys are doing great, though!"

Elise didn't think that Jeff actually said that thing about worms. She'd just misheard him. She climbed the metal stairs to the piler operator box, where the day-shifter scowled at her.

"Try not to fuck it up too much," he said, and Elise couldn't tell if he was looking her up and down because he was checking her out or because he was thinking she'd fuck up his piler with her feminine ways. The day crew walked off—Elise counted seven men. There should have been ten. She shivered in the clothes that refused to fully dry.

Bon Jovi was singing "You Give Love a Bad Name" when she took the controls. Elise breathed and it felt like the first breath she'd taken in two days. All the tension washed out of her, lactic acid flowing in a river from her muscles. She'd been thinking about going home as though *this* was not her home. As though the buttons and the gears and the halogen lights glowing across the rumbling beet bodies were not the floors and doors and ceiling of her house. Her body. The radio DJ recited some new study that found people were willing to work for less money if they found more meaning in their work, then urged listeners to visit the station's website and enter to win tickets to see Luke Bryan at the Fargodome, then played a commercial for Farmers Only: "You don't have to be lonely, at Farmers-Only-dot-com." Lonely? Who was lonely? Elise laughed aloud to herself.

Below, Elise watched Jai huddle into himself in the cold, scarf pulled up over his mouth and nose, hands in the armpits of his windbreaker. He pulled down his scarf to drink coffee from his thermos. Jai and Ryan moved slightly off-tandem as trucks pulled in, trotting up to the truck windows, taking the tickets and marking them, running over to the sample taker. They ran out of sample bags but Ash pulled up in the skidsteer with more, taking the filled sample bags with him when he left. It was all working so well.

Everything shuddered to a halt. No beets rained from the conveyor belt into the funnel, no dirt was shaken into the dirt box, the conveyor belts were not pushing the load toward the pile. Only the lights stayed on.

Elise clutched the sides of the control panel. This had never happened before. The guys on the ground turned their faces up to her like supplicants. She was afraid to push any buttons. She was afraid that it was somehow her fault, that she had broken the piler. *I'm sorry*, she thought, to the machine, to the beets. *I'm so sorry.* Dysphoric, heart hammering, she called Jeff on the walkie-talkie.

"Ope! On my way!" he promised. "Mainstreet" played on the

radio. She turned it off. She refused to look at the ground crew, only stroked the gears and fingered the buttons. She didn't deserve to control the piler. She didn't deserve to add to the pile. A sob caught in her throat. She wanted to kiss the control panel back to life. She wanted to give it whatever it wanted. She imagined parting her legs and straddling it, gyrating it back to life, until it hummed and vibrated beneath her. Mouth around the knobs at the top of the gears. Nipples against buttons. She'd ride it until it was good again, until the conveyer turned back on, beets clearing like a blood clot.

The operator box shook with Jeff's weight on the stairs. He struggled to open the door against the wind, throwing himself inside. Elise's dry lips cracked open, and she tasted blood.

"Okay now, let's see," he said. And without telling Elise what he was doing, he flipped an unlabeled switch on the control panel, then pressed the red power button. The machine kicked back into life, a lurching relief. Elise could have dropped to her knees, kissed and licked the padded mat she stood on.

"Should be okay now," Jeff said. "But this one's been a little finicky today, so give her a little space between the beets. She'll shut down again if she thinks the belt's too loaded down, even if it's not. Like this." Jeff demonstrated the pace at which Elise could safely run the belts. It was simple, and when Elise took over, Jeff nodded at her skills.

He stood beside her for a while, looking out the window at the pile.

"That's a lot of beets," he said.

He was right. It was a lot of beets. Now he was an unwelcome addition to the symbiotic relationship between herself and the piler. Watching her change costumes between scenes. He smiled at her, that unassuming and eager smile. When Elise returned it, her lip cracked again, an iron tang on her tongue.

48

DAWN CAME, BUT ONLY IN THE TECHNICAL SENSE: another thick cloud cover overlaying the sky. Elise took her last break, picked the *V*-marked bags out of the trunk and dropped them into the port-a-potty bowl.

She was barely able to follow the plotlines of *Pretty Little Liars* anymore, watching the same episode three times that night, once per break, before she felt like she knew what had happened in it. The episode was mostly about how the detective whom the hot blonde liar's mother slept with in season one (to get the hot blonde liar out of trouble for shoplifting) was trying to pin the dead best friend's murder on the hot blonde liar, and the gay liar's murdered girlfriend's cousin went on a date with the suspicious not-blind character. But then a game of Ouija implied that the dead best friend might not even be dead. She might be alive, hiding out in Minnesota working as a sample taker for the beet harvest.

It wasn't that Elise no longer enjoyed watching *Pretty Little Liars*. It was just so hard not to stare out the window and yearn for those distant piler lights. Her damp clothes felt like they had frozen to her flesh. There was another *You Are a Sugar Beet* pamphlet lying on the floor of Jai's car. Did everyone but Elise get a copy of it? Elise read by the light of her cellphone flashlight: *You may be beset by sugar beet maggots. Larvae hatch from eggs laid right beside you. They move straight to your nutrient-dense body, scraping at you with their mouth hooks. With your skin pierced, you bleed sap into the soil, moistening it so that it hardens around you. You may sur-*

vive the maggots but you will have lost favor with us, as we judge your scarred, post-infestation body subpar.

Gross. She put it down. Elise was not a sugar beet. She knew she was *not* a sugar beet. She touched the bruise on her neck, gently, lovingly. Elise could learn to love herself, someday. She just needed the headache to go away first, and she needed the piler for that.

In the morning, Elise handed off the controls to the same thin guy with the salt-and-pepper cowboy mustache and the nicotine-stained fingertips. He turned the radio off.

"Another day of cleaning up—" he started.

"Whatever," Elise said before he could finish, pissed off that this guy was going to be working her piler while she was gone. What could he have possibly done in his life to deserve it? Elise had *suffered*. She was still suffering. Elise was the queen of self-control. In the last thirty-six hours, Elise had only eaten iceberg lettuce and black coffee. She was growing suspicious of the scalehouse sugar. If the packets were only 15 calories, that wouldn't be terrible—but what if they were *more* calories? What if Salt of the Earth Sugar was secretly putting calorically dense filler particles into their sugar? What if there were worm eggs in the sugar and the worms were eating their way through her tooth enamel and that's why she had a cavity for the first time in her life?

At any rate, she'd stopped putting sugar in her coffee, which made the coffee gross—suffering! Elise had earned her place.

Before she made the trek back to the scalehouse to clock out with the rest of the guys, Elise strolled down to the pile. She wanted to gauge how much it had grown since the beginning of her shift. How proud she should be of herself. She couldn't tell, actually, at all, but she knew there had been growth, and that the growth was thanks to her. She imagined herself getting smaller as the pile got bigger and her heart filled with hope. Above her, the boom creaked back and forth in the wind. She imagined it falling, splitting her scalp open, her blood leaking into the pile. It was not an entirely discomforting thought.

The pile was so tall now, and so wide. The beets were like atoms, their bodies both individually discernible and indivisible from the whole. The color palette ranged from white to yellow to brown to black. The pile reeked of earth and was beautiful and Elise thought of climbing to its summit and lying on her back to watch the stars move across the sky, soft protrusions massaging her aching shoulders. Kissed all over by bodies as ugly and as beautiful as her own. And then perhaps she would sink down. Slowly metabolize into the pile itself as dawn croaked on the horizon, slip deeper and deeper so that she'd never have to face another day. She'd be safe within the pile, safe with the beets. Safe, and sweet.

Elise reached out and touched the pile.

The pile beeped.

It was a car alarm, and though Elise looked over her shoulder to see if someone had driven up to the piler, she knew that was not what was happening. The car alarm was coming from inside the pile. None of the day shift guys even seemed to be hearing it. They weren't even looking at her. Elise stepped closer, pressed her ear to the mass and listened to the steady, familiar, urban bleat. Though the beets themselves were hard and sturdy, the pile gave slightly, caving to the weight of her head. She listened, hoping the beets might speak to her over the sound of the alarm. But they were silent, and Elise could not spend the next twelve hours embracing the pile. It would arouse concern, and she might be forcibly removed and told not to return. She pulled away, gazed at the beets in the cold morning light.

Something green was pressed neatly against one of the pile's brown and white and gray lumps. Some kind of rot? She scratched her neck.

No. A twenty-dollar bill, blown against the beets, shockingly clean. She peeled it off the pile, wondrous at this reward. Around Andrew Jackson's head, someone had written *I <3 Oblivion*.

49

ASH SUGGESTED THE CREW GO TO SPAGHETT ABOUT IT on the way back to camp, "to celebrate" Elise finding the money. Elise couldn't refuse, lest she become a bummer. She would just get a salad. And throw it out. They played that Smiths song on the way there. Halfway through the song, her credit card company called, cutting Morrissey off mid-whine. She ignored it, apologized, pressed play again. They all screamed: "Heaven knows I'm miserable now."

Opening the door to the restaurant sent a pair of beets bouncing across the lot. Elise had forgotten the smell, so distinctive she imagined there must be some air freshener that corporate provided to all their franchises: roasting garlic with a sharp overtone of yeast. It wasn't an unpleasant smell. That morning, it smelled really very good. Elise let the guys order first, thinking that even though she was just going to get a salad and not eat it, she still felt exposed ordering in front of them. She was vaguely aware that spending her sole money here was exactly the sort of thing her parents would expect, their constant assessment that she was always being the worst, most reckless version of herself. And what would Tom have said? What *could* he say about Elise spending her own money while he treated himself with his parents' credit card?

Fuck Tom, said two voices at once, the beets and Elise's own, harmonious for once. He was such a fucking piece of shit for leaving her here. He'd always been a piece of shit. All those things he'd written to that friend in that fucking message she'd found.

His stupid band, the stupid music he played, god, it was so bad, so awful, and she'd just sat around acting like it was great because she wanted to be supportive, but she shouldn't have bothered, she should have told him straight-up that he was making music for teenage boys in the suburbs who weren't getting laid so they had to beat each other up instead. "You're a talentless hack," she pictured saying to him. She pictured grabbing his collar and pulling his face right up in front of hers so that spit fell on his face when she yelled.

A new text from "pure id": Burt says ur fat n bad in bed so ha ha hope u

"You gonna order?" the cashier asked. The guys were clearing the beets off one of the red-and-white-checked tables.

"Yeah," Elise said. She was just gonna get a salad. What had she gotten last time? With Cee? Cannolicakes (650). They had been so sugary it hurt. She rolled her tongue over her tooth. *No pain, no gain.* Just a salad, though. She stepped forward, eyes still on the menu so she wouldn't have to look at the cashier. Just a salad.

"Cannolicakes," Elise said. This was bad: she was swinging back the other way, a predictable outcome she never predicted. Elise always maintained the delusion that whatever good thing she was doing, she could do it forever. She saw something else she wanted. "Can I also get, uh, a garlic bread breakfast sandwich? No meat, just the eggs and tomato and whatever." The garlic bread breakfast sandwich had 830 calories, but there'd be less without the meat.

Tom was such a fucking bastard. If Elise was going to get to do anything good forever, it should have been him. Them. What they were doing.

The cashier finished punching buttons. "Anything else?"

"Fettuccine fries," Elise said. 390 calories. She imagined getting back to Burt and finding Tom there, waiting for her, how sorry he'd be and how she'd scream at him, how she'd tell him that his chance had come and gone, how he was a fucking fuckboy scumbag. And a liar. How she'd been right, actually. That was the wild thing. That season she'd spent panicked and fuming about Tom falling in love with another girl? He *did* do that. He *was* a cheater. She'd spent so much time feeling guilty, tiptoeing around conflict because she knew how much of his patience she'd already used up, and all along—all along—the whole time—forever—for years—she'd been fucking *right*.

"Okay, I got cannolicakes, garlic bread—"

"And the deep-fried eggplant Parm sandwich," Elise said. She didn't look at the calorie count. The little green numbers on the cash register display changed. "And a tiramisu. And a Coke." A joke: supersized Big Macs, extra-large fries, *Diet* Cokes! America hated fat people and it wasn't fair and Elise hated it and she hated her body for not just being a normal body that could look good no matter what she weighed. No, Elise's body was *special*. Elise's body was *stupid*. The numbers changed again. The numbers were not calculating calories. The cashier waited a moment.

"That it?"

It wasn't. Elise wanted more. She wanted everything on the menu, everything she could eat. She wanted to lay out a buffet for herself, eat it all in one sitting, eat up her money the way Tom had eaten up her twenties. Wasted her fucking time. Acted, always, like he was so noble for working so hard to save up so he could earn his own fortune or whatever without ever admitting that the only way he could do that on his barista wages was if he let his parents pay for things he was pretending to pay for while Elise really did pay for the things she shared with him with her own money that she could have been saving to finally show her parents that she was good, she *was* good, she was just as good as anyone else, she wasn't bad, she wasn't a bad person, she was always trying she just wanted a break she wanted to have fun she wanted—

"Ma'am?" The cashier's hand was out, palm up. Elise handed over the twenty. She went to the table to sit with the guys. These fucking guys, weren't they all so *great* and so *nice*, and wasn't she *lucky* that they were so *great* and so *nice*? She sat down at the chair someone had pulled over for her, the leg of the table taking up most of her legroom so she had to sit at a slight angle.

The *great* and *nice* guys talked about how everything smelled like beets now, even their hair after a shower. How the girl in the scalehouse was kind of an idiot. They parroted Jeff with his strong accent: *Real good! On my way!* Elise was in that shitty dive bar in Albany where she and Tom had spent a lot of time, *their* bar, where they knew what was on the jukebox and where, now that Elise thought about it, they'd first admitted to having feelings for each other. Elise, in her mind, sat in the corner booth with Tom. And he begged for forgiveness, and she screamed in his face. And then she hit him. And it felt so bad, but so good. She hit him and screamed and she hit him and screamed and he kept popping back up, happy to take more.

She was just so angry. The guys could feel the infrared waves of her rage surrounding her, bouncing off them. Her energy was bouncing off the plate glass windows. The food came, and so much of it was for her, and she was eating all of it, getting ricotta on her garlic bread (who cared) and popping the lid off the soft drink cup so she could take big swallows of Coke (whatever) with her mouth still full, her body aching to be given all she could afford to give it. Ricotta was pus leaking from a cyst. All Elise could taste was broad spectrums of flavor: sweet, salty, fatty. She didn't ask for a napkin but someone gave her one anyway. Oh, because she was crying. She blew her nose between bites and swallows, after the mozzarella topping the fried eggplant Parm sandwich (like she gave a fuck anymore) snapped against her lips, before she dipped a handful of fettuccine fries into the Alfredo sauce (shut up shut up shut up), getting the sauce on her fingers, wiping her fingers on the garlic bread sandwich, Alfredo like straight-up cum, eating the garlic bread sandwich and the fried eggplant Parm in tandem, one in each hand, switching between them each bite, thousands of millions of calories accumulating beyond the scope of mathematics, beyond the seams of her body, an infinite atomic calorie count.

Yes, said the beets. *Eat, good girl, eat.* She took, she took, the beets wanted her to take and so she did. The beet pile would let her get fat. The beet pile wanted her fat and full. She could eat forever, sugar sparkling into unending orgasmic growth.

Someone in a uniform was standing nearby now, their hands clasped in front of their chest, asking questions. Ryan was telling the person that it was fine. They were talking about her. Weren't they always? Wasn't everyone always talking about her? Behind her back but still within earshot, laughing? Tom made it that way, he'd made it so that she was ripe for being talked about, he'd turned her into a piece of gossip—and that made him such a fucking bastard. She deserved better. She was the one who could do better. He deserved to get in a fucking car crash and go straight through the window and die in a ditch where no one found his fucking body for weeks. He could die, he could die, he could just fucking die and Elise would laugh in his cold dead face, laugh so hard she puked.

Elise shot up from her chair, tripping over a beet as she ran for the bathroom. As soon as she leaned forward over the toilet, the food shot out. A sharp-edged mush, spicy with garlic and mostly still recognizable. She held herself up by pressing her hands to the sides of the stall as she purged, not even needing to finger her throat to do it. Like magic, it was coming up all on its own. Down to the ricotta, which slipped out like phlegm and plopped sadly into the porcelain. Elise's throat was raw, her skin flushed and tingling, sinuses clogged. Sweat at her hairline and on her neck. Cee's hat fallen on the floor. But it felt good, to be empty like this. Felt good to flush the vomit. To rub cold water against her eyes, sip it from her cupped hands, gargle and spit into the sink.

She emerged a new woman, someone who'd never think of being angry or violent, even in the safety of her own mind. Someone at peace with what had happened to her. The restaurant's three employees were hanging together in a cluster behind the cashier, watching her move across the dining room to the table of silent dudes, where she gathered her trash, and theirs, and threw it all out. She still had the tiramisu in its disposable round cup. She took it with her as she left, the biting wind stinging colder on her still-damp face and fingers.

She gave it to Cake. It made him happy. She peeled off her still-not-quite-dry clothes, marveling at the red irritated skin underneath them. She put on Tom's soft shirt, his comfy sweatpants. She took several aspirin, lay down, and let her many pains lull her into something not unlike sleep.

50

ELISE WOKE TO SNOW. ONE OF THE SNAPS THAT HELD Burt's cover in place had unsnapped, and for some reason the zipper was not fully zipped. Snowflakes blew into the camper each time the wind gusted against it. The flakes melted as soon as they landed, a dark dampening of the frayed carpet. Elise watched this for a while. Her cavity was getting worse; it was probably infected. She'd sleep until the aspirin stopped blunting the edges of the pain, wake up, take more, wait for it to kick in, sleep until it wore off. She'd gotten, maybe, two hours of real sleep. The pills burned in her empty stomach.

Beside her, Cake groaned as he scratched behind his ear, his eyes still closed. Elise thought she saw a little black dot jump on his back. She eased herself out of the sleeping bag and onto her feet. Cake was awake, then, so sudden it was like he'd only been faking sleep. He stretched and yawned, tail wagging. A happy little dog. Elise envied and appreciated him, wiped two measly tears from the corner of one eye.

Elise layered up and let the dog out, stepped down from the camper to re-snap the snap only to find that it would not snap closed; she couldn't figure out why, because she wasn't an expert in snaps. Elise was only an expert in egomaniacal self-hatred, the dark art of inventing new and spectacular ways to feel bad. The snap was broken. So was the zipper. Again. Or maybe Tom had never actually fixed it. Had Elise only imagined it, those few days—how many days had it been? Was a day a day, or was a day a night?

She left it because there was nothing else she could do. From the looks of things, day shift wasn't back yet, which meant Elise might still get to go to work. Her breath came out in puffs of cloud. The only gloves she had were her thin yellow mud-caked work gloves, so she wore them. Clutched her little shower caddy and went up the hill to the bathrooms. Elise loved snow. She liked listening to Bon Iver and making oatmeal on a snowy morning. Tom hated Bon Iver and liked to tease Elise about being basic. Pretty rich coming from a guy who listened to Thrice. Elise had always accepted the teasing because she thought Tom knew more about music than she did.

Someone was crying in the shower. Elise could hear the sobs over the falling water. Elise considered turning around and leaving the person to their sorrow. The idea that it might actually be herself in the shower, some kind of surreal déjà vu or astral projection, flitted through her mind.

On the inside of the bathroom door, someone had written *talented!* with an arrow pointing to the phrase *solo blumpkin*. Elise put her stuff down on the little ledge under the mirror. There was the bruise. Her constant companion. A pet she stroked for its comfort as well as her own. Maybe people thought Tom had hit her. She kind of liked the idea of people thinking that. Who didn't hate men who hit women? And Elise wanted the whole world to hate Tom the way she did. She missed him, though. Her heart and stomach were equally empty, but the emptinesses were inverses of each other: good stomach, bad heart.

She wanted to see who was crying in the shower. Sam, maybe? No—Sam was gone. *Where, though? Where is everyone going?* Everyone was going home.

Home to the beet pile, she thought.

Elise retreated into a stall. She pulled her feet up off the floor, sitting on the toilet with her knees under her chin. She waited. Maybe it was Cee crying in the shower, maybe she'd come back. Maybe Elise was Cee, had been all along. Probably not, but maybe.

Elise pulled out her phone. Lydia had texted: Tom??? Which meant people knew. Elise was not ready for people to know. She wasn't even ready to know. She didn't want to know anything. She imagined everything she knew, everything she had ever known, coagulating into corporeal form. A Big Boy, bursting out of her head like Athena. Elise went to Google. She hit ignore on the credit card company's phone call. She went to Walmart.com. She toggled menus until she got to *women's shoes*. Elise always sorted by *price: low to high* when she shopped online. Even though she wasn't shopping, the instinct was strong. As was her finger-itch to add things to her cart. She filtered down to *boots*. The boots Tom bought her were on the second page. They cost $89.99, which was more than Elise had ever spent on shoes in her life, even when she was a kid and her parents were buying her shoes. Elise's pink boots weren't pink anymore; they were mud-colored, the laces crusted and stiff. Elise wondered if Tom's mom was paying for her boots.

Elise googled *rash that turns into bruise.*

"Henoch-Schönlein purpura," said one result. "Urticarial vasculitis," said another. Elise would never be a vet tech. She was bad at science. "Sugar worm," said another. She clicked that one and read: *a relative of the common ringworm (Tinea corporis), the sugar worm (Saccharovermis corporis) is a rare mold-like parasite that lives on the cells in the outer layer of skin, reproducing asexually via burrowing spores. Unlike common ringworm, sugar worm infection is spread only by contact with airborne waste products of industrial sugar processing. Sugar worm infections are identifiable by the appearance of hive-like rashes that will leave significant and permanent bruising. There is currently no treatment for sugar worm infections.*

Elise covered the bruise with her hand.

Perhaps this wasn't what she had. Maybe it was one of the other things. She backtracked to the results page. Still the person was sobbing, the water still running. Elise knew that the hot water in the bathroom only lasted about ten minutes, and probably Elise had entered the bathroom twelve minutes ago. The Wi-Fi was taking forever. The screen switched, again, to an incoming call and she hit, again, ignore. Was she still infected? Was this a fucking joke? How could the bruise be permanent? How could there be no treatment? It was 2014. Wouldn't the FDA have something to say about this? The EPA? The local community board or PTA? She was going to have this bruise *forever*?

Finally, the results page loaded.

But there was no link to the page about sugar worms. It went right from "Urticarial vasculitis" to "7 Signs a Skin Rash Could Indicate Something Serious." She clicked that link. Nothing about sugar worms. She went back again. Waited, again. She repositioned herself, fitting herself sideways on the toilet with her feet pressed against one side of the stall and her neck and the back of her head pressed against the other. It wasn't long before this position became untenable, too. How could this person continue to sustain that level of weeping? Elise was, surely, the most heartbroken person in the entire camp. And she was infected with moldy sugar chemicals, or whatever the fuck it said. She pulled down at the screen to refresh, which only started the waiting all over again.

She planted her feet on the ground, took off Cee's snapback, and leaned forward, resting her forehead on the stall door. She typed "sugar worm" into the search bar. There were threadworms, which lived in the large intestine and absorbed sugar, but they didn't cause rashes. And pinworms, which were the exact same worm but with a different name. And lots of pictures of gummy worms. But no fungi called sugar worms that were related to ring-worms and caused permanent bruising. Glass dust stabbed into the meat of her thumb as she slipped it across the crack in her screen. She grunted and stuck her thumb in her mouth.

Elise couldn't wait any longer. She used the toilet and flushed, knowing that whoever was in the shower would have to hear it. But nothing changed: same sobbing, same rate of water falling against the tile floor. Nothing changed as Elise brushed her teeth, washed her face, combed her hair. She lathered her hands in the institutional pink foam soap and reached through the hole in Tom's shirt to rub the soap under her armpits. Put her work gloves back on, re-zipped her jacket, went to the door. She paused with a hand on the knob, one last chance to find out who was in the shower—but at that moment, someone opened the door from the other side, pushing Elise back.

"Oh! Sorry," Aya said.

"No, my bad," Elise mumbled. "Y'all back early?"

Aya nodded. "Probably they'll cancel night shift, too."

"Cool," Elise said, slipping out the door that Aya still held open.

"Hey, hey," Aya said, stopping her. "You okay? I heard you crying."

Elise clenched her jaw. "That wasn't me. They're still in there."

Except when she and Aya stood in silence, Aya looking at Elise and Elise looking at the ground, she didn't hear any sobbing. The bathroom was dark, moist, and quiet.

51

DINNER WAS HOT DISH: TATER TOTS AND CHEESE AND creamy soup and shredded slices of ham layered and spooned out in generous portions to everyone but Elise. Elise filled her plate, instead, with lettuce. Mike still wasn't there, and Elise, genuinely curious, asked the woman who came out to restock the red plastic cups when he was coming back.

"I'm . . . not sure," she said before retreating behind the swinging door. Perhaps she thought Elise was obsessed with Mike and that it would be dangerous to give out too much information. Elise filled her red cup, still beaded with water from the dishwasher, with a throat-stinging powder-based lemonade-proximate drink. It had calories but Elise had no idea how many. The words SPECIAL TREAT flashed in neon in her mind. The lemonade bit into her tender gums.

Aya and Chet and some of the other day-shifters chose a table close to the Mainers' table so they could trade gossip. Elise did not feel ashamed about what had happened at Spaghett About It. She felt contentedly empty. She no longer gave a shit what the cool Mainers thought of her. The time when she might have been able to impress them had long passed. Maybe she wasn't at rock bottom, but she was surely too deep down to bother trying to climb back up.

With the laundry done and payday looming over their heads, spirits were high and people talked about going "out"—to the American Legion, probably. When Chet asked about Tom, apparently just noticing that Elise was alone, she fought the urge to pretend Tom had never existed: *Tom who?* Instead, she said: "He's doing his own thing." She surprised herself saying it like that, all breezy and cool, pretending to be the kind of person who could let go so easily. Pretending to be the kind of person who could survive this. Was this the worst thing to ever happen to Elise? What else would win that prize? The crush who said he just felt sorry for her, bullies throwing food and coughing *TrimSpa* at her, half a decade of starving herself, Creeps McGee, or the long, intense withdrawal from the medication she could no longer afford once she lost her student insurance? Even though she preferred to slide downhill on the smooth, glassy surface of her self-loathing, Elise had the capacity for endurance.

Then again, none of it felt particularly awful compared to what other people went through. Elise had always had privilege, resources, a safety net. Just because Tom was rich did not make Elise or her family poor. She needed to call her mom. She felt like a bad daughter.

Someone said something about Mike, and Elise tuned back into the conversation.

"He got picked up on a domestic violence charge," said the girl Elise thought was named Murph.

"Third strike," Aya said. "So he's probably not coming out anytime soon."

"Shit," Ryan said through a mouthful of hot dish. "Really?"

"How do you know that?" Elise asked. This could be just a nasty rumor, couldn't it? Wasn't it *likely* just a nasty rumor? How could any of them possibly know for sure that's what happened? None of them *really* knew him.

"One of the breakfast people"—Murph jerked her head toward the kitchen.

"You know his ex-wife has a restraining order against him? And their kid?" Chet was the one to add this. "Last year there was this big scene in the middle of dinner when his kid came by here for some reason and then his ex showed up and then the fucking cops came."

Elise leaned back in her chair and pressed her fingers against her eyeballs, massaging them through the lids. There were little veins in there, in the eyelids. And bugs in her eyelashes. When she opened her eyes again, Ash and Jai were staring at her, nervous, as though waiting for her to steal the food off their plates and hoover it down and then puke it all back up onto the table. Elise felt like crying. Why was everything bad always getting so much worse, all the time, forever?

Now everyone was talking about how so-and-so had run off on so-and-so. Elise picked at the remains of her salad. The gossip she really wanted to know was who'd been in the shower. She wanted to know how they did it, how they sobbed for that long. They must have emerged spotless.

52

THE BEER AT THE AMERICAN LEGION WAS SKUNKED.
Bud Light by the pitcher, almost undrinkable. Almost. To make
up for it, the bartender poured them a pitcher of Grain Belt, on
the house.

"It's on me, guys," Elise said when she brought the new pitcher
back to the table. A joke. It made the guys smile. Her friends? Yes, her
friends. They were paying for her to drink. They were very nice guys.

In two days, she'd have enough to cover the overdraft and
plenty more. The money would come and fix everything. She'd
buy her friends beer and dog food and a Spaghett About It buffet.

Elise was drunk, her stomach empty but for three beers and
all the aspirin. Her eyes felt lazy, her tooth didn't hurt, her mind
finally loosening the death grip it'd been holding since Tom left.
Tom. Tom was gone. Tom gone. Elise accepted the shot of brown
liquor Jai placed in front of her, held it in the air alongside all the
other shots and said, "Long live the beets." The thing about brown
liquor is that some part of Elise always expected it to taste like
apple juice, and it never did.

Old white men sat around the bar in groups of three or fewer.
Elise and the Mainers and Murph, who'd tagged along, were the
anomalies in several ways: in number, in raucousness, in dialect,
in fashion. Though their clothes were *mostly* utilitarian and stank
of beets and soil, they were still not *merely* utilitarian; they had
the class-appropriating edge of East Coast millennials. Elise wondered if the locals hated them. She wondered if wondering was why

the locals would hate them. *Don't worry*, Elise thought, gleefully. *I hate myself, too!* On the jukebox, a country singer sang about getting drunk with a barefoot girl in the bed of a truck. Actually, there wasn't a jukebox. It was just coming from wherever the music was coming from.

Elise wanted a cigarette. So did Murph, who was rolling one on the table, and Jai and Eric. They went outside, where it was snowing lightly but steadily. Elise really wanted to listen to Bon Iver, and when she said so aloud, Murph laughed, but not in an agreeing way. Tom would've reacted the same. Whatever; Elise didn't have to put up with that anymore. Elise was free! Elise didn't want to get too emotional, make another scene, so she focused on her cigarette. *Enjoy it*, she thought, *enjoy the moment. Return the dirt.*

"Do you think the beet pile is eating people?" Elise said out loud, not having planned to say it but realizing once she said it that she'd been thinking it for a while. "Is that why everyone is disappearing?"

Murph and Jai laughed. Murph was good-looking with generous proportions, a body Elise would prefer over her own even though it was not a thin body. Elise was the only person on earth who needed to be skinny to be worth looking at. It wasn't fair, it was just the way it was.

Back inside, snowflakes melting into their hair like lice burrowing toward the scalp, Elise noticed a table of three boys in the corner of the bar. The only other patrons under fifty, she guessed. They watched her and Murph and Jai walk back toward their table. All three were corn-fed, husky with muscle, the ghosts of acne on their chins, looking too young for the beers in front of them.

There was a new pitcher on the table, a beet bobbing around the bottom, smiling back at her. The conversation had lapsed back to back-home gossip exclusively of interest to the Mainers.

Elise drank to fill the space. She played with her phone for a minute, pretending there was something interesting in there, something besides a big crack and increasingly concerned messages from friends and statically unhinged texts from Linnie (the most recent was just the skull and water gun emojis repeated in a pattern for several lines, which probably constituted a threat but they were emojis so not very threatening) and pictures she now had to decide what to do about. She didn't want those pictures to exist—the ones of Tom, of her and Tom, of things they had found photographable together. The pictures were inside the phone. She put the phone down, and when she looked up, the three corner boys were standing over the table.

"Hey," one of them, a blond, said.

Elise's immediate reaction was not a warm friendly feeling but something on the scale of fear. She imagined the boys watching them, judging them to be from elsewhere, judging them to be something other than good Republican Jesus-worshipping folk and deciding to show them a thing or two. Elise wondered if she was the only one feeling this awkward intimidation. What was the right way to feel? How did Eric and Jai feel? Or Murph, who looked a lot gayer than Elise did?

"Hey, man, what's up?" That was Ryan.

"You guys here for the harvest?" the same blond guy said. The table nodded en masse. "That's cool. Buy you a pitcher?"

Elise felt like an asshole.

There was a redistribution of space, a shuffling of chairs to one side or the other to accommodate the boys. The blond one wound up right next to Elise. He smelled like body spray. His name was Luke and he went to the local satellite branch of "U'v'M," same as Sydney the scalehouse girl. Elise asked if he knew her. He did. It was a small community.

"My dad works the harvest, too," Luke said. "He drives truck."

"Why do y'all say it like that?" Elise asked. Luke was kind of handsome and she liked his name. Luke; it seemed so wholesome. " 'Drive truck'?"

Another shot appeared in front of Elise and she wasn't sure where it came from but she was grateful for it. Imagine if Tom saw her now: flirting with this cute college boy. Living it up, having fun. All the fun she should have been having all those wasted years with him. Luke's smile revealed that he must have needed braces when he was younger but never gotten them. She supposed he could still get braces now. People did that, sometimes. Adults with braces.

"I don't know," he said, making eye contact and keeping it. "Just do. Always have."

"Does your dad drive truck the rest of the year, too?" Elise asked.

Luke nodded and picked up the shot that had appeared in front of him, too.

"Long-haul, though," he said. "He's supposed to be in Texas right now, actually. He stuck around to finish out the harvest. The money's too good."

And then everyone had their shot and everyone took it at the same time and it did not taste like apple juice. The table was getting crowded with empty shot glasses and pint glasses and people's phones.

Luke wiped his mouth with the back of his hand. "So where you from?"

"New York," Elise said. Then added, "Brooklyn." She thought that would probably impress Luke. Didn't everyone want to leave their cow town and go to the big city? Wasn't everyone from New York City sophisticated and cool? She was insufferable. She wanted another cigarette. She wanted to refill her pint glass. She wanted

Luke to put his hand on her thigh and she wanted his hand to be bigger than her thigh and she wanted him to be impressed by the size of her thigh. Elise blinked.

When she opened her eyes, she was on top of Luke in a blue bedroom. The sheets really needed washing. Luke's hands were on her hips, moving her up and down, and she was making all these noises. Which he didn't want her to do, she realized, as he flipped her over and put his hand over her mouth. She was very dry, and it was a miracle that Luke's dick was inside her at all.

"Please," he whispered in her ear. "My parents."

So she closed her mouth and focused on the feel of his dick moving in and out of her very dry pussy. She was nauseous and getting kind of upset. The first sex she had with someone other than Tom couldn't be like this. Shouldn't be like this. She had to enjoy it. She grabbed Luke's hands and brought them to her neck. But Luke just looked at her, confused, his hands limp around her throat as he continued pumping away.

"Squeeze," she said. He looked dubious, but he did it. It worked, was working. Elise closed her eyes; nausea fading under the swell of her arousal as he squeezed, a feeling, hard like a beet stuck in her throat, followed by the rush of a body thinking it was in danger. Her struggle underneath his heavy body matched the pace of his thrusts.

"You're . . . a dumb whore?" Luke whispered, assuming that if Elise wanted A, she must also want B. "You're a stupid . . . bitch. Holy shit, holy *shit*. Is that okay?"

It was neither okay nor not okay to Elise. She wasn't process-ing it at all. Her mind was black and red with pain and panic. It kept going back to the beets. The pile. Luke's dick thickening and engorging, rounder and harder and starchier inside her. His body bulbous, bulging. The air vegetal, the dirty sheets dirty with real dirt. She pulled his mouth down onto her mouth, tasted greenery and loam.

Luke was very good at choking her, but she had to smack his arms to get him to let go before she passed out. Then she had to grab his wrists to get him to do it again. The bruise on her neck was especially sensitive, pain like a mellow purple light coming from below the other pain. Momentum inside her, the bed lifting, the beets resisting gravity. Elise forced herself to keep rising, hydraulics hissing at the lift. Luke had beets for eyes. They gleamed down at her. They fell down on top of her. She cried out, but it was silent because of Luke's hands squeezing her throat. Having him inside her felt like nothing, but at least she was finally wet. The beets shivered in the bed, refusing to let go, refusing the momentum. She tried to lift. She wanted them to come. She opened her mouth to take them in. She touched her breasts, hard and round, hands coming away dirty. She grabbed Luke's ass, fingers digging into the roots, knuckle-deep into the pile, she pulled down at the beets to get them loose, begged them: *Just let go, just let go, just come down, ready, waiting, return, ready, more, need more, we need grow, dirt, we need—*

But then Luke grunted out the phrase *holy shit* and stopped moving, and he let go of her neck. He dropped to his elbows on top of her and breathed hot beer into her face. The truck blinked out of existence, taking the bedful of beets with it. The piler dissolved. The dirt turned back into human filth. The pile faded out of her reach.

Elise turned her head to the side. The pillow smelled bad. She was limp now, too. She closed her eyes, nausea creeping back in as Luke rolled off her.

Elise didn't know or care what he did with the condom after. Had there even been a condom? Fuck, she was wasted. She was still thinking of the beets. How they weren't men, how they couldn't disappoint like men could. How they weren't women, either, so she didn't need to question the motivations of her wanting them. How they were bodiless. How they made her bodiless. How much pleasure that promised.

"Holy shit," he said. "I've never had a girl want that before. That was hot. I hope I didn't hurt you too bad?"

"Hurting too bad is the point," she answered, still facing away from him.

After a moment, she felt his arms encircle her. She put a hand under the pillow, which was how she always slept, and rapped her knuckles against a beet. Frustrated, she pushed it down onto the floor, where it thudded dully. Then she felt bad. She loved the beets. She reached down and picked up the beet and slipped it under the sheets, pressed it between her legs.

"Are you okay?" Luke asked.

"Why wouldn't I be?"

"You just seem kind of upset," his voice came from too close.

Elise just wanted to be home, in her own bed. She wished Luke would turn into a dog. Cake never tried to hold her like this, just curled up in the space behind her knees. How had they gotten here? Was this house, Luke's parents' house, within walking distance from the bar? How badly had she embarrassed herself? Had she come on to Luke, or had he started it with her? Why did her knees hurt so much? Whose job was it to wash these sheets and why hadn't they done it? She grinded herself gently against the beet, but she could tell that it wasn't going to get her anywhere. Not with Luke behind her like that.

"I'm fine," she said. "Let's just go to sleep now."

A minute of silence.

"You wanted that, you know. You did. You wanted to come

back with me. You know that, right?" There was a mild panic in his voice. He was soberer than her.

"I'll leave," she said, observing the headache that was still somewhere in her frontal lobe. She wouldn't leave; she couldn't. She was stuck in that bed for the time being. Elise was always getting herself stuck places she didn't want to be. She wasn't going to throw up, she could tell, but she wished she could. If she were home, she'd make herself puke to feel better.

"No," Luke said, seeming genuinely upset by the idea. Then, trying to save face: "I mean, you don't have to. Sorry."

"Then go to sleep," Elise said. "Go to bed."

Luke was quiet after that. He started to snore gently. Elise could make out, in the moonlight coming through the window, the messy boyness of the room. All the blue. He had a collection of truck ads taped in a line across the wall. A poster-sized ad for Jägermeister. A flyer, corners torn from where it had been taped somewhere else, for Florida Georgia Line at the Fargodome. She closed her eyes against it all. She wanted sleep more than she could ever remember wanting anything. She was so sick. Confused and sad. She didn't know this boy. She couldn't remember getting here. She wished, longed, to be in the piler; to be laid down gently and lovingly against the pile. She wanted to be asleep so she didn't have to be sick and confused and sad.

For once, she got what she wanted.

53

ELISE WOKE UP HUNGOVER AND OUT OF HER MIND. Thirsty, roiling. Luke was still asleep when she literally rolled out of the bed—her limbs not responsive but her spirit overwhelmed by the need to be away from this young body baking hers under the blue comforter. Why was he so feverishly warm? Elise landed on her knees and forearms. Her knees hurt in a sharp, stabbing way, and when she got her legs out from under her, she found both kneecaps were badly skinned. The curtains had fish on them. And were blue, around the fish. There was an alarm clock on the table beside the bed, but it was knocked over. Elise didn't know where her phone was. She didn't know where her wallet was. She didn't know where she was. She didn't know who this kid was. Trucker's son. It didn't matter, did it? Elise bet he didn't know her name, either.

"Elise?" the trucker's son's voice, sleepy and confused, came from above her.

God's voice, Elise thought, and laughed. Laughing made her want to puke. She crawled toward the desk against the window under the fish curtains and dragged herself up from the ground into the rolling desk chair. The trucker's son's desktop was crowded with agricultural textbooks and the detritus of several blunts and a bunch of chewed-up generic clear black pens and their chewed-up caps, and that same fucking *You Are a Sugar Beet* pamphlet that was following her around, and a half-eaten sheet of those candy dots on paper, the eaten half all jaggedly opaque in places where one of the sugar blobs had pulled some paper up with it, and Elise wondered if the trucker's son ate the paper with the dots, and if he did, if he actually kind of liked it. Like she did. Her cavity ached. It didn't matter.

She picked up the pamphlet.

She asked: "Where is the bathroom?"

He looked a little put off by her request. He rose, blanket falling from his bare chest. Was he good-looking, now, in the morning after? Elise didn't think so, and she didn't care. It didn't matter.

That's right: his parents. *Please*, he'd said the night before. *My parents.*

"Did I do that to you?" The trucker's son looked equal parts stricken and proud as he pointed to Elise's neck.

She reached up, touched it with her fingertips. The bruise.

"No," she said, putting a little extra venom in the word. *How dare you think you could do this?* "Bathroom."

"Down the hall," he said. "On the right."

Elise got up. She was naked. Naked in front of this boy. First since Tom. Her beet breasts and stretch marks on her thighs. The belly that curved over her pubes. Her clothes were all the way across the room. Her bag was overturned, her shit spilling onto the carpet all around it. Cee's hat poking out from under the bed. Cigarettes and lighter several feet away from each other. Her first instinct was to check how many cigarettes she had left. Tomorrow was payday. It didn't matter.

"I have to put clothes on?" she asked the trucker's son. She knew why she asked this question, the obvious answer to which was *yes*. To make him feel bad. She hoped it implied something like: *I am a sexy older woman and I'm not used to having to get dressed after nights like these, I am used to padding nakedly and sexily into a dude's bathroom, but I can't do that here, trucker's son, because you're a little boy who lives with his parents.* How dare the trucker's son be young. How dare he live with his parents. How dare she be there.

"You can, uh"—the trucker's son pointed to a dresser beside the door, half its drawers half open.

There was a glass tank full of dirt on top of the dresser. She got closer and saw the dirt in the tank moving. She swayed, heart palpitating, blood sour in her veins. A worm emerged from a dirt tunnel, pressed its pink body against the glass, then squirmed back into the dirt.

The trucker's son's wardrobe was a color wheel of flannel, and shirts with beer logos on them, and custom-printed fraternity shirts. The one on top said FOR A GOOD TIME, FILL UP TO HERE WITH BEER. There was a picture of a pint glass and an arrow pointing to the top of the pint glass to show where to fill for a good time. She put on a pair of boxers from a different drawer. All the while, the trucker's son was watching her. He'd lain back down, covered himself once more with the blanket. According to the clock, it was half past eight. That didn't matter. She brought the sugar beet pamphlet with her.

The hallway was not decorated. It was a plain hallway. Green walls. Bare wooden doors. Coffee smell. There were people talking somewhere in the house, voices low but angry. Elise pressed one hand to the wall to steady herself as she walked. She passed an open doorway on her left, saw the kitchen through it. At the kitchen table, the trucker, sneering down into a cup of coffee. At the sink, the trucker's wife, quietly sobbing. Or two entirely unrelated people who had nothing to do with the trucker's son, who were just in the kitchen to spook Elise as she walked past, two people whose four eyes barely registered her presence as she dragged her unwieldy body down the hallway. The man's voice started up when Elise was out of sight. She paused to listen.

"I can't reason with you. You're hysterical. You're a fucking—I fuckin' stayed *for you*. Let some punk kid take the goddamn rig just so I could be here another week. It's not enough for you, though. Nothing's ever enough. I don't have to put up with this shit, Linnie, and you know it and that's why you're such a crazy bitch. I could do better, I could get any cunt in this fucking town, couldn't I? Couldn't I? Look at me, Linnie, and admit it. You're lucky I put up with your shit."

The bathroom smelled like pecan pie and dry rot. She cupped water in her hands and drank from the tap. It tasted like beet stink but was good against her tongue. She saw her face in the mirror: her makeup was all fucked up, her tangled greasy hair above it, making her look feral. She liked it. It looked like she felt. A caged thing finally let loose. The demonic interest on a payday loan finally come due. A beet bouncing out of a truck, rolling down a ditch, determined to propagate on the side of the highway.

There was a family photo across from the toilet. There was the trucker's son, with the two people she'd seen in the kitchen, but actually there were two of the trucker's son in the photo. And two identical little girls. Elise studied the photo, which was taken in front of some anonymous marbled blue backdrop with soft lighting, everyone in churchgoing clothes, dresses for the girls.

She sat on the toilet, taking a leisurely hungover shit. It was one of those spine-tingling beer shits. It made sounds hitting the water. She read from *You Are a Sugar Beet*: *At the processing plant, you will be sent through a slicer, where razor-sharp blades will neatly dismember your root body. Your flesh exposed and gleaming, you will be bathed in boiling water. Your cells, denatured and ruptured, bleed sugar into the water via osmosis and diffusion, leaving your more corporeal body as bland, beaten, sugarless pulp.*

The rest of you, a sugary, starchy juice, can be evaporated, concentrated, crystalized and whipped. Such violence. The bathtub was full of beets. In the medicine cabinet behind the mirror, there were no little orange bottles of Vicodin or Xanax, but there was a nearly full bottle of Children's Delsym 12 Hour Cough Relief, grape-flavored. It was the good kind of cough syrup; the right kind, with only dextromethorphan; no acetaminophen or guaifenesin or phenylephrine, all of which would make you sick. Elise took the cough medicine out of the cabinet. Her tooth hurt. She hated it. Thought about ripping it out, roots and all, bleeding out the infection that made her jaw boil with pain. The cough syrup smelled like cough syrup.

"The snozzberries taste like snozzberries," she said aloud. She'd never had trouble chugging Robitussin back in her freshman year of college. Other friends would throw it up. Was it Elise's nearly always empty stomach, her body screaming for calories in any form, that made it so digestible to her? Or maybe her long intimate relationship with puking? That was a good conspiracy theory about herself. She drank the bottle in a few loud gulps. It tasted like Dimetapp. Elise thought about texting her mom: remember Dimetapp? But that would be weird!

No one was in the kitchen when Elise made her way back down the hallway. But the coffee cups were still there, steaming. In his bedroom, the trucker's son had fallen back asleep but he woke up when she sat on the edge of the bed.

"You look good in those," he said. He meant his clothes. "Last night was . . . crazy."

"Yeah," Elise said, though the trucker's son was wrong. Last night had not been crazy. This morning was crazy. The light coming through the fish curtains was crazy. The shit she just took in his bathroom was crazy. Chugging cough syrup was crazy. The way her heart was beating so fast was crazy, the deep deep sinkhole where her serotonin had gone, making her mind and body react to everything like it was a threat, was crazy. If everything could hurt her, then didn't that mean that nothing could hurt her? That nothing mattered? That there was no matter, a simulation, dissociation deep enough to see the world for what it was: one thing, reflected in infinite funhouse mirrors to make it seem like humans and worms were different things when, of course, they were not. Elise was so hungover she wished she was dead. Those were Cee's words. Cee was so hungover she wished Cee was dead. Cee as Elsie and Elsie as Elise.

A door slammed somewhere in the house.

"Get back here, Linnie! You crazy fucking *bitch*, I'll fucking leave right fucking now, you hear me?" The man's voice was slowly getting harder to hear as he moved through the house, away from the trucker's son bedroom. "I'll leave, I think that's what you want, I think you want me gone so you can tell all your little bitch friends what a fucking asshole I am, right? You fat fucking *slut*. I *should* leave you for her, I—"

Another door slammed, cutting him off, and a moment later a truck revved to life.

"My parents are crazy," the trucker's son said.

Elise couldn't tell how he actually felt about them because he was smiling but blinking rapidly. Elise was a New York State Museum facilities manager's daughter. She knew the trucker's son's name was Luke. She felt sick of herself in a fun new way. Who did she think she was, really, with her meaningless degree and her roach-infested apartment and her loving parents and her criminal record that was only clean because she was seventeen when she was arrested? Was Cake okay? Where had he spent the snowy night? The same place he spent all the nights when she was working: somewhere. He'd be hungry now, though.

"I've got to get home to feed my dog," Elise said.

"You have a dog?"

"Sort of," Elise said. Then, decisively, "Yes, I do. His name is Tom."

54

IN THE TRUCKER'S SON'S TRUCK, ELISE BURPED GRAPE and closed her eyes.

"What's your dad's name?" Elise asked. She already knew his mother's name was Linnie, because that was the name his father had been yelling.

"Hmm?"

"Your dad's name. What's your dad's name?"

"Burt. Where's your place?" Burt and Linnie's son asked. Burt. Burt! Elise knew a Burt. "Well, it's in the park, right? But which is it?"

"It's a green camper," she said. A nap was a promising enterprise. Burt and Linnie had ruined her life. "Just wake me up when we get there."

But he didn't have to, because she woke up when the pickup stopped. She hadn't really been sleeping, anyway. Suspended in semiconsciousness, rocking back and forth between hangover and nothing. She could have used something greasy and fried, but she wasn't sure she'd ever eat again.

"This one?" the son asked.

"Yes," Elise said.

There was the dog, leaping toward the pickup as Elise got out. The camp was quiet: day shift at day shift, night shift asleep. The ground was muddy with snowmelt. Tom's clothes hardly even looked like clothes anymore, more like aberrant soil formations.

Tom's paws left perfect dirt prints on Elise's jeans when he jumped up on her.

"Hey, buddy," Burt's son said, too enthusiastically. Elise did not know why he'd gotten out of the truck at all. "Hey, buddy, how ya doing?"

After the single night away, the camper felt cold and lonely. Elise turned on the space heater and poured dog food into a bowl. Home sweet. Tom jumped inside to eat. For some reason Burt's son followed. She sat down on the bed. He looked at it, then looked around the camper.

"This place is cool," he lied.

"Okay," Elise said.

He went to sit down on the bed beside her but at the last moment jumped away. Elise did not know how to ask him what he was doing here. The world was starting to scatter. *Was* he here? Was he real? Wow! Was she Elise, or was she Elsie?

"Shit," he said. "Are those fleas? I think I saw a flea."

Elise looked. Sure, maybe. Why not?

"Sure, maybe," she said. "Why not?"

"Um," he said. She could read the desperation all over his face: how badly he wanted out of this situation, how he was young enough to not be very hungover and wanted to spend this morning smoking a blunt and going to McDonald's. How maybe it wasn't all that cool that Elise let him choke her. How maybe the bruise on her neck wasn't some edgy, poetic story.

"You can leave," Elise finally managed. She dug her phone out of her bag and plugged it in. "Sorry. You can leave."

She turned her phone on. U ok? Eric had texted. Then: plz. Then: im gonna get famous doing interviews on the true crime podcast about u. Then: idk just text back. Then, from Ash: I'm sure you're fine but text when you can anyway just so we know we don't have a situation on our hands. They already did. Elise was a situation.

I'm ok, she texted Eric. She didn't respond to Ash. Eric could tell Ash. It didn't have to travel far, that text. Just hop across the campground. She hoped Eric was sleeping, that he wouldn't text her back and she'd never have to answer for her own actions.

"Are you . . . sure?" Luke was picking at a pimple next to his nose. She didn't know what he wanted from her, now. Sex, again? She couldn't fathom it. "Are you gonna be okay?"

"Yes," Elise said. Why did he care if she was going to be okay? Elise wasn't even real. She needed him to go before she disappeared. "Please. Leave."

Luke crouched down in front of her. Tom was watching them, licking his lips of crumbs, drooling a little bit.

"C'mere," Luke said, taking her chin in between his thumb and forefinger and pulling her face against his. She could tell he was trying to kiss her sweetly but it was just wet. When he pulled away, he said: "You're so interesting."

"Okay," Elise said.

She just wanted to be alone with the dog. With her dog, Tom. She pressed play on her phone to start the Bon Iver album and lay back on the thin vinyl mattress. First she heard the broken zipper going up, then down. Then she heard the truck start. Then she heard the truck drive away, car wheels on gravel road. She let all the vowels in the world dissolve so that she could be Elsie without having to be Elise.

55

ELISE REMEMBERED THIS: THIS. THIS IS WHAT IT WAS like. There was the dog. She pressed her nose against the dog's flank and took a deep breath. Smelled dog. Doggy. Dirty, earth dog. Cute wagged his Tom tail and smelled not like beets. She pulled her face away and lay flat on her back staring up at the green canvas ceiling. Green. Canvas. Ceiling.

She stood up. Walking felt like falling. She couldn't do it straight. She sat down. She regretted this decision.

She lay down. Her body was many layers coming apart, but breathing deep still felt good. She was shaking but she wasn't sure if she was shaking. She had sand in her mouth. She was a sandbag body. Everything is a memory, she knew. Even the things. Even the sleeping bag, a memory. All the sandbag layers of memory touched. Ocean body. Ocean floor body.

The sandbag spilling out. The waves pull the sand back out to ocean. Elise hated the ocean. Tumble dry. But in college. Being watched. Wriggling. She was a sugar. Beet maggot. She was infected. She had a parasite. She groaned and curled and fetal-cringed. Sketch on the floor of Elise and Tom. She picked it up. Should she eat it? She put her lips on it. Touched it to her tongue. Elise was looking down a long black hole and all down the hole were her layers of her self standing overlapped. *That's what it looks like inside yourself,* Elise thought. *This is what it looks like inside yourself.* Elise wanted to kick the rest of her down the hole. The cavity. She wanted to helium-lift away. She wanted her life to not belong to her. All the girls alive inside her adding so much weight, weight, weight. A cavity.

Elise was a sugar beet worm. Elise was trapped in the camper. She touched her head and hit the hard hat. Elise's heart was beating hard but hollow. The fuzzy drumstick against the big drum. Being watched in the room with the costumes. Clutching her hard hat head. Felt flesh and hard hat were the same. They were fucking right in front of her. Tom and Cee made of dirt.

"I didn't leave you," Dirt Tom said through his beet lips. "I'm waiting for you, Elise."

"You know why we had to go," Cee said, her beet eyes kind. "I know you know."

Elise did know. Elsie knew. The pain began to subside. Elise knew how strong the pull was.

"You chose it over me," she said with her worm lips squirming, absorbed into the rest of her face.

"Only for a while," Tom said, reaching for her. Caressing her cold plastic hard hat hair. "Come now and be with us."

She already was with them. She was them. In the pile, they could be perfect. Together. Start over as nobodies, no one else inside them keeping them guarded and weak. They could fill each other entirely. Be only one. Elise leaned into their dirt bodies and let them embrace her. Felt the urgent pleasure of the beets entering her mouth, her stomach, the soil caking the backs of her knees, a cooling balm against the eczema. Felt how it could be. How it would be.

No, though. Tom the dog put his head on her hip. Tom was gone because Elise was a hard hat and not Elsie. She was a parasite with parasites inside her. She was wet dirt on her cheeks. She wanted to burrow into a little hole of blackness. Tunnel like the worm she was. She burrowed by pulling the sleeping bag. The sand all shifted heavy. There were fleas. The space heater hot. She was tripping very hard. Elise, crying, but it wasn't Elise and she wasn't crying. Who was seeing her anybody? Elise on the ocean floor tumbling. She didn't know how long. Too long. The sugar worm bruise forever, the earthworker ouroboros, she'd do anything to make it stop. She grabbed her hard hat head and pulled. Flesh fused plastic pulled. Screaming at the pain not the pain that was in her head, hard hat head, flesh from her forehead pulling with the plastic, blood run face, skull bone, girls inside push push push at the skull, the headache, the hard hat scalp skinned from her skull, held in her hands, full of blood, her hair bloody with blood from where the top of her head was ripped off and making room for the others, every Elise screaming at once with worm lungs worm stomach beet heart beating beating beating heart.

56

ELISE WAS NOT *NOT* TRIPPING WHEN IT CAME TIME TO carpool to work. If she had to describe how she felt, she would not be able to. How she felt was like this: the world was not very real, but much less fun than a cartoon world, and also she was still hungover but now she was constantly hovering half an inch above herself. She took some aspirin. Maybe a little more than recommended. She should have slept. She should have eaten something. She tried, in the car on the way to the site, to eat the sandwich that someone who wasn't Mission Mike had prepared for her and which the guys had collected for her since she'd missed dinner, a sandwich that only had peanut butter on it, but she could only taste the existence of the food, the grainy matter, the stiffness of something besides nothing in her mouth. But at least her eating disorder wasn't saying anything to her, that voice still sandbagged at the bottom of the roboocean. She smoked a cigarette between bites. It made her heart beat very fast. She looked like hell, makeup still smudged on her face, eyes red and bagged, lips chapped, nose crusted, pores huge and full of dirt. The beets would still want her, she knew. She sat in the backseat with Ryan, who leaned in when he spoke to her.

"Hey, were you okay last night?" he asked.

She swallowed a mouthful of matter. She was confused, but she would have been confused by the question even if she weren't already confused about everything. She was still wearing Burt's son's beer T-shirt. Elise couldn't look out the window because it would make her sick. She had to look at Ryan, whose brows nearly met in the center and who had a nose ring. Had she always known that? Had he always had a nose ring? Born with it? Could he tell that she was also Elsie, in addition to being Elise?

You aren't, though, something said.

You're better, you're us, said somethings else.

"Why?" "she" "said."

"I just feel like we could have looked out for you better," he said.

In the front seat, Eric and Jai were talking about something else, but Elise got the feeling that they weren't really talking about anything and were in fact listening to Ryan make this apology. Outside the window, all the fields were on fire. The sky was charred clouds. The haze was the pure heat of flames. Scarecrows lit up like pyres. Whole families of rodents blistering, crisping, dying. The last of the world's food was burning up, the dry, sandy, lifeless soil grateful to be put out of its misery. The soil remembered that once, it was wet and dark and filled with fungus. It remembered prairie grasses and bison shit, snowmelt and rain. It remembered the worms; all those beautiful worms. It remembered when the things sowed in it were worth reaping.

Elise blinked and everything went back to normal: dusty pesticide clouds and the beautiful floating will-o'-the-wisps of machinery headlights.

"It's fine," "she" "said." She still didn't know what he was apologizing for.

"But everything turned out okay?" Ryan asked. "You can tell me if it wasn't okay. We can find that guy, you know?"

"It's fine," "she" "said," beginning to understand that Ryan was apologizing for letting Luke take her home when she was so drunk. She knew why. But he was just confused, because Elise's body wasn't Elise's the way other people's bodies were their bodies. Elise's body was just a problem. It had belonged to her parents first, then to an eating disorder, then to Tom. And look what had happened to it as soon as it was back in Elise's possession. She'd thrown it in all these awful directions. She was better off without control, she was better off sharing the space of her body with everyone and everything else. She ought to be Cee. "I'm not your responsibility."

"That's not—" Ryan started to say. Then he released her, leaning away. "I just want you to know that, you know, I'm here. We're all here. For you."

"You're one of us," "she" "said." Dropped her cigarette out the window. She didn't know why she said it, except that it felt right.

And Ryan nodded, though he looked slightly confused.

"Sure," he said. "Of course."

There was the Big Boy. Elise pointed and said, "That's my husband," but it wasn't as funny as when Sam said it. No one even laughed. It was the worst moment of Elise's life.

57

THE PILER LULLED ELISE INTO A STUPOR SO DEEP SHE transcended not only her own so-burdened identity, she abandoned the realm of distinct corporeal forms. When she maneuvered the levers, her palm opened up and swallowed the knobs and the shafts. When she pushed a button, it continued downward infinitely, swallowing her finger, then hand, then arm, then torso and neck. The dirty glass was clear for Elise because she was the glass. She could see everything the machine saw: every angle of the people working it, from above and below at once, and she could feel the beets roll and tumble along her conveyer belt body, and she swung her neck back and forth slowly and steadily like a pendulum depositing beets into the pile. Her tooth didn't hurt because she didn't have teeth, only gears. To be Elise was to be the machine was to be.

Elise understood, now, how the piler yearned for the pile. How the piler achieved enlightenment through its agony: the suffering of the machine under its impossible desire tumbled into a state of acceptance so full that it continued and continued to do the work of building the pile even though each beet added to it reminded the piler of its inability to be the pile.

The pile was a paradigm of impermanence. It was both the pile and not the pile: the still frozen mountain of beets and the absence of beets as they were taken away. The pile was the sweet release of the accumulated self: all the tons of decisions and desires, and all their eradication. It made Elise wonder, if operating the piler meant being the piler and being the piler meant complete satisfaction, then how much better would it be to be the pile? Could being the pile be *better* than being the piler?

Yes, Elise, the beets murmured as they passed along all her perfectly functioning mechanisms. *It's even better in the pile. In the pile, you have no wants, only endlessly met needs. In the pile, your every flaw is flawless. In the pile, you are always wanted by everything. It's heaven. It's waiting for you.*

No wonder Tom and Cee had chosen it. She knew, for sure, what had happened. It all made sense: Tom and Cee, always talking with their heads bowed close, talking about how it felt to operate the piler, how they wanted to be part of the pile. Perhaps they had been waiting for the day when day shift would be released early so they could return to the site undetected, or perhaps it had been entirely spontaneous. Elise could feel how the piler felt when Tom and Cee had driven Tom's car straight into the pile.

Elise refused her break when Jai offered it the first time.

"Really?" he asked.

Elise was too busy being the dirt box, eating the dirt shaken off the beets, to discern if there was annoyance in his tone.

"You can take my break for me," Elise said. Her voice was both her voice and the voice of the piler.

"Huh," Jai said.

And when he came up again sometime later, Elise said the same thing. And the next time. Twelve hours wasn't long enough. Elise wanted forever.

But the next person who came up into the piler box wasn't Jai. It was Jeff. His cheeks were ruddy from the walk over.

"How's it going up here?"

"Great," Elise groaned in her rusted metal voice.

"I heard you've been working straight through the night. You okay?"

Elise wondered how he'd heard about that. Had Jai told someone? Blurted it out in the scalehouse?

"I'm fine," she said. "We're understaffed and I can handle it."

"You know, I used to operate pilers," Jeff said.

Elise did not care about that information.

"So, I get it," he said.

Elise did not care about that information, either, if it was information, which she didn't really think it was.

"Hey, do me a favor, kid. Look at me," Jeff said. Elise did. She rotated her boom to the left so that she could face him. "It's easy to lose yourself in work. Trust me, I know. You've got a lot of things going for you in your life, you know?"

"You don't know me," Elise rattled, which was true because Jeff did not know Elise, but also because Elise was also not knowable because she was not Elise. She was the piler.

"I don't need to," Jeff said. "You're young. You've got a family, right? I can tell you're not like some of these other folk."

Maybe Jeff meant that Elise was not a homeless crust punk. Maybe he was racist and meant that she wasn't a brown-skinned migrant worker. Either way, he was saying that, in his mind, Elise was not disposable. A great big compliment; or it would have been if Elise wanted to be not disposable, which was not what she wanted to be. She simply did not want to be.

"You got a family, right?" Jeff repeated. Elise's family was in the beets. "You wanna tell me about them? Or maybe, I don't know, a cat?"

"A dog," Elise said, surprising herself by speaking at all. It was the first time she'd thought of Tom all night. While Elise was not, Tom was. That was undeniable, a wrench thrown into her moving parts.

"A dog," Jeff nodded. "Try to keep him—her—them in mind

tonight. Why don't you come on out, take a break, and think about what you and your dog are gonna do when you get home after your shift."

Home? Could she and Tom go home together? With her harvest money—she'd get paid the next day. Then more money, two weeks later. She could bring Tom back to Brooklyn. Get a pet-friendly apartment. She'd work as hard as she had to, pay the rent, keep him healthy. He could chase the roaches away. She would come home and Tom'd be waiting for her on the couch. Elise dropped her hands from the controls and slammed back into her body. She regretted it immediately. Her tooth sent shooting pains down her jaw. Her brain bulged and throbbed against its cage. Her lungs and liver and kidneys and heart all hurt.

"Ope! That's real good," Jeff said. "Now you come on out. Think about your dog. They need you, don't they?"

Tom wasn't in the beet pile. Elise's heart flexed around the thought of leaving him behind. She couldn't do that to him—not after he'd already been left behind once. Tom was a good dog and deserved better than that.

"Okay," she said quietly. "Just a little break."

Jeff retreated down the stairs, passing Jai on his way up. It was hardly three seconds later that Elise emerged from the operator box, but she didn't see Jeff walking back to the scalehouse. It was possible that he was at the other piler, giving Eric the same speech. But it was also possible that he'd never been there at all.

58

IN THE CAR, SHE PUT ON THE NEXT EPISODE OF *PRETTY Little Liars*—it started with the liars sitting around a campfire at a campsite, asking their new crust-punk neighbors if any of them knew or had seen their supposed-to-be-dead best friend. The artsy liar's adult-teacher-boyfriend was acting shady, the way the boyfriends always were, but it always turned out they had good reasons to act shady. Elise thought about Creeps McGee. A teacher, too. She was flayed open and defenseless, memories buffeting her hard as the wind. Elise still didn't know why he'd targeted her, if he'd targeted her—or had he found ways to watch all the girls changing, when they left rehearsal early for dental appointments or stayed late to get high in the parking lot, then sneak around backstage, giggling. Recently she'd tried to find him on Facebook, just to see if he was still teaching, but there was no trace of him on the internet. It was like he'd never existed at all, like Elise had just made him up in her memory. Part of her *fantasy world*. That was what her mother had said, anyway, when Elise finally told her, purposefully accidentally letting it slip as they drove together to the mall. Her mother had been silent a moment. Elise thought, in that moment, that she hoped her mother didn't think Elise was making it up—that she didn't think Elise was too fat, actually, for anyone to want to watch her change.

"Elise, are you *sure*? Because sometimes, you know . . . sometimes you live in a fantasy world."

Elise opened Jai's car door in time for all the puke to hit the gravel. She gagged until her abs ached, then retreated back to the car, laying her body long across the backseat. Thirty minutes later, she woke up with an awful pain in her neck. If the nap had done her any good, it was lost on Elise, who could only feel how bad she felt. She wanted back in the piler. That was the only place she knew she'd be safe from what she'd done to herself.

But when she approached the piler, it wasn't running. Elise's heart hammered. Had the boom got stuck? Had the conveyor jammed again? Was she broken?

No, the crew was just locking out in preparation for cleaning, Jeff standing beside Ryan with his slight stoop and his sincere, guileless smile, overseeing in his lackluster managerial way. The wind had died down. It was still cold as hell. Ash and Jai stood by the metal ladder.

"Wait," Elise said. "I'll do it." Her desire for relief was unspeakable. It had been years since she cleaned out the dirt box.

"That's a lot of beets," Jeff said to Ryan as Elise jogged toward the stairs to take the shovel from Jai. She followed Ash up the ladder and through the hatch and into the dirt box.

Where it was warm. And dark.

The ambient heat of the machine cut through Elise's constant chill, reminding her that there was a time when she was not cold. There was a time when she was as warm as the planet itself. And her mind as dark. The air was wet and thick. Elise and Ash stood back-to-back, stabbing the heaps of soil that had accumulated on the metal walls.

Return the dirt. Return the dirt. Return the dirt. Return the dirt. Return to the dirt. Return to the dirt. Return to the dirt.

The more Elise and Ash breathed, harder and harder as they labored, the wetter and thicker and more suffocating the air grew. Sweat streamed down Elise's temple. She went to wipe her brow but stopped before the back of her hand could hit her hard hat. *Return to the dirt.* Elise kept stabbing and pulling, the dirt coming off and off in satisfying lumps.

But there was something wrong. *Return* to *the dirt.*

The more dirt Elise dug out, the more dirt built up on the walls.

There was less space now than there had been when Elise entered.

Elise pulled down another layer of the wall and her ass bumped up against Ash's.

Return to the dirt. Return to the dirt. Return to the dirt. Return to the dirt. Return to the dirt. Return to the dirt.

It was an invitation, or it was a command. Each clump obeying gravity fell down into an abyss that opened beneath Elise's feet. Each clump created two new ones. She heard Ash breathing, his carbon dioxide carried on humid breath. The soil, Elise thought, would have oxygen in it. She scraped dirt from the wall and her spine met Ash's. The air was hot. The air was heavy. *Return to the dirt.* The walls touched Elise and she struggled to lift her arms enough to pull down another shovelful. The walls pressed against her chest. Her shoulders ached with the convoluted twists she needed to make in order to keep digging. *Return to the dirt.* The walls trapped the shovel above Elise's head. She began to dig with her hands. She felt Ash's heartbeat. She felt the soil's heartbeat. All the worms' heartbeats. She had no heartbeat.

Return to the dirt.

The pockets of air that remained were mostly water now. When Elise tried to breathe, her ribs compressed around her lungs, she drew in her own waste, Ash's waste, the gases condensing to droplets in the heat. The soil would have oxygen, though. How else could the beets grow? *You are a beet,* the voice said. *Return to the dirt.*

Elise continued to make feeble scraping motions with her nails. She and Ash were crushing each other now. Elise looked up. The white specks in the dirt were like stars. The white specks were worms. Elise scraped. *Return to the dirt.* Elise tried to breathe and couldn't. Elise opened her mouth and leaned into the soil. There was no way to get rid of it all. It could not be emptied. There was nothing to do but accept that. She took the soil between her lips. She let it tumble down her throat. It squirmed inside her, infinite worms laying infinite eggs. She breathed in the soil. She breathed. She ate.

"Looks good to me," Ash said.

Elise coughed, dry and loose and rattly. She was holding the shovel. There was dirt around her feet, up to the ankles of her not-pink boots. Ash clapped her on the back.

"You okay? Got a little dirt in your throat?"

Elise's lungs ached, her back surely bruised from the pressurized contact. But the dirt box was cooling down, fresh air rushing in as Ash opened the hatch. The nausea, the exhaustion, the pain rushed back. It was better in the dirt, it was. She wanted to lie facedown on the floor. She wanted to go back. She wanted to return.

59

TOM WAS NOT IN THE CAMPER WHEN ELISE GOT BACK to camp. Elise would have waited for him to notice she was back, to hear the popping of beets under car tires and come running to be fed, but she couldn't. It had been hard enough sacrificing the control panel to the disgruntled-as-ever day shift guy. She'd slept the whole way home. She needed to sleep more. She filled his bowl and put it on the floor of the camper, near the door flap with its broken snaps and zipper. He would scratch and whine when he wanted to come in and eat. She changed into Tom's luxe sweatpants. She thought about some other version of her, currently lying in Tom's arms, the two of them having left together and driven all the way back to Brooklyn and their good little desperate lives. Climbing into her sleeping bag, with only a moment's pause to miss Tom's curled-up body beside her, she moved seamlessly into sleep.

As she slept, an invisible miracle took place between Salt of the Earth Sugar (subsidiary of Damballa Foods, subsidiary of Cartill Inc., d/b/a Walker-Moloch-Rolfson) and S. R. Arndt-Beherit & Co., d/b/a Beherit Financial Services. Money from the former, processed by an automated clearinghouse, was deposited by the latter into Elise's account. Neither the servers nor the code responsible for the transaction were relieved when the incoming money filled the hole in her bank account. Neither was Elise when she woke up and thought: *It's payday.*

She thought she would feel something more, but she didn't. As it turned out, being overdrafted for nearly two weeks hadn't actually had any effect on her life. Unless it was why Tom left, which it wasn't, maybe only as an excuse. Her parents had never found out. Her bank had not bothered her with threats of closing the account. She had not missed out on any fun, because there were people here who, impossibly, were fond of her, and also because there was no fun to be had besides generic camaraderie. Which was a lovely thing that Elise enjoyed. And now Elise had money—a lot of it. Enough to keep the apartment for another month, long enough for Elise to figure out what she'd do next, how to make a new life with and for Tom.

She couldn't even check what her non-overdrafted account looked like, exactly how much money she now had, because even though her phone had been charging the whole day, it would not turn on. She was not sure what time it was, but it was early. The sun was high and bright over the wind.

Tom's food sat untouched. Elise frowned. Had she slept through him whining and barking to get in? Did he think she'd left him, too? Could he smell the food through the canvas, hungry and cold, while Elise baked herself dry in the sleeping bag with the space heater going full blast? Fleas jumped across the place where Tom used to sleep.

She unzipped the door. The wind was bearing down on the camp, blowing a landslide of beets downhill. Her hair swept across her face, blinding her. She couldn't pull her hair back before it was snatched out of her hands and blown over her eyes again. She put on Cee's snapback. No dogs at all, anywhere. Cars in front of all the campers—day shift was back early. The wind had torn the fabric awning off an RV, the green-and-white-striped canvas flapping wildly like a flag.

Arin's truck was gone. There was an impression in the beets where it had been reversed off the campsite and onto the road.

"Tom," Elise yelled, but the wind carried her voice away. She kept trying: "Tom! Come here, Tom!"

She paused.

"Cake," she yelled again. "Cake?"

Could anyone hear her? Anyone at all? Nothing and no one responded. A newspaper circular for the Lapeer Motor Inn blew against her shin. Elise kicked it off.

Since Sarah had left her that note, then it should be Sarah that Elise talked to. She imagined the conversation going well: *Yes, Sarah might say, we let Tom in because of the wind. Here, do you want to take him back? Or we can keep him tonight while you're at work.* Except they wouldn't call the dog Tom, because that wasn't the name they knew him by, though it was his name, as much his name as Cake had been. Dogs did not really have names, so any name you gave them was as good as any other. Dogs lacked the burden of continuous identity. They didn't have to be anyone but who they were in the moment.

Elise knocked. Sarah struggled to open the door; the wind caught it and slammed it against the siding.

"Shit," Sarah said, over the wind.

"Here"—Elise grabbed the handle and tugged it as Sarah stepped aside to let Elise in. Elise had to hold the door closed while Sarah leaned over her shoulder to lock it, or the wind would have blown it open again.

"Jesus Christ," Elise breathed, realizing now in the spacious warmth of the RV just how awful life was in Burt. Was this an actual heating system they had? Was that a dining room table? There was a window over the table with a frilly baby blue gingham curtain on it.

Josh looked up from his phone, smiled at Elise.

"A truck turned over at our site," Sarah said, leaning with her arms crossed against the tiny sink. "They sent everyone home. You probably won't have work, either, unless this passes soon."

"Oh shit," Elise said, not caring about this story, only caring about Tom, but capable of behaving like a good, normal human. "Was everyone okay?"

"Yeah," Josh said. "Lucky the bed fell away from the piler. But it was a bitch trying to clean it all up in this wind. And the truck is still there, as far as I know. Dunno how they're gonna get that sumbitch back up."

"I actually came over here to see if you'd seen the dog around," Elise said. "He never ate his food? And it's so windy?" Elise imagined Cake struggling against the wind, digging his paws into the dirt, clawing at the earth before being lifted and swept away. She could not seem to take a breath deep enough to fill her lungs.

"Oh," Sarah said, beaming. "I guess my note didn't survive, huh? Figures. Arin got in touch."

Elise went cold all over, like she'd been shoved outside.

"I guess he met some local dude who drives long-haul and he had to get a load to Houston, but the dude wanted to stay and work the harvest s'more, so he's splitting the deal with him. So, yeah, you know, Zed took his truck down to meet him."

"Oh," Elise said. There was pressure behind her eyes. "But."

Sarah was smiling like this was good news. Josh was looking at his phone again, hand digging into a bag of plain Lay's Ruffles chips. Their life seemed so exquisitely quotidian.

"I'm sure he's glad you took care of him, though," Sarah said.

"Who?" Elise blurted. Sarah's smile faltered. "I mean—but he left?"

"Um."

"He left the dog," Elise went on, aware that she would be unable to keep from crying. She wasn't sad so much as angry. That was the worst—so mad you start crying and then no one takes you seriously. In the linoleum hallways under the fluorescent lights while everyone watched. "He left Cake behind. He just disappeared. He left the dog."

Now, Sarah shifted. She went from leaning on the sink to standing straight, arms crossed tighter now.

"He didn't really *leave* Cake," Sarah said. "He knew we'd take care of him. He left his truck. It's his dog, Elise."

"How can it be his dog?" Elise said, voice thick and distant.

Josh was staring at her. Sarah looked over her shoulder at him.

"Listen, I'm sorry, but just because you put out some food doesn't mean he's your dog either," Sarah said. "And honestly, you wouldn't understand what that dog means to Arin. He's had a tough life. He knew someone would take care of Cake, and someone did. What did you expect him to do, anyway, just stick the dog in the back of a semi?"

"But he left him," Elise choked out. She burned. Everything Sarah said was a stupid excuse for a guy who abandoned his dog with no word about when he'd come back. Arin had disappeared. He'd just run away. He'd left Tom out in the cold! With no food, no water! Tom could have run into the street and gotten hit by a car, or frozen to death in the woods! "You can't just . . . you can't do that!"

"I can see this is really upsetting to you," Sarah said. "But I'm sorry. You're just going to have to deal with it. Maybe one of the puppies . . ."

"He left," Elise yelled. Her nails were digging half-moons into her palms. "He left! He left! He left!"

Elise thought of Tom: the woodsy stinky smell of his fur, the way he slept like a donut in the space behind her knees, the way he cocked his head at sounds from outside the camper, pawed at her face when he wanted her to scratch behind his ears. One time, he was sleeping with his nose under his tail and woke himself up by farting in his own face. That had been the first time she'd laughed since Tom left. She thought about being the type of person who would leave all that behind without telling *anyone*. Who would just run away. Who would abandon, at their convenience, something that loved and trusted them.

"Here"—Sarah was suddenly holding a glass of water out to Elise. "Drink this. Calm down. Do you think . . . maybe this isn't about the dog?"

Josh rolled his eyes. Elise's instinct was to grab the glass of water and throw it against the wall. Fleas. She still had fleas in her bed. It was too warm in here, too nice, too full of good things. The carpet that she wanted to rip up. The curtains over the sink that she wanted to drag down. The boyfriend's eyes she wanted to claw out. The bag of chips she wanted to shove down his throat. The fire she wanted to set, letting the wind finally do what it seemed to want so badly to do: catch the flames and carry them across camp, take everything and everyone with it, cinders caught up and carried across town to burn the movie theater, the turn-of-the-century houses, the American Legion, the Buck Barn, the gas station—a big explosion there at the gas station—spread to the beet sugar processing plant and the Walmart and the acres and acres of pesticide-fogged cropland, melt the smile off the Big Boy's dirty plastic head, incinerate the whole flat fucking face of this barren goddamn wasteland.

Everything but her piler, her pile.

Elise only realized she'd left Sarah's trailer when she heard the slam of the door hitting the siding again. Hair in her face. Indentations in the grass where Arin's tires had been. Everyone else cozy and warm in their half-decent spaces. Elise seeing, for the first time, how shitty the little green camper was in comparison to what everyone else had. Everything about Elise was shitty compared to everyone else. Tom was probably happier on his way back to Arin. Tom was probably happier without her. Tom was probably already with her, in a way. If he was with Cee. And Elise was Cee, some version of her. Elise was lying back on a hotel bed, under a crisp white comforter, a room Tom had paid for, his head between her thighs letting her take as much as she wanted from him.

Something hit Elise in the back of her calf. She looked down: a beet, blown down the hill. She hardly felt it but she still screamed. Loud and hard, but the wind only blew louder and harder to remind her that her pain didn't matter. No one cared.

Elise couldn't fathom crawling back into her moldy little flea-ridden bed. She was wearing Luke's T-shirt, and Tom's sweatpants, and Cee's hat. Her anger melted, dripping downward into soggy, fetid grief. She didn't have the energy to fight the wind even for the few yards that lay between Sarah's trailer and Burt. She turned, instead, in the direction the wind was blowing. She started walking where the wind directed her to walk.

60

THE WIND PUSHED HER UP THE HILL TOWARD THE MIS-
sion, then past it. Past a Payless that had popped up overnight, a
poster in the window for BOGO sugar beets. The wind rushed her
toward the county road that led to Eldritch, passing first through
the shopping district—Spaghett About It, Buck Barn, gun store,
credit union, check-cashing place, Walmart, ag store, Hobby
Lobby, another gun store, Hardee's. It took Elise through the end
of the afternoon and most of the sunset to walk her way out of
Robber's Bluff proper into the nebulous non-place of "farmland."

There were no trucks coming or going. Elise thought that
any truck that tried to drive against the wind would be caught
in a stalemate, wheels churning in place, sinking into the carpet
of beet guts. Any truck that was going with the wind would be
lifted, wheels and axles off the earth, blown bed-over-cab toward
the biblically near horizon. There were clouds. There was a dirty
light. There was the film of foggy dust hanging over the fields.
Elise had never learned if it was pesticides, or water, or dirt. She'd
wondered every day and never asked anyone. Maybe Luke would
have known. Or Sydney. Maybe everyone but Elise knew.

It was cold, of course. When had it ever not been cold? If not
externally, then internally? Elise's feet hurt. Her construction
boots were so caked in mud and beet clumps that it was like walking on heels. But the pain didn't bother her. She thought: *No pain,
no gain!* The hems of Tom's sweatpants dragged along the ground,
soft fabric gone crusty and torn to shreds. Always, her life had

been so messy, so constantly moments away from disassembly. But now! Now with the wind on her side! She could sew up her life at last, so tight and clean the seams would be absorbed back into it. For once, her life would have flesh protecting it. For once, she'd be who she *was* instead of who she happened to have been. Elise was so tired. How much would she weigh without all these girls inside her? She knew the answer: She'd be light enough. Finally.

She imagined leaning back into the wind, lifted and carried the rest of the way. Cee's snapback blew off her head and Elise watched it get carried away, a smaller and smaller speck until it disappeared into the haze. The last best promise of a life where she had made different decisions, done different things. The part of her that was Cee was too far away, now, to reconcile.

It surprised Elise when her phone buzzed in her pocket, because she had not taken her phone out of the camper, because it had not turned on when she tried to turn it on. But now she pulled it free. Texts from people who had not yet learned how much better their lives would be without her. She swiped them all away. She cut her thumb on the crack in her screen.

There were new texts from "pure id," too, but Elise didn't read them, barely even registered the same old words repeated: fat ugly whore. She tapped out her sole reply: I fucked your son. Then she went to the website for her credit card, which was an impossible thing for Elise to be doing because she didn't have a data plan and there was no Wi-Fi. But she went there anyway, and she paid more than the minimum. She dropped the phone into the beets on the side of the road. She was winning, at last. She was the winner.

There was something else in her pocket. Paper, folded: the sketch Sam had done of Elise and Tom. Elise tore a piece off and put it in her mouth. She chewed and swallowed. Strip by jagged strip, she ate the drawing, let it fill her stomach. Energy for the long walk.

The Big Boy's eyes were no longer looking off to the side. They looked straight at Elise, followed her as she made her slow, plodding way past him. The lights inside his pupils were flashing in a rhythm Elise recognized as Morse code. She paused for a minute, watching the long and short blinks. The cold burned her cheeks and the tips of her ungloved fingers. Elise didn't know how to read Morse code, but she knew that the Big Boy was blinking the lyrics to the Smiths. The Big Boy was miserable now. Not Elise! Elise would never be miserable again.

Something familiar fluttered up against her boot. The now-familiar family beamed at her. The little girl was bleeding from her mouth. Or maybe it was beet juice. Red dripped down into the white powder in her cupped hands, turning the top of the mound pink. Elise read in the flashes of light that came from the Big Boy's eyes. *Now, you are ready to be granulated, packaged, and shipped across the nation. Finally, you have fulfilled your purpose. You've abandoned the long fiction of a singular, independent, boundaried body. You have been ripped into so many directions, dissolved into so many solutions, that you have discovered the diffuse pleasures of having no body, no boundaries. You, sweet beet, have been transformed in a way humans can only dream of. Through disintegration, you have transcended.*

Elise tore the pamphlet into strips and ate them.

She started walking again. It was deep night in the Midwest. No shapes rose blacker against the not-black sky, there was nothing for all the world's nightborne mysteries to hide behind, not even a moon. Not even, because of the clouds, stars. When cars occasionally passed Elise, they did not stop or slow for her. Perhaps the drivers did not see her.

~ 61 ~

ELISE FELT SO GOOD. AND BETTER WITH EACH STEP.
She was closing in on the end. She could feel the pull of the pile
at her chest, thick strings of desire reeling her in. And then there
was the turnoff into the gravel lot. The scalehouse, empty. The
port-a-potty, knocked over by the wind. It had landed on its side,
the door hanging open, and Elise could smell the waste and blue
water that slopped out of the tank. But only for a moment. The
wind carried her away from it, without carrying the smell. It was
a kind wind.

Elise's knees shook as she walked across the cracked pavement
toward the piler. Finally, a shape. The lights were off. It stood, noble
and quiet, its energy dormant. The piler looked over its shoulder at
her approach. She could feel its satisfaction at her arrival. She was
doing the right thing.

Her phone buzzed again. Impossibly, again. She'd dropped her
phone on the side of the road. Elise did what humans do when
their phones buzz. She pulled it out and looked at it. The background photo was a photo of Elise with beet eyes, a smiling mouth
full of sugar. Her tooth ached. It was five in the morning. Her
mother was calling.

Elise stopped walking.

It was six back in New York, so it wasn't so odd for Elise's
mother to be awake. But why was she calling? Elise's comfort dove
fast into fear. Bad news? Why else? Elise could not feel the finger that pressed the screen to accept the call. She did not feel the

phone against her cheek. The wind tried to push her. Over the pile, Elise saw something happening in the sky.

"Hello?" Elise's voice was thin with uncertainty, and the absurdity of the moment: soon she would hear her mother's voice.

"Elise, oh, it's so nice to hear your voice," her mother said. "I'm glad I caught you! I thought maybe you'd be on a break . . ."

It did not sound like anything was wrong. Elise stared at the pile, at the sky above it that was subtly, strangely opening up.

"Is everything okay?" Elise asked. If only her mother had called fifteen minutes later. Now all Elise's certainty was ebbing. Perhaps this was not the right thing to do, after all. Perhaps it was a trap. Perhaps she should just go home. She had the money now. She could just go home. What if her body was not so irredeemable? What if the credit card company could go fuck itself? What if she *was* loved, by someone, somewhere? What if there had never *been* any worm eggs in the sugar?

"Everything's just fine," her mother said. "I just realized, boy, it's been a while. I guess you've been busy, huh? Hard work?"

"Mom," Elise said. Elise's mother was one of the only people who knew all the Elises inside Elise. Though she didn't know all of them very well. There were several Elises inside Elise who were a mystery to Elise's mother, but in practical terms, Elise's mother knew them. Elise wanted to ask, then: Do you think it's worth it? Are they worth the weight? *Am I?*

"You sound a little funny," her mother said. "Or is that . . . what's that noise?"

Elise wasn't sure what noise her mother was talking about. The noise of the wind had ceased to be a noise.

"Um."

"Is this a bad time?"

"It's fine," Elise said, the pressure on her back increasing. The wind was getting frustrated. The sky opening up above the pile was turning green.

"Oh, okay. So, how's it going?"

There was much, over the years, that Elise had not told her mother. Elise had often told her mother that everything was fine when things were not. She didn't want to worry her mother. She did not think her mother understood her. Elise wished never to hear her mother use the phrase *fantasy world* ever again.

But Elise did not want to lie to her mother then. She caved to the wind, just two steps forward, toward the pile. The sky over the pile was moving. Bands of colored light. Maybe this time her mother would see Elise the way Elise wanted to be seen—as a real inhabitant of the real world with real needs who needed help, so much help. She needed help more, even, than she needed rent money. She was all aspirin and heartbreak and hunger.

"Not great," she blurted out. The words were a form of collapse, and Elise gasped with them. "I think I'm in trouble."

The wind pushed, angry. Elise choked at the effort it took to not move forward. The sky went blue and green—it was so beautiful. Terrifying, beautiful.

"Oh, Elise," her mother's voice crooned.

The wind kicked Elise's legs out from under her, sent her toppling forward onto her knees—Elise managed to keep her hand with the phone in it up to her ear. This was a bad idea on the wind's part, because now that she was lower to the ground, it had less sway over her. Elise leaned back, onto her haunches, curling up into herself, closing her eyes against the northern lights someone had promised her so long ago.

She didn't have to do this. She could go home. She could just go home. Let her mother put the fresh flowers beside the bed. Fresh linen pillowcases on the pillows. Let her friends take her out for Vietnamese food. Watch movies under a blanket. If she did this, she'd never find out what happened in *Pretty Little Liars*. She didn't have to stop breathing, did she? She could keep breathing. She could learn to live with all her other selves. She could learn to live in her imperfect body. She could learn to save money, she could get out of debt. She whimpered, eyes gluey with tears. Through her eyelids, she could still see the spectral glare of the sky, frightening, tempting, beckoning her forward.

"I'm sorry, honey," Elise's mother said. Then she sighed. "You know, I knew something like this would happen."

Elise's jaw clenched. The stone rising in her throat slid back down, dissolved into her empty stomach. What had her mother imagined? Was it this? Was it the voices, the worms? The profound abandonment? The dirt box—had Elise's mother really known about the dirt box? No, in truth, whatever Elise's mother had imagined could go wrong was so tame in comparison. Her mother had imagined Elise losing a job. Running out of money. Getting injured. Something her parents could, begrudgingly or not, save her from. Something Elise could thank them for, learn from, and thrive in the wake of. Elise and her parents did not live in the same world. Elise found her jobs on Craigslist. Elise had student loans that would outlast her. Elise would be sick for the rest of her life unless she did something about it now.

Elise let the phone fall from her ear. Elise's mother knew this was going to happen because Elise's mother knew all the Elises and knew that they could never escape futility, the defining characteristic of her life. Elise's mother kept talking through the phone but the wind picked up the noise and carried it away. Elise blinked up at the sky over the pile, now more beautiful than blinding, now more sincere than seductive. How silly she'd been, those few moments of doubt. The wind had not been angry, after all. Just a little exasperated that even after everything, Elise thought she might know better.

The solution was not to *learn* to *live* with the other selves. It was not to *adapt* to her body.

In penance, Elise crawled the rest of the way. Hands and knees. A worm. She approached the pile. It had grown so much since that first shift. It was so powerful now. Even the wind left it alone—the moment Elise reached out her hand toward it, the world stilled. Her frozen, unfeeling fingers could feel the beets. It was like feeling the world's skin. Elise was directly under the northern lights now, bathed in them. Sparkling.

She could get even closer.

She climbed.

Even if Elise fixed all the problems with herself, there would still be everyone else to reckon with. People were always looking at Elise. They were always seeing her the wrong way. They were always looking at her as a liability, a burden, a mistake they would someday be done making. With pity. With contempt. With lust. Without permission.

Hand over hand, Elise pulled herself up the pile. Pressed her body to the bodies, the divine pleasure of contact. She let her tongue loll so that she could lick and kiss and taste the pile as she simultaneously moved up and into it.

If Elise couldn't be seen the way she wanted to be seen—all of her, together, no dead weight, no other self, just Elise just trying to fucking *live*—then she wouldn't be seen at all. She was tired of the need for control, the holding back, cornering herself and suffocating herself and shrinking herself down into some consumable product, a provider of satisfactions, a fucking artificial sweetener, all the good always just making everyone's coffee palatable without allowing herself any substance. Any calories.

Each handful she went higher, she felt herself inching closer to everything she'd ever wanted, everything she'd ever lost. The weight began to melt. The lights smiled on her. Smiled pale, wide. Elise moaned as her breasts turned into beets. Her hips pushing into the pile.

Elise wasn't anyone else. She *was* all the selves she'd ever been, and if she couldn't be all those selves without suffering, then she wouldn't be anything at all. She lived in her body, just her, only Elise, and she could leave her body if she wanted to. And she wanted to. All of the Elises wanted the same thing, maybe for the first time ever, they sighed in unison. No one heard it and no one had to.

She was halfway to the top. If she never got there, it would still have been worth it just for these little ripples of perfect loss: there went the minimum payments, there went the hangovers, there went puking in restaurant bathrooms. There went Elise. There went Elise. There went Elise. Shed like pounds. Easier and easier to lift herself up. Closer to the sky. Deeper into the pile. Elise grabbed and pulled and gasped as her legs, all the way up to her knees, became the pile. Freer now, faster. The night was crystallizing around her, sky cauterized with color. Elise was level with the boom, heard it whispering its love to the pile. To her. Elise groaned as her pelvis finally disappeared, her troublesome stomach released at last. She was crying. It was ecstasy. How stupid she'd been to wait this long. She was almost there. Another handful. She was up to her shoulders. She remembered nothing before the harvest. There had never been anything but the beets. A light from the sky held itself out to her, promising. There were no more beets to pull herself up with. She lifted the one hand she had left and accepted the help.

For a second she was the roots of everything. All of it entered her open mouth, traveled through her into the pile. Elise screamed, trembling, at the impossible, undying pleasure and pressure and the endless atomic uniformity of being: to be everything at once was too much to take.

Which made it all the sweeter when the sky let her go and the last of Elise sank into the pile and was released, and weighed nothing, and was no one.

Acknowledgments

THIS BOOK WAS WRITTEN ON THE ANCESTRAL LAND of the following peoples: Shawnee, Potawatomi, Delaware, Miami, Peoria, Seneca, Wyandotte, Ojibwe, Numu, Wašiw, Newe, and Nuwu. It takes place on land seized from the Dakota people. I stand in solidarity with the fight to return sovereignty to these populations.

Thank you to Maggie Cooper, who never gave up on this weird little novel (and, more importantly, never ran out of beet puns). The entire team at Aevitas rules.

Thank you to Drew Weitman, who provided the most exciting plot twist of my life.

Thank you to Jill Bialosky, Laura Mucha, Amy Robbins, and everyone at Norton.

Thank you to Michelle Herman for helping shape the architecture of this book, and to Nick White for cheering me on.

Thank you to the many teachers who have encouraged me: Elissa Washuta, Marcus Jackson, Kathy Fagan, Sara Jane Stoner, Vivian Lopez, and Loren Tunick, among others. A special thank-you to Matthew Burgess, who might be an actual angel.

Thank you to my friends at Ohio State University and Brooklyn College, all of whom helped teach me to write (and how to human). I hope you know who you are, and if you don't, please ask me and I'll tell you if you are or aren't.

Thank you to Amy and Jenna, whose company has made my life better.

Thank you to Zoe Mays, because friendship is magic.

Thank you to Mary Hanrahan, who has always provided unwavering support.

Thank you to my parents, for being good parents.

Thank you to Carly and Ryan, without whom this book literally would not exist.

Thank you to Lydia, who has always been good at endings.

Thank you to William, who I love more than anything in this life or the next.

Thank you to the dogs, who cannot read.